D0063661

DEADLY,
CALM,
and
COLD

Also by Susannah Sandlin

The Collectors
Lovely, Dark, and Deep

The Penton Vampire Legacy
Redemption
Absolution
Omega
Allegiance

Also in the Penton Legacy World
Storm Force

Written as Suzanne Johnson

Sentinels of New Orleans
Royal Street
River Road
Elysian Fields
Pirate's Alley

THE COLLECTORS

DEADLY, CALM, *and* COLD

SUSANNAH SANDLIN

Montlake
Romance

This is a work of fiction. Names, characters, organizations, places, events, and incidents are either products of the author's imagination or are used fictitiously.

Text copyright © 2014 Susannah Sandlin
All rights reserved.

No part of this book may be reproduced or stored in a retrieval system, or transmitted in any form or by any means, electronic, mechanical, photocopying, recording, or otherwise, without express written permission of the publisher.

Published by Montlake Romance, Seattle
www.apub.com

Amazon, the Amazon logo, and Montlake Romance are trademarks of Amazon.com, Inc., or its affiliates.

ISBN-13: 9781477826812
ISBN-10: 1477826815

Cover design by Kerrie Robertson

Library of Congress Control Number: 2014912197

Printed in the United States of America

To the real denizens of Lincolnshire and especially Swineshead, England, whose lovely town and rich history I unmercifully rearranged in the making of this book. No one will come and dig up your lawns.

CHAPTER 1

One step forward, a dozen steps to the rear. Welcome back to the idiot's club.

Samantha Crowe scowled at her reflection in the mirror of London's lavish Bridestall Hotel bathroom, its gleaming Italian marble frame mocking her pale face. Make that her pale, worst-hangover-in-history face, a pasty oval surrounded by a blond mop of tangles and pierced by two bloodshot green eyes.

They weren't bloodshot because she was hungover—at least not entirely. They were bloodshot because she'd slept in her contact lenses. Because God forbid the man she'd spent the night with should see her in red-framed geek glasses. Correction: the guy she'd slept with after only knowing him a week. The man who'd wined and dined her, flashed a lot of money, and hung on her every word.

That in itself should have been a red flag upside her headful of stupid.

A man for whom she'd broken her own no-men-until-after-grad-school rule, only to awaken and find him gone, luggage and all, without so much as a "screw you." Then again, his lack of communication was quite a literal "screw you" minus words.

Her brains had apparently oozed out her ears while she was listening to his pile of flattering horse manure. Rich American businessmen didn't fall for plain-Jane grad students who tended to prattle on about their research. It wasn't even sexy research that would lead to a cure for cancer or baldness, but obscure medieval history, for God's sake. She'd probably bored him into fleeing.

"Face it, Crowe. Bad man choice? You got skills." Oh well, at least she'd gotten dumped inside a five-star central London hotel; it could've been in her own fleabag studio flat in Bayswater. That would have happened to Carolina Sonnier, the name and person she'd left behind ten years ago, when she was eighteen. Caro was an equally bad judge of character when it came to men; too bad when she'd changed her name she couldn't have implanted some kind of jerk radar.

Last night? Not going on her curriculum vitae.

A knock on the hotel door prevented her from more positive self-talk, which she wasn't very good at anyway. She opened it to find a chipper, immaculate, dark-suited hotel employee with a cart covered in shiny silver-domed dishes.

"I didn't order anything. You must have the wrong room." Sam's stomach growled as if on cue, reminding her that she had consumed nothing solid in more than twelve hours. But she'd looked up the hotel online, and the small suites like this one cost more than a thousand pounds a night. She doubted breakfast was within her fellowship-stipend budget.

A chill of panic rushed up her spine. What if Gary Smith, her one-night hotel stand and six-day love interest, had taken an early exit and left her to pay the oversized tab, with an overpriced meal as an exclamation point at the end? Talk about screwed.

"Oh, no, I assure you this is the correct room." The room-service guy was way too cheerful. "A full English breakfast courtesy of Mr. Smith, madam. Shall I bring it in?"

Well, okay. Things were looking up. *"Courtesy of"* usually translated as *"paid for,"* right?

"Go for it." Sam stepped aside and mentally tallied the cash she had left in her bag so she could at least tip the guy before dodging out on the bill, in case she was wrong about that translation. She pulled out a five-pound note and slipped it into her pocket while the waiter uncovered eggs Benedict, meats, breads, potatoes, more breads. She'd be swimming in carbs the rest of the day.

"Mr. Smith apologized for his early departure but asked me to assure you all the expenses have been handled and to personally deliver this." The waiter pulled a thick manila envelope from beneath the food-laden plate and handed it to her, smiling when she awkwardly traded it for the folded fiver. Poor guy; she hoped his tips the rest of the day made up for hers.

As soon as he'd disappeared down the carpeted hallway, she put out the "Do Not Disturb" sign, checked her cell phone for the time, and then consulted the hotel information card posted on the back of the door. Checkout wasn't for another four hours, so she had time to eat and shower in elegance before returning to her minuscule apartment.

Now that it appeared Gary had at least thought enough to order breakfast for her and leave a note, her mood improved rapidly. She was still an idiot, expecting flowers and violins when the guy was apparently thinking more last-night-in-London quickie, but that was her pattern, wasn't it? Thus the grad-school rule. Now she was going to change it to the no-more-men-period rule. She wouldn't be the first spinster to grace the halls of academia; in fact, it was almost expected.

She rolled the tray near the window and pulled over a cushioned chair. She'd been too nervous the night before to make much note of the room's decor except for an overwhelming sense of gray, but now that she studied it, Sam realized the color scheme seemed inspired by a dense black-and-white tapestry with a lot of horses and hounds. This fabric covered the walls and the bed and the back of the chair, and the furniture gleamed with an antiqued-silver finish. Even the bust of the horse's head sitting on the window ledge had the patina of aged silver.

How *veddy* British upper crust. Conservative, stuffy, and almost dizzying. Might as well enjoy it while she could.

Sam laid the envelope on the tray and shoveled eggs and sausage, toast and potatoes onto a plate as if she hadn't eaten in a week. Everything in London cost a fortune, way more than back at Louisiana State University, and her one-semester research fellowship didn't afford her much more than whatever the corner market held in its clearance bins—that and her morning coffee indulgence. Poverty was proving to be a good diet tool, so she couldn't complain. How many people had a chance to live in London for four months, doing nothing but academic work for a master's degree? Never mind that the way she'd gotten here hadn't exactly been on the up-and-up. She would more than make up for it with her research results.

Curiosity outweighed hunger after a couple of bites, though. That envelope looked awfully thick and heavy—way more than a simple we'll-always-have-our-six-days-in-London good-bye note. It was a simple brown business rectangle with a metal clasp on the back. She ran her hands across it, then slid a nail underneath the flap to pop it open. It had been sealed well—not like one might fasten a hastily dashed-off, spur-of-the-moment note.

Weirder and weirder. Sam's sense of unease returned—the one she'd had when she'd awoken to find herself alone in the room, with the drawers and closet empty and no sign of Gary's luggage. Even the champagne stand and glasses he'd already had waiting in the room when they got in from the restaurant last night had been removed.

Something wasn't right.

She pulled out the contents, noting a folded white sheet atop what looked like a stack of photographs. She set the paper aside, confusion turning to hot anger when she saw the first image in glossy eight-by-ten detail. What kind of sick joke was this? That perv had sent her photos of . . .

Hot anger froze into icicle claws that sank into her heart and compressed her lungs. The photos were of her, with him, in this room last night. She recognized the shape of his body, but the face wasn't that of Gary Smith. It was someone else, someone she'd come to London to forget.

Fingers numb, heart racing, she flipped past image after image, more than half of them showing things she didn't remember doing. No doubt that it was her, though. Her face was always visible—not to mention everything else. By contrast, Gary Smith's face wasn't in any of them. Not a single one. Only the face of the man from Baton Rouge who hadn't been anywhere near the Bridestall Hotel.

Her memories of last night were fuzzy, but they weren't that fuzzy.

Underneath the last photo, which showed her head thrown back in what looked like pleasure, fingers twined through the man's hair (his face conveniently hidden), she found a smaller envelope.

What kind of sick freak had she been with last night? And by God, she'd faked that orgasm because one thing she *did* remember was that he'd been rough and clumsy, his mouth a virtual Grand Canyon with lips and a tongue. He'd been all about his own pleasure with little regard for hers. Except he apparently had an agenda.

How had he gotten pictures of David? How had he known about David at all when she'd left him and all the mess of their affair behind her in Baton Rouge?

Sam's fingers shook, partly from shock but just as much from anger, as she set the smaller envelope aside and unfolded the note. It wasn't on hotel stationery but plain white paper like one might find in any office setting in the world. Nor was it handwritten but printed on an ordinary ink-jet printer, by the looks of it. None of this made any sense whatsoever.

Oh God. Her focus froze on the salutation, just two words: "Dear Carolina."

No one outside a couple of juvenile court workers and a teacher back in Louisiana knew that Carolina Sonnier, juvenile felon with a three-strikes arrest record, was now Samantha Crowe, normally self-controlled graduate student with horrendous judgment in matters of love and sex.

How the hell could he have found out about Caro? She'd buried her other self behind sealed records and a carefully created web of lies.

Her lungs struggled to breathe under the weight of panic, and the walls that had seemed elegant a few minutes ago now threatened to suffocate her in their black-and-white textile excess. She didn't want to read any more, not here, not in a room he'd paid for and gone to a lot of trouble to set up for this sick joke.

I have to get out of here.

She stuffed the photos and papers back into the envelope and tucked the whole bundle into her oversized purse. Crammed her feet in the stupid heels she'd bought for her big night with the rich American who'd chatted her up at her corner pub only a week ago and—miracle of miracles—had seemed genuinely interested in her. Interested in her mind as well as her body, she'd thought. She had been upset after a text message from her mom, had gone to the pub to unwind, and had been bulldozed by the lavish attention, especially when he wanted to see her again, night after night.

On some level, she obviously still believed that interest from a well-groomed, wealthy man would prove She had been finally moved beyond the mean streets of New Orleans's impoverished, crime-riddled Eighth Ward, where violence and drugs would suck you down and then spit you out like last week's gumbo.

All the attention from this man had proved was that, once again, she'd been an absolute fool.

Looking around the room to make sure she'd left nothing but her self-esteem behind, Sam tugged down the hem of the black dress she'd thought such a tasteful and practical purchase before she left Baton Rouge. It had been intended to see her through any evening events she might need to attend while in London.

Well, she'd had an evening event, all right.

She kept her gaze trained on the marble floor when the hotel doorman greeted her and opened the heavy, glass-paned door for her to exit the lobby onto the city street, busy at midmorning with traffic and shoppers, tourists and business people. Common sense told her the doorman couldn't possibly know she wore last night's dress, couldn't know the shameful contents of the envelope in her purse, but her nerves screamed otherwise. For all she knew, every hotel staff member had gotten a copy. Not that they'd understand the full significance of the expertly doctored photos.

The hour it took her to travel across town to Bayswater by bus and tube helped slow her heart rate and give her some perspective, sitting there among tourists and commuters and students all going about their normal business. She had freaked out and run before reading the letter. Gary Smith obviously had money, judging by his choice of hotel and the cash he'd thrown around all week. He'd claimed to be a venture capitalist, and if he had half a brain, he'd realize a grad student wouldn't make good blackmail material. Unless he demanded payment in history textbooks and the occasional romance novel, she had nothing Gary Smith could possibly want.

Maybe Gary was the one in trouble. Maybe he was the target and she was the pawn.

Seriously, Samantha or Caro or whoever you are. Get a freaking clue. What are the chances his name is even Gary Smith?

She silenced her inner nag, whose strident voice had tried to warn her a few times that Gary Smith was too good to be true. Instead, she clung to the perverse hope that the man was a victim of violence rather than a sociopath, hanging on to that possibility until she arrived at her studio apartment in a decidedly middle-class-going-funky neighborhood a few blocks and a world away from Kensington Palace.

By the time she reached the top floor, she'd convinced herself she should be worried about him. Gary might be hurt. This could be some kind of bizarre ransom demand. After all, London was a huge city. It wasn't like the mean streets in her hometown, where the criminals often knew the victims, or even the political pathways in her current city of Baton Rouge, where most of the criminals worked in the state capitol. Gary was a rich American, and that made him a target.

She jiggled her bag to get at the key ring in the bottom, still un-accustomed to carrying only one key. She had no car to lock, no office to lock. Just a mailbox key that also fit into the lock of an attic room so tiny that if she stood with her legs apart, one shin could touch the edge of the undersized twin bed and the other the ledge of the narrow futon that served as a sofa. The flat also boasted one cane-bottomed chair and a small round table that held her laptop, a kitchen where she could reach everything without moving her feet, and a bathroom too small to turn around in. All that luxury for only $1,500 American a month and "quite an amazing steal," the leasing agent had insisted when she'd rented it online.

She let herself in and collapsed on the futon, refusing to open her purse until she'd recovered from her eighty-eight-step climb—she knew because she counted them every time she went up or down. She kept thinking it would get easier, but after almost three months she still was gasping lungsful of air by the time she got to the sixty-step mark.

Finally, armed with a bottle of water, she reopened the packet, removing the photos and the smaller envelope, setting them all beside her on the faded red cushion of the futon. Again she unfolded the paper, and though the words "Dear Carolina" still sent chill bumps washing across her arms, she continued to read this time.

Dear Carolina:

Thank you for sharing ad nauseam your research and theories on the whereabouts of the crown jewels that England's King John had the misfortune to lose back in 1216. Now it's time to back up your claims. You have thirty days in which to locate the jewels.

Obviously, she was suffering from stress-induced hallucinations, because she couldn't possibly have read that right.

Sam read the first paragraph again, and it hadn't changed. Forget about Gary the Perv. He was now Gary the Certifiably Insane Freak. Find the crown jewels lost eight hundred years ago? The man was psychoballs.

Sam rattled the paper in frustration before lifting it to continue reading:

> *On November 15, your time will expire. If you have proven successful, you will be compensated for your efforts once the crown jewels have been turned over to me.*
>
> *If you have failed, the contents of the attached folder will be delivered to the dean of the LSU Graduate School.*

That son of a bitch. Sam set the letter aside and got up to pace the small patch of worn carpet between the bed and futon. Gary, or whatever his name was, shouldn't have made the mistake of underestimating her. She had changed her identity, her background, and her whole life, then worked her ass off to not just have a different kind of life but make it a good one.

If she had just been alone in the photos—or with whoever Gary Smith really was—she wouldn't care. It would be embarrassing to have her assets—and everything else—splashed all through the history department. Her face heated at the thought of her professors and classmates seeing the photos.

But even when it was eventually proven that the photos had been doctored, it would be too late. Once they were out, David's career would be tainted beyond repair.

And to think she'd wasted brain cells worrying about this frogsnout being in some kind of trouble. Find the crown jewels that every treasure hunter and his dog had been trying to discover for almost a thousand years? And do it in a month? Right.

She stomped back to her seat on the futon to finish the letter, hoping it had a way for her to contact "Psycho," as he would forevermore be known to her.

> *Should you decide the photos are not enough to entice your cooperation, maybe the contents of the smaller envelope will convince you. That, too, will be delivered not only to your dean but the university president, your student newspaper, your academic sponsors, and anyone else who might be interested in knowing that you fucked your way into that prestigious fellowship you're so proud of.*
>
> *I'll be watching you, even as I continue to relive the pleasure of last night. You have more sexual talent than your plain looks suggest. Best piece of ass I've had in a long time, and I mean that with all sincerity. Guess Professor David Thompson thought so, too. I hear he's up for the deanship next year; pity for him to lose his career over you. You're good, but you aren't that good.*
>
> *Yours,*
>
> *"Gary"*
>
> *P.S. I hear your mother is in need of a new drug supplier. Perhaps I can help.*

Heat spread across Sam's face and neck, and her hands seemed to operate independently of her numbed brain, refolding the sheet of paper and reaching for the white envelope. It was about a six-by-nine, but thick with folded papers. She closed her eyes for a few moments when she saw what they were, then forced herself to flip through them. She didn't stop to read the details of the court records that were supposed to be sealed, but she saw enough to know it was all there. What she'd done to survive. How she'd been caught. Made an example of. Served time.

But her arrest record wasn't what that last paragraph referred to. No, it could only refer to something Psycho couldn't possibly know. Yet, he obviously did.

Bile rose in her throat when she saw the last three pages that were clipped to the arrest reports. She threw the folder on the floor, scattering obscene photos and the ugly details of her life—all her mistakes—across the thin, cheap rug that covered the hardwood.

Not all her mistakes. Her biggest mistake had taken place last night in Suite 202 of the Bridestall Hotel.

She made it to the lavatory just in time to lose her expensive breakfast—far more expensive than anything posted on the room-service menu. Acid burned into the lining of her esophagus as she collapsed to the tile floor, her back against the sink, her feet sticking out into the living area. And she could still see them, those last sheets of paper.

They were crystal-clear printouts of pages from her private journal, pages in which she'd gone on and on about how guilty she felt that she'd slept with David, her grad-school adviser. Sam had thought they had something real, right until the moment she'd overheard a colleague asking about the wife and kids he'd neglected to mention.

When he'd tried to buy her silence by putting together a highly embellished recommendation packet that would win her the fellowship to continue her research in England, she'd been hurt enough, and stupid enough, to go along with it. Not to guarantee her silence— she was too ashamed of that affair and her own stupidity to ever tell anyone.

She'd taken it because she was hurt. She'd taken it to punish him and to get some distance.

David had used and hurt her, but Sam knew she had to own her bad choices. She didn't want to ruin his career, and this would do it. Universities could put a positive spin on a student from a disadvantaged background. Even a criminal background could be turned into a bad-girl-makes-good story since hers weren't crimes of violence.

But the greatest college PR spinners couldn't save a professor who screwed a student, or who manipulated records and recommendations to pull in a research fellowship. Maybe she could have earned it on her own, but now she'd never know. She'd told herself it was okay, that her research would prove she'd deserved it.

Now, Psycho had enough ammunition to ruin them both.

Finally, through the fog of her shock came the creepiest sensation of all, the thing that sent chills up her spine and wrapped tendrils of fear around her numbed brain.

Gary Smith had gotten her journal, and her journal was on her laptop hard drive.

Her laptop was always in this room or in her messenger bag, at her side. She'd never left it alone with him.

He had been here.

CHAPTER 2

Swamps. He couldn't escape them.

With every step across the rugby field, Brody Parker sent chunks of mud cascading off his feet and legs like Pigpen in the old Charlie Brown cartoons. He stopped at the edge of the field and beat the football against the sole of each shoe, knocking off as much of the thick brown muck as he could before getting into the matchbook-sized car sitting at the closest end of the parking lot.

In Florida, people called this kind of land a swamp. Here in Lincolnshire, they called it a fen. Which was nothing more than a fancy name for swamp.

"I still say this isn't proper football, Parker!" Jet Worthington shouted through the window of an even smaller car parked several yards away. "You Yanks are nothing but thugs in uniforms."

Brody scratched the side of his head with a middle finger and heard an appreciative laugh from the rest of the guys who were still walking off the mud pit they called a field.

"We might not look as pretty, but we tackle like men!" he yelled in return. "Same time Saturday?"

"Right then."

Brody was the lone American living in *ye olde* esteemed village of Swineshead, population about two thousand on a good day. Today, like every day, he spent a few seconds thanking God that he'd found it, or that someone had found it for him. Thanking God that even with his reconstructed right knee, the one he'd be bathing in sports cream for the next few hours, he could indulge in an occasional game of football.

It still amazed him that this close-knit community had accepted him, even welcomed him. Most of the residents had deep, centuries-old roots here going back to when Christ rode a donkey, but they had taken him to be exactly what he claimed: a distant nephew of old Parson John Jessop, whose own family had deep, deep ties to Lincolnshire and neighboring Nottinghamshire.

The parson had died seven years ago, a confirmed bachelor at the petrified age of 103, and unless it was sometime in the Stone Age, his DNA and Brody's had never crossed paths. Brody had never heard of the man, or the town, until a week before he "inherited" the ancient Jessop cottage in the middle of Nowhere, England. Brody had arrived with a new name, British citizenship papers, a suitcase of clothes with price tags still attached, and the little white VW that had been covered in mud almost from the moment he entered the county.

Swineshead was the perfect spot for a man like him, and to his eternal surprise, he found himself happier and more content than he had any right to be, all things considered. He'd managed to convince Jet and a few other regulars at the local pub to let him try to enlighten them with lessons in American football one or two mornings a week. They even pretended to enjoy it. They weren't friends, exactly, but helped stave off the worst of the loneliness. Most of the time.

Brody took a longing glance at the Grainery on his way through town but decided against stopping for an early dinner. He was starving, and they made a fine burger not so different from what he might get back home in Florida. At least it was close enough to satisfy the occasional bout of homesickness.

Not that Florida had been home for a long time, and not that it would ever be home again.

He was way too muddy for polite company, however, so he continued onto the village's narrow high street, past regal, old St. Mary's Church and the local art gallery where some of his own work was on display, and then worked his way east along Abbey Road. These weren't the bucolic, rolling green hills of England, for sure—Swineshead sat too near the fens that stretched between where the River Welland and the River Witham converged near the North Sea.

So it was flat and often wet—kind of like south Florida without the heat and stifling humidity.

But home had never been the sweet shade of green this place would turn in spring. The fields and pastures stretching away from either side of the narrow road would be painted in bright, rich grasses and blanketed with white-and-yellow patchworks of wild-flowers. Even this time of year, when the weather was dreary and the fields brown, the memory of the green to come struck a chord of peace somewhere deep inside him. It triggered contentment and hope—two things he'd never expected to feel again when he'd been ferreted out of the US.

That color was why he'd been unable to resist taking up painting after arriving in town. He'd thought all his artistic impulses had been browbeaten out of him as a kid. Now his landscapes and character studies sold well enough to support him and let him avoid mean-ingful work that would put him in close proximity to other people. Artists were solitary, and except for the occasional pint at the pub and the odd game of football, Brody needed to keep his life as soli-tary as possible.

A half a mile east of Swineshead, just past the former site of the medieval Cistercian abbey, he pulled into a drive that ran between two groves of trees whose leaves were beginning to carpet the ground in orange, red, and gold. The road to the Jessop cottage was more a rock-strewn path than a driveway, which suited him perfectly. Unless one knew where to look, one wouldn't find it.

Brody stopped the car where the loose gravel ended. To the left, a dirt path led through a chest-high brick wall to a small clearing surrounded by trees. Ahead lay a narrow opening in a seven-foot wall built of the same tan-and-gray brick as the house. The roses, for which he could take no credit, were dormant now, but they'd bloom again. They'd been here when he arrived and would probably be coloring the landscape long after he died, hopefully as aged as old Parson John.

He tossed the football in a bin a few yards from the back door and stopped to pull a couple of dead leaves off the ivy that draped the bottom half of the cottage. Toeing off his muddy athletic shoes, he took a careful look around for killer spiders, of which the old house seemed to have an abundance. He'd almost as soon face a guy with a gun as a spider, not that he'd admit that to anyone.

According to his British contact, who'd found both the house and the alleged ancestor Jessop, the cottage sat on two acres and dated back to the 1600s, when it had begun life as an almshouse. Before that, the land had made up part of the original holdings of the now-long-gone Swineshead Abbey. It was only forty miles southeast of Sherwood Forest, and Robin Hood's bad King John had a place in Swineshead history, as anyone well into his pints at the Black Dragon Pub would be willing to tell you.

The almshouse bit was more than ironic. Until his paintings had begun to sell, Brody had been in danger of needing charity himself. He continued to take an occasional tenant in the small apartment over the detached garage he used for storage; he still didn't trust his artistic skills enough to support him without a backup plan.

Brody crossed the postcard-sized, neat courtyard toward the door, glancing up out of habit at the camera peeking discreetly from the ivy. The small security light, a pinhead-sized glow he could only spot because he knew exactly where to look, wasn't green as it should be. It blinked red.

What the hell?

He swallowed a rise of panic until common sense kicked in. He hadn't made much noise other than closing the car door. Whoever had tripped his security system, if the intruder were still here, might not have heard him, which would give him an advantage.

And it might be just that—an ordinary intruder. Not someone after him specifically. He'd been here for seven years undetected; no reason to think that had changed.

Brody moved quietly back to the car and popped open the trunk, reaching in to remove a small-caliber pistol from the covered well that housed the jack and tire-changing assembly. England wasn't like the US when it came to firearms. Here, normal citizens—especially football-playing foreigners with bad knees pretending to be artists—didn't carry guns.

Brody had two but didn't advertise the fact lest anyone wonder why he might need them or, worse, start checking into his past. His .45 was tucked inside a hidden compartment in the frame of his sofa.

He kept this baby for emergencies, which today's circumstances might or might not be.

Leaving the trunk open for the sake of stealth, he peered over the wall to the small, hidden parking spot in the clearing. At the sight of a dark-blue sedan, the drain of adrenaline from his muscles was immediate. What was Cynthie doing here?

His British contact, Cynthia Reid, was the only person outside a couple of FBI agents who knew his true identity—or what used to be his true identity. For all intents and purposes, and according to the *New York Times*, the man from Miami, Florida, known as Nathan Freeman was dead and six feet under. But Cynthie rarely made the two-hour drive from London without calling first.

She'd also never before used the key to Brody's house. Something didn't feel right, and Brody's scalp tingled as the hairs on the back of his neck rose in warning. It was his body's old danger antenna, rusty now but still working, pumping adrenaline back into the same limbs from which it had so recently receded.

Avoiding the loose stones of the path, he went to the door, walking as quietly as he could. He slid his fingers around the knob and turned it slightly, stepping to the side as the door swung open on well-oiled hinges.

All was silent, but for the distinctive click of a gun's safety being released.

CHAPTER 3

"You're a lunatic. You said you had a simple surveillance job. Get someone to photograph you with that unfortunate girl, you said. Take the photos to a trusted source to get them altered. Now you want me to traipse around rural Lincolnshire making sure she follows orders? You'll get us both killed, or worse."

"You can find some pawn to do the traipsing for you. Besides, what's worse than being killed?"

Tom Nelson stood at the hotel window overlooking another rainy late autumn day in London, his hands restless as they moved from his pockets to straighten his tie, then tug at the lapels of his jacket. "What's worse than death? Exposure. Prison. You know—ruin."

"Don't be a drama queen." Brent Sullivan—or Gary Smith, as his own recent pawn knew him—swiped a finger across the screen of his new tablet computer, watching as the brilliant little machine read his fingerprint, verified his identity, and popped up his latest e-mails ranked by importance.

Another swoosh of his finger. Nice. The new operating system worked well. The applications his people had developed for it would earn him another billion by this time next year *if* his investment panned out and it got snapped up by one of his tech-design competitors. And his hunches usually proved true.

"It's a good offer," Brent said. "The risk is minimal. You find someone to watch the girl, check in on her occasionally, and let me know what's going on, make sure she gets what she needs to do the job. Exert a little pressure if she wanders off course. Ten percent's a big cut for thirty days of work. Easy peasy."

With a few more swipes across the touch pad, Brent transferred a seven-figure sum from his home account in San Francisco to his London bank, and then to the account number Tom had given him. It should be plenty to cover the man's 10 percent of the value of the treasure he was seeking, plus expenses. Paying him up front would ensure he did as he was told, honorable old bastard.

Brent wasn't worried about him coming around. He'd grumble awhile, then he'd do whatever he was told. They'd done this dance before and the result never changed. Tom was C7, and once a member, always a member.

Besides, Tom loved the rush as much as the rest of them. The C7 were the Collectors, an exclusive club of seven adrenaline junkies with a taste for competitive games, unlimited money to raise the stakes, and the balls to play God with other people's lives.

No, make that five true junkies. One had died, and Tom Nelson was a charity case.

"Easy peasy. Bloody hell." Tom scrubbed a strong, blunt-fingered hand through his salt-and-pepper hair and returned to where Brent sat at the suite's dining table. Still damp from his two-block walk in the mist, his hair lay plastered to his head except for a few strands his fidgeting had formed into a spiky helmet. But he remained a physical presence in his early forties, still looking every bit the street detective he'd once been, right down to the ill-fitting black suit and skewed tie.

Brent resisted making Columbo jokes. Tom didn't have much of a sense of humor and probably didn't watch reruns of old American-detective TV shows.

After bouncing around MI5 and its home office, the detective now worked in the hallowed halls of the recently formed National

Crime Agency as part of an organized crime unit. He had a convenient set of skills for any C7 needs in Great Britain.

And Brent's quest was a huge one. After all, if one were scheming to obtain one of the most sought-after treasures in British history—and do it right under the noses of Parliament and the God-Save-the-Queen herself—who better to help than someone highly placed in the British version of the FBI?

Tom slumped in the straight-backed chair and poured himself a cup of coffee. "You could've afforded a spot of tea, you cheap bastard."

Brent stifled a small smile. If the man was grumbling about tea, that meant he was already caving in. "Coffee's good for you." The caffeine might improve his disposition.

"What is it you're after, Sullivan?" Tom rummaged in the basket of baked goods that had been delivered an hour ago and extracted a muffin. After slathering enough butter on it to harden the arteries of half of London, he settled back in his chair. "C7 members seldom take on partners when they identify the treasure they're going after. You declare your thirty-day period and shut everyone else out. Is this one personal, or do you just have so many millions to throw around that you don't mind dropping a crumb or two my way?"

Brent topped off his own coffee, absently rubbing at a drop that had spilled onto his jeans. This hotel room, the one he'd actually been staying in for the past seven days while in London, was much nicer than the one he'd rented as Gary Smith for last night's sexual Olympics.

"Ten percent's a fucking fortune with this job," he assured Tom. "This is major. Maybe you'll luck out and I won't need you beyond last night's little photo session and a few phone calls. But I'm leaving England tomorrow and need someone in place to keep an eye on things. Just find yourself a contact in Lincolnshire by close of business and stay on top of the situation. You can always call me on my private line if something else comes up."

He dug in his pocket and slid a disk across the table. "There's your own personal copy of last night's porn debut by my alter ego Gary Smith. You set it up to be photographed and got the photos doctored; you should at least get to enjoy the results. Plus, you'll have them on hand in case Samantha Crowe needs to be reminded of what's at stake. Nice work, by the way. They're pretty damned graphic, and it would take a trained eye to tell they'd been doctored. You kept my face out of it completely."

Tom chewed slowly and didn't crack a smile. "What about your arse?"

Brent laughed. "My ass looked absolutely spectacular, of course." And his target for last night, the mousy little Louisiana graduate student named Samantha Crowe—or at least that was the name she currently used—should have the fruits of their efforts in her hot little hands by now. No doubt the breakfast he'd ordered for her was tasting more than a little sour.

Tom took the disk and slid it back toward Brent, his bottom lip curled. "No thanks. Share them with someone with a greater interest in your arse. You're not my type, and I doubt that girl will forget your threat."

"*Our* threat. You're such a proper old fart." Brent slipped the disk into his laptop sleeve, watching as Tom sipped his coffee. The man's hands shook slightly, and Brent wondered, not for the first time, if the guy were losing it. He'd been against bringing the agent into C7 from the beginning but had been outvoted.

It wasn't like Tom had joined out of any deep-seated desire to play treasure hunter. He'd simply been desperate to pay off a big gambling debt before his wife found out, and he'd been willing to trade his skills for a cut in C7 so they could continue to live well beyond their means. The members who had wanted to include him thought his law enforcement experience would come in handy, especially for surveillance and background checks.

If Tom were developing a pesky conscience, however, he'd have to be eliminated, and not just from the Collectors. Brent wondered if he needed to hire someone to watch his watchdog, to make sure Tom didn't balk.

"You got a problem with the organization, Tom? Is C7 getting too hot for you?"

"Of course not." Tom's steely blue-eye gaze settled on Brent. "I just don't like the timing. Tell me what you're after so I'll know it's worth the risk. We all agreed that C7 was out of business until this unpleasantness with your secretary of state was a year past. It's been only six months."

"Our *late* secretary of state," Brent corrected. The cofounder of C7 and a Texas oil billionaire who'd gotten too greedy, the former secretary of state and presidential hopeful was no longer among the living. Facing political ruin and criminal indictment, he'd shot himself, or so everyone believed. "The media's accepted the suicide story and moved on, and that's good enough. We're safe and clear."

He set his coffee aside and pulled a file folder from the stack of papers on the edge of the table. "The feds attribute the secretary of state's suicide to a trail of tax-evasion charges he couldn't shake. The house of cards had started to fall, and he took the coward's way out before C7 could be exposed. Or so the story appears. I wouldn't know for sure, of course."

Tom narrowed his eyes, and Brent waited for him to ask the cop question: Was Brent behind the man's supposed suicide?

After a few seconds, however, Tom simply nodded. "I don't want to know any more about it. Not a bloody thing. If you're willing to risk starting up the C7 games again, I guess the rest of us will have to play. Although now I suppose we're C6."

Brent knew the detective didn't like him, or any of the other C7 members, but as long as Tom Nelson did as he was told, Brent didn't give a rat's ass if he were popular. "We'll be seven again soon. I'm flying to Cartagena tomorrow to recruit a new member. The deal's all but done. He's rich, not to mention a mean son of a bitch. Perfect for us, in other words."

Tom's thin lower lip thinned even more, and the deeply carved lines on either side of his mouth compressed as if he'd sucked too hard on a lemon. "Is it drug money we're courting now? Do we really want to bring in someone who's made his fortune that way?"

"You're hardly in a position to judge." Brent's anger rose, sharp and hot, but he hid it behind a raised eyebrow and a smile. Sanctimonious British prig. A lot of people underestimated Brent Sullivan, and he always proved them wrong. Always. If they got in his way, he removed them. It was as simple as that. Tom was on thin ice.

Brent might only be thirty, but he'd grown up on the wrong side of the San Francisco Bay. Hard work and a willingness to take risks had moved him "from the outhouse to the penthouse," as the saying went. He wouldn't apologize for it, and if his hands had gotten dirty, who the hell cared?

Small-minded Tom Nelson thought the C7 games were about money and finding lost treasure, but he was dead wrong. The games were about power, pure and simple. The power to take big risks. The power to force people into doing things they wouldn't normally do—people like Samantha Crowe and, yes, even people like Tom Nelson. The treasure? That was a bonus.

He feigned a jovial smile. "C'mon, Tommy. You're as greedy a bastard as the rest of us, admit it. You like that fine house you and the wife live in. The vacations every summer. Plus, this is a treasure you'll want to be in on, being as you're such a fine English gentleman." Brent slid the file folder across the table, tapping the top of it before leaving it for Tom to open. "You asked for details, but remember. Once you read it, you can't unread it. And ten percent's all you're getting."

Tom's conscience appeared to have finally gone on holiday or had been beaten down by curiosity. Drug money and exposure apparently as forgotten as last week's lottery number, the hand he reached out to flip open the manila folder was steady as the Rock of Gibraltar. He scanned the folder's contents with the practiced eye of someone accustomed to reading police reports, looked up at Brent with a frown, then took the file to the window. He pulled out a pair of reading glasses and pored over the folder's contents again, slowly, with his back to the room. Though the American forms probably differed from the ones Tom was accustomed to reading, the language of background checks was universal, so there was no doubt Tom would understand it all. Samantha Crowe, or Carolina Sonnier, had amassed quite a dossier in her teenage years.

The detective closed the folder and returned to his chair. "So you have an American student with a rather sordid past, questionable ethics, and a research project that centers around a spot in Lincolnshire. This is the star of your blackmail photos? What could she possibly know that you'd risk exposure of C7 this soon after the secretary of state's suicide?"

Brent grinned. "The research, Tommy, the research." He leaned forward. "If her hunch is true, what I'll get from this particular game will twist your fellow countryman's knickers, or whatever you call them. You should like that."

Tom's eyes took on a wicked glint, the most enthusiasm he'd shown so far today. There was no love lost between the NCA agent and the other British C7 member, a bored, philandering—but extremely wealthy—member of the minor peerage whose arrogance was anything but minor. "If it makes Lord George Andrews unhappy, then I'm for it. What's this oh-so-valuable thing you're trying to acquire?"

Brent had been so certain that Tom would eventually cooperate, he'd already called Lord George and the other members of C7 to start the time clock. According to C7 game rules, he had thirty days to get his hands on the treasure before the other members could either start looking or give up the quest if it proved too difficult. Every day for a month, unless the treasure were found first, he had to pay a million bucks to be split by the other C7 members. It was chump change, and this treasure would recoup that $30 million many times over.

"Think back to your history lessons," he told Tom. "You're familiar with the story of bad King John?"

Tom poured more coffee and loaded it with so much sugar he might need a fork to consume it. No wonder the Brits had bad teeth.

"Of course," Tom said. "Evil lot, he was. And almost gave us to France." Anything smacking of the French, Brent had learned, automatically counted as a sin to a true and proper Englishman.

"That's the one." Brent leaned forward again and spread his hands on the table, his blood stirring at the idea of what he'd learned from Samantha Crowe. And to think it had all been happenstance. He'd wandered into a pub out of sheer boredom his first night in London for a series of business meetings. He'd struck up a conversation with a rather plain girl after he heard her American accent.

She'd blown his mind with the possibilities that her theories opened up. So he'd spent the last six days avidly courting her, playing the role of the adoring suitor, just to find out what she knew and how sure she was of her hunches.

Brent loved following hunches: big gambles, but also big rewards.

"Next question: What's he most famous for, your evil old King John?"

Tom frowned. "Hell, Sullivan, do you know how long it's been since I studied history?" He tapped a finger along the side of his coffee cup. "Let me think. John signed the Magna Carta, of course. He was the baby brother of Richard the Lionheart. The bad guy in all the Robin Hood tales. The landowners hated him, and he was a right steady bastard. As I recall, he even . . ."

His voice trailed off, and his eyes widened. "As I recall, he even lost the bloody crown jewels. You think this Samantha Crowe"—he laid a hand on the folder, almost caressed it—"can help you find the royal crown jewels missing for almost a thousand years?"

Brent leaned back in his chair and grinned. "We'll find out, won't we?"

"Bloody hell." Tom sat back and shook his head. "Just one more question."

He handed the folder back to Brent. "You're getting to be better known in public circles these days, what with the recent magazine articles and such. What's to say, even if the girl succeeds, she won't recognize you one of these days when she's flipping through a bloody magazine? I agree, it's a huge prize if she finds it. But is it worth the risk?"

Brent shrugged, putting the file in his briefcase and snapping it closed. "It's only a risk if the girl lives to tell about it, Tom." He smiled at the deep frown on the detective's face. "And rest assured, she won't."

CHAPTER 4

Brody didn't wait for the pistol to appear or, worse, to be fired. As soon as he heard the sound of the safety being released, old instincts took hold and he charged in the door at full speed, his head down like the medieval-style battering rams the reenactors used over at the fairs in Sherwood Forest. Even a small-caliber pistol could kill at such close range, and he'd shown a remarkable gift for survival. He didn't plan to stop now, plus Cynthie might be in trouble.

Within a few seconds, Brody's head-butt slammed into the shooter's midsection, the gun went off with an ear-piercing blast, and they crashed to the old, scuffed hardwood floor. Brody's weight landed on his bad knee, sending shards of pain all the way up to his hip. On the other hand, he didn't have a bullet hole in him yet.

His assailant got a knee in the groin before he pinned the asshole beneath him . . . and found himself looking into a familiar pair of hazel eyes.

His adrenaline levels, which had been shooting up and down like a roller coaster since he'd seen the blinking security light, took another dip.

"Cynthie, what in God's name are you doing?"

"What am I doing? You're the one who just tackled me like one of your bloody American footballers." Cynthie Reid closed her eyes and puffed out a shaky breath—not that she'd ever admit it was shaky, at least not to him. "Why are you sneaking in like that? Didn't you see my car? I could've blown your brains to King's Lynn."

"I wasn't expecting to be met at the door with a gun. I thought you were a burglar." Brody rolled off the petite brunette, climbed to his feet, and reached down to help her up before taking a quick survey of the entryway. "Jesus. You shot a hole in my wall."

"Swineshead doesn't have burglars, and I'm sure your wall has seen worse." Cynthie stepped into the doorway and looked out, then grabbed Brody's arm and pulled him inside. She closed and locked the door before retrieving her gun from the floor. "Were you followed?"

Brody stared at his friend in disbelief. *Yes, friend.* Cynthie had been his lifeline for most of the last seven years, doing everything from brokering art sales, about which she knew nothing, to buying the pistol Brody now stuffed in his waistband—delivered with a lecture about not being caught with it. If he was caught with it, she'd deny knowing anything about it.

And yet here she was, holding not a tiny pistol that looked like a toy but a lethal fourth-generation Glock, near as he could tell. Her hands were steady, but Brody knew the agent could handle a firearm as well as he, but he couldn't resist plucking the pistol from her fingers before she did worse than shoot a hole in the wall of his entry hall.

"Paranoid much?" Taking a quick look out the window to make sure no one *had* followed him, Brody closed the curtains and turned on a lamp. "Better tell me what's going on, because, woman, you're freaking me out."

"That makes two of us, then, so it's only fair. I'm freaking *me* out. I detest guns."

"And yet there you were, waving one around like a badass American. It's a miracle you didn't shoot yourself." Brody walked into the adjacent kitchen and retrieved two sodas from the fridge, glancing around the corner at the front door lock, which was intact, and the ground-floor windows, also closed and locked.

At least he knew why the red light had been blinking; the security system was set to trip when a door or window opened, even with a key, and would stay on until he manually reset it with an alphanumeric code. He changed key codes once a month now. When he'd first arrived in Swineshead and installed the security system, he'd changed them every day, sometimes more than once.

He handed Cynthie one of the sodas and took the chair nearest the stone fireplace. It was Parson John's old relic of a recliner, covered in an ugly red-and-blue print that Brody thought displayed now-threadbare roosters and hens. But it was comfy and he couldn't bring himself to ditch it; it belonged here. Plus, for today's purposes, unless an assailant came down the chimney, it faced all the room's access points.

Cynthie sat on the sofa, her slender fingers clutching the glass soda bottle as if it might take a notion to fly away if she didn't hold on tightly. Her wedding ring clinked against the side. Wyland Reid, a manager at one of London's West End theaters, would likely not be amused to learn that his wife was running around rural Lincolnshire wielding a gun, despite her position with the NCA.

"Tell me what's going on."

"It's probably nothing, but I let my imagination run riot and here we are." Cynthie unbuttoned the dark jacket of the business suit she always wore to work but rarely after-hours, another sign she'd left London in a rush. Now it had dust bunnies hanging off it, from rolling around his entry hall floor.

And yet another sign of a hasty departure from the office: her dark hair was still pulled back in that twisty thing professional women seemed to like. She'd once admitted she wore it that way because it made her look more serious, maybe even helped overcome her petite stature and the large, earnest eyes that gave her a fragile look.

Despite her dislike of firearms and current attack of nerves, Cynthie Reid was not fragile. She was a pit bull in heels.

"I got an e-mail at work a couple of hours ago that I thought you should see."

Dread knocked out the last vestiges of Brody's postfootball happy mood. He watched her hand slip into her briefcase, rattling the sheets of paper as she pulled them out and held them toward him. He didn't want to take them.

As usual, she could read him like a first-grade primer. *See Brody run.* "Not looking at it won't make it go away, my friend. And as I said, I'm likely just being paranoid."

He sighed and ran a hand across his chin. He hadn't shaved this morning, and the stubble scratched his fingertips. The sensation was enough to ground him as he reached for the papers.

A lot of papers. An interoffice memo had been sent to alert National Crime Agency workers in Cynthie's department that there had been a breach of electronic files.

Brody looked up. "Decipher this for me."

She sipped her soda, then leaned over and set the bottle on the coffee table. "Agents in my division are notified if any background files pertaining to us or our contacts are accessed. Normally, it's easy to see who checked them and why. This one was from an unknown source, so we were alerted as a precaution." She gestured to the papers. "Once I saw the list that had been pulled, I printed it out so you could see what you thought."

Brody riffled through the remaining pages, which contained a list of names. One of them was his. "Give me the short version and I'll read the rest more closely later."

Cynthie's posture relaxed a little as her voice took on more of her usual in-charge-and-taking-no-prisoners tone. "A 'minor irregularity' is what my NCA director called it in the memo, bloody bureaucrat. But someone pulled the names of all the people in Lincolnshire with MI6 files."

Brody whistled. While MI5 handled domestic matters and had been rolled in with the new NCA, MI6 was like the CIA. It didn't mess with small-time hoodlums and petty thieves. Just international criminals, suspected terrorists, and, well, people like himself. "Special circumstances," as his situation had been called.

He scanned the list of names. "This many criminals live in Lincolnshire?"

Cynthie laughed and shook her head. "You of all people know how these things work. They're just like your federal agents. MI6 keeps files on all kinds of people for all kinds of reasons, some of which are utterly ludicrous, no doubt."

No doubt, indeed. "I see I made the list, though." Brody Edward Parker, age thirty-three, dual American and British overseas territory citizenship, residence Swineshead, Lincolnshire. "Did our mystery hacker access the sealed files? There's nothing here to tell them much more than they'd find in a phone directory."

He didn't like it. Not one bit. But there was no reason to panic yet. "Anything to indicate who pulled it? Anything to make you think it has something to do with me?"

"No, there's no reason to think you're involved, and as far as I could tell, no sealed files had been hacked. I just don't like any hint of a security breach. Call it a bad feeling."

Brody arched an eyebrow, and Cynthie threw up a hand in defense. "I know, I always tell you feelings are for people too lazy to do the legwork. But you have a good thing here, except that you need a woman. I don't want to see you displaced again. Forewarned is forearmed and all that."

"Displaced is a nice way of putting it." New name. New identity. He couldn't go through it again. Wouldn't. He'd been willing to say good-bye to Nathan Freeman when it became obvious there was no other choice, but he liked being Brody Parker, long-long-lost great-great-great nephew of Parson Jessop, late of Swineshead. "Keep your ears open and stay in touch. I'll dig around online and see what I can find out about some of the others on this list. Why did you drive up here instead of calling?"

"Since you're not paranoid, I thought one of us should be." Cynthie's eyes had lost their anxious look and regained their usual glint of mischief. "Besides, you didn't answer your phone, and Wyl has flown up to Edinburgh for a couple of days. I was bored and thought it would give us a chance to catch up. I hoped you might have some additional pieces for me to place in that new gallery of regional art opening over in Nottingham. They've been asking for more." Uh-huh. His NCA contact doubling as art agent had been awfully paranoid when he arrived home, but he got no sense that she was holding anything back. Even iron-vested agents could get the willies, although he'd thought Cynthie immune. "Glad to have the company. We can take dinner at the Grainery."

She hesitated, flicking a glance down to his bare feet, over the muddy shorts and T-shirt, and up to his unruly mop of dark hair that probably held its own share of mud. "I don't know if you're quite a proper dinner companion, plus you got mud and"—she brushed a dust bunny off her jacket—"stuff on my suit."

"What if I promise to bathe and loan you a clothes brush?"

She laughed. "Then you have a date."

"Give me ten minutes." He went into his bedroom, pushing the door shut partially before tugging his T-shirt over his head and tossing it on the floor.

"Brody, I forgot to ask—"

He froze in position, his back to the door. Damn it, Cynthie had followed him. She'd seen his back. Seen the ugliness he showed to no one. Ever.

Brody's first impulse was to turn around and pretend everything was normal. His second impulse was to pull the shirt back over his head. He did neither, his limbs cemented in place. He closed his eyes and took a deep, steadying breath. "I'll talk to you after my shower, okay?"

"It's not so bad, Brody." Her soft tone held pity, and he hated that. "I knew you'd been burned."

Knowing and seeing were different, and he had no intention of discussing it. "Give me ten minutes, okay?"

"Right then."

Only when her footsteps grew faint enough for him to be sure she'd gone back into the den did Brody exhale. It would be fine. Cynthie wasn't a date, or even a vague romantic possibility. She was a friend, happily married, and he'd trusted her with most of the ugly details of his life. He had a lot of them. His tortured, mangled skin was just one more.

They'd have dinner, chat, and he'd fix up his spare room for the night; the apartment over his garage needed cleaning out. Then he'd go into the little room off his bedroom where he kept his security monitors and computer. Once he fired up his laptop, he'd try to figure out why the hell someone wanted to see who in Lincolnshire had MI6 files and what they might be looking for.

CHAPTER 5

Tom rubbed his eyes and glanced at the clock on the wall of his den, then at his wife, who'd curled up in an armchair. "You shouldn't have let me doze off, love."

Donna Nelson looked up from the computer printout she'd been reading and smiled. Despite the knots of worry tangled in his gut, Tom couldn't help but smile in return. Her affection and patience and acceptance warmed him, even after twenty years of marriage. Especially after the past twelve hours.

"You needed the rest, Tommy. Not that those two hours of sleep will keep you alert today—and you're going to need to be alert."

His mistake had been lying down to read, but every one of his muscles felt as if it had been pounded flat and run through a pasta press. He'd gone the emotional equivalent of a marathon in the past two days, from being summoned by that crude upstart Brent Sullivan and treated like so much trash on his shoes to being ordered into that sordid business with the girl in the hotel room as if he were no more than a low-rent private eye, and all for what? So a pup with more money than God, and as crass and arrogant as anyone Tom had ever met, could potentially walk away with something that belonged rightfully to the people of England?

All the while, good old Tom Nelson did the actual dirty work of leaning on the pawns as well as hiring someone to help him do the leaning. Even if it were to earn him a lot of money, it would be dirty money. Blood money. Sullivan had made that clear.

It ate at him from the inside out. The chances of the girl succeeding were slim, but that was almost beside the point. Sullivan would kill her, whether she succeeded or not, because she'd be a loose end the man thought he could eliminate without consequences. Tom had seen enough of her files to know he was right. No one would mourn the death of Samantha Crowe.

Tom wanted out of C7, he was drowning in guilt, and he wanted nothing more to do with the likes of Brent Sullivan. He just didn't know what to do about it.

Sullivan had been clear on what he *should* do, though, hadn't he? Made it clear that Tom was only included in C7 by the others' charity and their need for the services he could provide. Made it clear that however much the authorities thought the American secretary of state's death was a suicide, it wasn't—and let that be a warning. Made it clear that the greed and weakness of character that had led Tom to join C7 in the first place now had him trapped.

Remaining in C7 was onerous. Leaving C7 would be lethal.

If they were willing to kill the bloody American secretary of state and presidential hopeful, they'd not hesitate to have a midlevel NCA investigator knocked off.

After his meeting with Sullivan, Tom had spent the next couple of hours walking the streets of London, paying no mind to where he was going. He kept reshuffling the problem of the C7 like the same worn deck of cards that had been his downfall, hoping he could deal them onto the gaming table in a new configuration that would give him a way out. He kept coming up with the same losing hand.

The city sidewalks had been slick with mist, the day shrouded in the rain-soaked fog that had become a London weather cliché. He'd ended up at Nelson's Column, a place he often walked to remind himself why he'd chosen to work in law enforcement even as the London agencies formed and reformed, shuffling him from post to post. He'd gone along and taken whatever they handed him: duty and all that rot.

Only today, instead of beaming down with dignified pride as he usually did, Tom's great-great-great-uncle Admiral Lord Nelson frowned down on him in heroic disapproval. A true relation of mine, he seemed to say, would never have allowed himself to be trapped in such a situation.

In the end, Tom had gone to the only person in whom he dared confide, the one for whom he'd sold his soul to avoid having her discover his weakness for gambling and cards. They'd sat at the kitchen table where they often took their meals. After hearing him out, his story told in halting sentences and bursts of apology and regret, Donna Nelson had shaken her head, her hair still as red as the day they'd married, but for the tiniest hint of gray.

She'd made a few comments about fools and gambling. She'd paced awhile and left the room, no doubt to console herself in the bedroom they'd recently had redecorated. They'd lived well beyond what his job could afford, both of them. It wasn't an excuse, but just a fact.

Eventually, Donna had returned to the kitchen with red-rimmed eyes, made him tea, and sent him back to work with the suggestion that he put his cyberintelligence training to work by riffling through the MI6 files for a suitable pawn.

She, meanwhile, would research the bad old king and his lost treasure.

As it turned out, there was a boatload of theories about what happened to the crown jewels back in 1216. The American girl's ideas were no more far-fetched than many of the others.

Donna had been all business so far, but he needed to know how she felt. Not about the mess; it was quite unforgivable. But about him, because much too late, he'd realized he had underestimated her strength and her capacity for understanding.

"Do you hate me, Don? I can't blame you if you hate me. I hate myself. Stupid." He sat up and waited for her answer, dread and hope mingled. Oh, he knew she didn't really hate him—couldn't hate him any more than he could ever hate her. But her disappointment in him, her lack of true forgiveness, would be just as painful. As he'd floundered in an emotional sea the past three days, since receiving that first phone call from Brent Sullivan, he'd come to realize that she was his anchor, always had been. He might carry the badge, but she had the strength.

"I know where to place the blame, and it isn't with you, at least not entirely." Donna set aside her files and came to sit beside him. He pulled her against him, inhaling the floral scent of her shampoo, taking comfort in the familiar curve of her shoulder pressing against his side.

"Do I wish you'd never become involved with that lot of bastards?" Her voice was silk, edged in steel. "Of course, and I'd have told you so if you'd asked me. We'd have handled it together if you'd come to me instead of hiding it. I know part of it's my fault; I pressure you to spend more than we should. I know that I complain about things around the house and you try to make them right. But not this way. We can do with less and I will help. You believe that, don't you?"

"Of course, love." Their home wasn't anything Tom cared much about, though he'd never tell her. He wanted a quiet, comfortable life with his fiery-haired wife, and he wanted to make her happy. Hadn't quite succeeded at that, had he?

Donna watched him closely. "Do you promise that you've stopped with the gaming? Pay me the respect of the truth, Tom."

"I haven't touched a card since the first job I did for that bloody lot of amoral arsewipes." Tom shook his head. "Ironic, really. They bailed me out of the mess I'd fallen into and then scared me so badly I didn't dare continue with those habits. Lost the taste for it."

He pulled her against him more tightly. "They have no souls, Don. Especially this Sullivan bloke. He frightens me, I have to admit, and you know that I don't frighten easily."

Donna sat quietly for a moment, and he thought she'd drifted off into her own thoughts. Then her shoulders stiffened, her back straightened, and she turned to face him. "We have to go through with our plan to get you away from them, as we talked about last evening. It will work, but only if you're willing to be as soulless as they are. Just this once, Tom. We'll beat Brent Sullivan at his own game and set a trap for him. We'll worry about what happens to the crown jewels when and if they're found. But you know what will have to be done."

She made it sound so simple when it wasn't simple at all.

"Don't forget." Tom leaned forward. "Brent could contact the girl directly, so I won't have complete control. It's too dangerous for me to go to her and openly try to sabotage Sullivan. She might tell him in order to play us against each other, and that would sign my death warrant. Someone else will need to watch her, and we have to be very careful whom we choose to do the work for us."

Traipsing about the far reaches of Lincolnshire would *be* dirty work. It comprised part of an area called the Wash, one of England's largest estuaries and fed by four rivers. It was mostly fen and fog this time of year. Not so swampy inland, but still rural.

Donna leaned over and retrieved the stack of folders she'd been holding when Tom awoke. "These are the people who have additional MI6 records that are stamped as being sealed. They weren't in the files. What does that mean?"

Tom stifled a yawn. "Could be any number of things. MI6 is international, so the person might have committed some type of offense in his home country—that's most common. Or be on a watch list that's classified for MI6. Suspected terrorists, for example, or people who've been known to have connections to a suspected terrorist organization. Or it could involve someone who isn't a regular British citizen but is living here permanently under some type of international arrangement." He took the stack from her. "How many are there with sealed files?"

"Only three in Lincolnshire. Two in Lincoln and one in Swineshead. If you branch out over the border into Norfolk, there are a couple in King's Lynn." She pulled a map of England from beneath the stack of folders. "How sure are you that this is the area where Brent Sullivan's person will be looking?"

"Absolutely sure. Swineshead in particular, so it's a spot of luck that there's a person there with an MI6 record. When Sullivan gave me the files to read, while he was busy gloating, I managed to go to the window and take scans with my phone." He'd also recorded their entire conversation. The self-obsessed toad hadn't even noticed.

"There weren't a lot of details on the girl's research," he said. "The files mostly contained reports of her brushes with the law so he could blackmail her, and a bit of improper university goings-on. But he'd made a few notes on the folder, enough to show she thinks old King John took the crown jewels with him to Swineshead instead of sending them along with his baggage train that sank into quicksand in the Wash." According to Donna's research, Swineshead had been almost on the coast back in those days. "This Samantha Crowe thinks the places people have looked over the centuries were off base."

The more he said it, however, the more unlikely the whole thing sounded. "Then again, wherever the old bastard's jewels are, they're probably buried under twenty feet of earth or water by now. Maybe we should just forget this whole thing. Let it play out. The chances of that poor girl finding anything are minuscule. And he's going to kill her whether she finds them or not."

"He won't kill her. Open your eyes, Tom. He'll order you to do it, and then where are you? A murderer." Donna's voice was hard and practical, and Tom's heart dropped into the soles of his boots. God damn the man. She was right.

"I won't. I've never done murder, and I won't start now." It went against everything he'd ever believed in. He'd sold his soul when he got involved with C7; he'd damn it to hell for all eternity if he killed on their behalf.

"Well, you can't try to save her either. I know it sounds cruel, but when Sullivan moves against her, you let it happen. It gives you more ammunition to use on him. We can't feel sorry for her, and we can't just sit back hoping she doesn't succeed."

Tom looked at the woman he'd shared a bed with, a life with, and wondered where this side of her had come from. She had feminine ways and gentle manners, his Donna. This woman was hard and practical; she frightened him almost as much as Brent. Almost.

"Listen to me, Tom. One mistake and we can lose everything, so buckle up and do it well. This is our best hope of getting you away from Sullivan and this C7 nonsense. We can't worry about what happens to the girl. Another opportunity to be on the inside of one of their schemes might not come around for months or years. It needs to be now, especially since someone in Swineshead has a sealed file. That's your way in, your way to find your own pawn to turn the game against Sullivan."

Tom closed his eyes, shame fighting with fatigue fighting with horror. "You realize what you're saying? If the girl finds the jewels, and yet we can't allow her to turn them over to Sullivan . . ."

"Then we will stop her ourselves, using our own pawn, and will set Sullivan up for it." Donna straightened the stack of folders with businesslike briskness. "We'll do what we have to in order to get you away from these bastards and protect our life and our home. First, though, you need to find the right person to do our mucking about in Lincolnshire. See if the bloke that lives in Swineshead has something dirty in that sealed file that you can use to control him. I looked up the address, and he lives near the site of the old Swineshead Abbey. He could be perfect."

She was talking about more blackmail, but that was how the C7 games worked, wasn't it? Find someone with a weakness to exploit. Same as they'd done to him, and now he'd be doing it to this guy in Swineshead.

"You're right, love. Perhaps he'll be a criminal who deserves a bit of arm-twisting." That would make things easier.

Donna gave him such a long, steady look that Tom wanted to crawl under the table. "I don't like it either, Tom, but it's the fastest way to get you out of C7. You don't want to be doing their dirty work for the rest of your life or until someone makes a mistake and you all end up in prison."

Tom fidgeted under her glare. "Don't worry. I can do what it takes." Oh yes, he could do it. The question was, could he live with himself afterward?

He looked at the folder Donna had handed him as if it might sprout a mouthful of daggerlike teeth and gnaw off an arm or leg. Then he sighed. "I'll retrieve his file. Tonight, we'll figure out how to destroy another poor bugger's life."

CHAPTER 6

The Bayswater Starbucks was Sam's one nonnegotiable habit. The menu bulged with a dozen types of brewed tea but only two nonespresso coffees, a simple roast and a decaf. She felt it her duty as an American to at least keep the employees' coffee-making skills sharp with a daily—or almost daily—visit. The breakfast assortment amused her, from the soy porridge and "Berry Good Bircher," which was basically oatmeal and yogurt, to her Sunday favorite, the "Sausage Buttie": Lincolnshire sausages on a soft roll with ketchup.

"But it's Thursday. You never order the 'Buttie' on a Thursday." The barista, a tall, emaciated blonde who'd likely never eaten a sausage in her life, much less one doused in ketchup and wrapped in a blanket of bread, flicked a sympathetic look over Sam. She probably was assessing everything from the blue circles under Sam's eyes—the result of no sleep in the last forty-eight hours—to the New Orleans Saints T-shirt to the messy ponytail she'd pulled her blond tangles into. "Then again, you look like you could do with some sausages. I'll even bring them to you."

"Thanks." Sam walked to the back and slid into a seat at the far corner table, then extracted her laptop from her satchel. Free wireless was another perk of the Starbucks, although Bayswater was awash in Internet cafés, and Internet access was one of the things that had finally pried her from her flat. She'd been sitting there for two days, afraid to leave, her chair propped beneath the doorknob.

She'd been trying to figure out what to do but had come up with no viable answers. Thus her desperate need for caffeine and Google.

While she waited for her computer to fire up and connect, she opened her bag and pulled out the mail she'd retrieved from the first-floor box on her way out. She'd only been in London two months and was on a limited-time student visa, so she rarely got anything beyond flyers and junk. Certainly no personal mail.

Most of her time in London had been spent in the British Museum, where she'd pored over the original Magna Carta—well, the English translation of the original Latin version. She'd inhaled every bit of trivia about the sad reign of King John, from the scholars who declared him the most evil king to ever walk the earth to the apologists who said he was misunderstood and his performance as king was underrated. The truth probably lay somewhere in between.

On the subject of the king's loss of his crown jewels, however, she'd found surprisingly little. Historians seemed to lose interest in a little thing like the disappearance of royal booty when the Magna Carta loomed so large.

Now that the ruin of her career—not to mention David's—was imminent, Sam had finally accepted that she had to abandon her traditional means of research, which was limited to studying obscure medieval documents, diaries, and account ledgers. Instead, she would spend her last month in England in the field. She'd have to pass on the normal research she'd planned to do in Lincoln and instead go to the village of Swineshead, maybe with a shovel or pickax. She'd be lucky if she didn't end up in jail.

Alongside her computer, she placed a folder containing train schedules and a map of England she'd picked up at a newsstand down the block. Once her food was ready, she propped the map against a plastic holder stuffed with sugar packets and ate while she

DEADLY, CALM, AND COLD

studied the area known as the Wash, just over a hundred miles north of London.

The most widely accepted theory about the lost treasure was that King John, en route to London from the north, had fallen ill and veered off to Swineshead to spend the night at the Cistercian abbey located there. He'd supposedly sent his baggage entourage with the jewels ahead of him through the swampy, unpredictable Wash. The baggage train had miscalculated the time of high tide and had been caught in quicksand. Everyone and everything had disappeared, sucked under. Animals, people, wagons, and jewels, including the king's scepter and crown.

Sam had another theory, and if she had any hope of proving it, she'd have to find a way to get to Swineshead with no car or money. And she needed to get there yesterday.

She wrenched her eyes from the map at the buzz of her cell phone. A text message. She didn't know anyone in England well enough for them to text her, and David had avoided her like the Black Plague since buying her silence with a boost to get this fellowship. They e-mailed terse, infrequent messages about her research and the progress of her thesis.

That left only two text options: her blackmailer and her mother, neither of whom she had much interest in hearing from. They both wanted more than she was able to give, were unpleasant to deal with, and had the potential to destroy her life.

Reluctantly, she reached for the phone. Dear old Mom had met her only child's news about this research trip with a "Who'd you sleep with to get that?" followed by a "Who's going to help me around this place?"

And damn it, she couldn't even claim a moral victory because of the way she'd gotten the money to pay for the trip. She'd just felt cheap.

Dear old Mom, who'd hit her up for cash before she left and had already texted her twice, including the drunken ramble that had sent

Sam off to the pub for her first ill-fated meeting with Gary the Black-mailer.

Dear old Mom, who'd find the cash to buy drugs or alcohol and pay her cell phone bill—but rarely managed to have enough to live on since Sam, her resident juvenile delinquent and enabler, had escaped into the world of academics.

The message was short: *Need rent $. Cm home whr U belong.*

Sam blinked back the tears that sprang up from nowhere and shoved the phone back in her pocket. She hadn't cried when the ass-hole blackmailed her, used her, and humiliated her. She hadn't cried when she discovered he'd gotten his hands on her computer. She'd been angry with herself.

So she wouldn't let herself crumble into a storm of self-pity over that stupid text. She'd never had the kind of mother who could be a confidante or a source of help. Elaine Sonnier had always been the needy one. Carolina was the strong one.

You still are strong, no matter what you call yourself. Don't forget it.

"Damn skippy," she muttered, pushing her plate off to the side and spreading the map in front of her. She thought big bad John had kept the crown jewels with him, and if so, she thought the most likely spot for them to be lost was Swineshead, on the grounds of the former abbey, and not farther south or east into the Wash.

She found the dot on the map and blew out a frustrated breath. Getting around was the problem. She could lease a car if she let next month's rent slide; if she didn't succeed in this idiotic mission she'd been given, she'd be crawling back to live in New Orleans's Eighth Ward and stealing what she needed to live on anyway.

Or she could take the train to Swineshead and maybe lease a car after she got there, if it was even large enough for a car-rental office. Another thing she needed to check on. Given a choice, she'd rather practice driving on the wrong side of the road out in the boonies than in London.

Pushing aside the map to find the train schedule, she noticed a white envelope amid the junk mail. Ordinarily, the idea that a real letter was in her mailbox would've been a nice break in her daily routine. Today, it filled her with dread; a little normal routine would be welcome.

The standard business envelope was plain and white and had absolutely nothing written on the outside, which was enough to start Sam's heart thumping erratically. It was thick with something— something bad, no doubt—and she wanted to open it about as much as she wanted to throw herself on the tube tracks in front of an on-coming Circle Line train. Maybe less. At least the train would put her out of her misery quickly.

I need more caffeine for this. She took her cup back to the counter and held it up to the barista.

"Oh, you are having a day, aren't you?" The woman gave her a wry smile and a quick refill. Sam stopped on the way back to her table and loaded the cup with sugar and cream. The fat and sucrose would add a nice topping of queasy to the "Buttie" now churning in her gut.

A few sips of hot comfort and a deep breath later, she picked up the envelope, tore off one end, and peered inside.

"Holy cow." Sam looked around to see if anyone was paying at-tention and then pulled out a stack of British pounds. A lot of British pounds. Not in small increments either. Blowing in the end of the envelope to inflate it, she looked inside to see if there was a note and was half relieved and half filled with dread to see there was.

She extracted the single folded sheet of white paper, again printed only with a generic ink-jet message:

Traveling money. Black Ford Fiesta parked a block east of Queensway Metro. Don't bother trying to trace the license. The clock is ticking.

A shiny black-trimmed car key was taped to the sheet below the message, "FORD" printed on its bow.

"Cheap bastard could've gotten an upgrade at least." She pulled the tape off, pocketed the key, and sipped her coffee. She should get in the car, drive out of London as fast as she dared without getting on the wrong side of the road and ending up in a head-on collision, and keep driving. She could be homeless in Edinburgh or Swansea or Liverpool as easily as in New Orleans, and she trusted her street skills enough to stay a step ahead of Psycho.

She only got stupid when men were around, which they weren't going to ever be again, ever. Especially that one.

She flipped open the train schedule, intent on finding the earliest train to the farthest destination.

"Mind if I join you?"

A forty-something Englishman in a dark suit, his black hair flecked with gray and a dark-gray raincoat over his arm, stood next to the chair opposite Sam.

"No, sorry. I'm on a deadline." The last person she wanted to talk to was a man. Any man. Even one that looked like somebody's uncle.

He pulled out the chair and sat anyway, draping his raincoat across his lap and moving the sugar container aside to make room for his cup of steaming something. Tea, no doubt. "It was a rhetorical question, I'm afraid."

Sam leaned back in her chair, trying to give off the most unfriendly vibe she could muster. In her present mood, it wasn't hard to do. "And why is that? Charmed by my stunning beauty? It couldn't be my witty repartee, could it?"

The man smiled, and it infused a warmth and likability into a face that at first had seemed stern and austere. Mostly, Sam decided, the guy looked tired. She knew the feeling.

"You are lovely, of course, but"—he held up his left hand, where a simple gold band caught the morning light coming through the Starbucks window—"I'm quite spoken for."

Sam snorted. "Like that matters to most men."

"It matters to me." English Hubby sipped his tea. "I'm here to receive an update on the project you're undertaking for our mutual acquaintance." His accent was clipped and precise. Businesslike. "He requested you keep me apprised of your progress and ensure me that you understood the nature of the time limits under which you've been placed."

Sam frowned. On some level, she'd hoped Psycho had just flown back to the States and planned to leave her alone for the next thirty days—make that twenty-eight and counting. Now he had a watch-dog. The situation just kept getting better.

"Not without some kind of evidence that you know what you're talking about," she said. "For all I know, you're an enemy on a fishing expedition. What is our mutual friend's name?"

The man chuckled and again he looked like someone Sam might trust under different circumstances. Of course, trust had gotten her in this mess to begin with. And he was a man. Therefore, no trust.

"Clever try, but all you need to know is that when you had your little mattress tango in the second-floor suite at the Bridestall, our mutual acquaintance called himself Gary Smith." He paused, and this time he didn't smile. "It was quite a performance."

God. Sam closed her eyes and fought down the swell of nausea that threatened to turn her local Starbucks into the site of a head-spinning scene from *The Exorcist.* This guy had seen those freaking photos, maybe had even been the one to have them doctored. She wanted to crawl under the table and chew her way through the floor and straight to hell, then pull him in with her. Or maybe she was already there.

"Who are you and what exactly do you want?"

"You can call me 'Tom,' and I want you to tell me what your plans are toward finding the items you've been asked to procure."

"The items I've been asked to steal, Tom." Like that was really his name. Gary and Tom. A fine, ordinary pair. "Might as well call it what it is."

The man didn't answer, just sipped his tea and gave her an inscrutable, calm gaze. He was very Zen, her new friend Tom. Also very cop-like. Sam had had enough experience with cops to know that most excelled in the long, calm stare down. She doubted Psycho had a cop on his payroll, however.

"Fine." The quicker she talked, the quicker he'd leave her alone. "I plan to leave London now that our mutual acquaintance has coughed up some money and a car."

Sam would swear she'd caught a momentary flicker of surprise cross Tom's face, but he recovered so quickly she couldn't be sure.

"Very good. I'm glad they arrived safely and on time. Where do you intend to go? Swineshead, I imagine?"

She held up the map. "Yep, or maybe Boston since there are more places to stay." From her limited research so far, Swineshead wasn't overrun with hotel options, even with her newfound wealth. But Boston wasn't far away.

"Not Boston. You'll waste too much time commuting. You must stay in Swineshead—since my understanding is that's where you think the items are located—and do what you can to immerse yourself in the community." He reached into an inner pocket of his suit coat, pulled out a folded sheet of paper, and pushed it across the table toward her.

Sam eyed it but made no move to pick it up. "You guys are big on note writing, aren't you?" And they weren't exactly love notes. "Just tell me what it says."

Tom nodded and looked out the window for a few moments, watching people hurry to and fro to begin their workdays, before answering. "You're angry, and you have every right," he finally said. "But our mutual friend isn't one you'd be advised to cross. Be as cheeky as you like with me, but if he contacts you directly, I advise you to say as little as possible. Answer his questions and don't opine."

Right. Because her new buddy Tom was all about protecting her, and she'd be happy to opine about that. "What's in the note?"

"The name of a man in Swineshead, an American artist, in fact. He often has an available room to let on short notice and will no doubt offer you a reasonable rent. As an added bonus, his home lies on a portion of the former grounds of the Swineshead Abbey."

Interesting, but suspicious. "Why the hell would I stay with someone you and my psychotic blackmailer picked out?" The man was seriously delusional. "I'll find an inn, but thanks anyway. I can visit this guy if it looks like his house holds any interest."

"That wasn't a request. Consider it an order directly from Gary Smith. Drive to Swineshead and find Brody Parker."

Tom pushed his chair back, stood, and slipped his right hand into his coat pocket. For a crazy instant, Sam was sure he'd be holding a gun when his hand reappeared, but instead he held a white handkerchief that he used to wipe off the table, the chair, and the cup he'd been holding. Sam's cop radar was pinging again; he was getting rid of fingerprints.

"Brody Parker," she repeated.

"He'll be expecting you by nightfall."

CHAPTER 7

The Black Dragon was filled with a late lunch crowd, or an early drinking crowd, although what constituted a "crowd" in Swineshead was relative.

Brody was participating in both late lunch and early drinking. For the past half hour, he'd been parked at a table near the bar, watching the locals knock back beer while he waited for his steak and ale pie. He'd already plowed through an order of chips.

The soft chatter of voices blended with the clink of glasses as more pints were filled and distributed. It gave the place a comfortable ambience to go with the coziness of all the dark wood and soft lighting. The really animated conversations, of course, took place outside the door and in the small parking lot, where the smokers had been forced to move when the country's smoking ban took effect.

"Son, do you realize your hands always have paint on them? Today, they're green." The pub owner, Greely, set a pint on the table in front of Brody. "You might meet some women if you had a proper wash." He squinted and leaned closer. "I think you have green paint on your chin, too."

"Hey, I've been out earning an honest living, okay?" Brody scrubbed his fingernails across his chin. "Not all of us can hang out at a pub all day."

He watched Greely return to his spot behind the dark, ancient bar and scrubbed a few flecks of green paint off his hands. His early-morning session had taken him southeast of Swineshead, where the land grew flatter and wetter, the patches of earth less stable, the landscape foggy and bleak this time of year. The wind coming off the distant water, with little to break its intensity, had been surprisingly cold.

He stifled a yawn. The past couple of days had been anything but restful. As soon as he and Cynthie had returned from dinner and he'd been convinced she was safely ensconced in his spare room, he'd gone into his security room and first verified on the camera footage that she was the only one who'd approached the house in the previous twenty-four hours, which had been a relief. Once he was satisfied that she was the cause of the security-system activation, he got online and studied the list of names pulled from MI6 files.

He'd concluded that the person on the list most likely of interest to authorities was a guy living in Lincoln, the county seat about thirty miles to the northwest. The man's Facebook profile had interests that included organizations rumored to have ties to organized crime, and the NCA and MI6 had units that dealt with nothing but the mob.

At least Brody hoped that was the tie and that his name on the list was mere coincidence.

"Earth to Brody." Greely waved a plate in front of Brody's eyes and set down a feast of steaming pastry and beef. "Forget the airy-fairy artist-muse thing for a while and join the real world. Who do your Waves play this weekend?"

Brody laughed and dug his fork into the steaming pastry. "It's the Alabama Crimson Tide, not the Waves, and they play LSU—Louisiana State University. It's a big game." Brody sipped his beer. He'd become an Alabama football fan out of necessity. He didn't want anyone to know he was from Florida, and Bama games were more likely to be streamed on the web. "You need a decent Internet connection in this place so you people can watch real football for a change. Most of the games are online."

This was a running conversation that always ended in good-natured sparring about whether the Fosdyke football club could beat the Crimson Tide. It was Greely's favorite topic next to complaints about national politics. To hear him tell it, Parliament was mostly made up of devil spawn.

Brody watched Greely return to the bar, stopping along the way to talk to a newcomer, a woman who looked completely out of place.

Linking his fingers behind his neck and flexing his stiff shoulder muscles, pretending to stretch, he gave her a longer look, trying to decide why she didn't fit in. Finally, he realized what it was: she looked like an American student. Jeans, running shoes, backpack.

The woman took a seat at the bar and kept talking to Greely, who like many pub owners was a bit of a philosopher and dispenser of local history and wisdom. The woman was waving her hands around; probably one of those people who couldn't string two sentences together without hand gestures. Over the noise, Brody heard "hotel" and "urgent."

No business of his. He turned back to his steak pie and shoveled the last bite into his mouth, noting a big swath of green paint he'd missed earlier. It trailed a verdant smudge from wrist almost to elbow. Oh well, it would just add to his reputation as the eccentric artist.

He felt her rather than saw her, a soft, accidental brush across his left shoulder as she stopped behind him. "Excuse me, but you're Brody Parker?"

What? Brody sat up straighter but didn't turn. He'd been right; she was American. Maybe even Southern, although it was hard to tell from a few words.

Greely showed up and reached for Brody's empty plate. "It depends on why you want to know, love, as to whether he'll admit it or not. If you're looking for someone to escort you on a scenic tour of Swineshead, you'd be better off with someone such as myself. If you're a bill collector, this big, silent hulk would be the one you want."

Using his foot to shove out the chair next to Brody, Greely added, "Have a seat. You already have a pint and Mr. Parker here detests seeing a woman drink alone."

Brody hated to be paranoid, but why would a strange American woman be asking for him, especially a day after a security irregularity at MI6? He tried to maintain a neutral expression as he watched her take the chair. She was pretty, going on average, with hair that swept the top of her shoulders in a fan of sunlight and honey. Red-framed glasses gave her more of a studious Marian Librarian look than one of a federal agent or an assassin, but that would be a brilliant disguise, wouldn't it?

She set her beer on the table and looked at him for the first time. Brody's breath caught. Whoever this woman was, she had the most perfect green eyes he'd ever seen, the color he thought of as Lincolnshire green and was forever trying to capture on his canvases. He could drown in that color.

When their glances caught, he'd been in the process of setting his pint back on the table after taking a sip. Instead, he set it down on his fork, knocking the utensil off the edge of the table with a loud-enough clatter to draw looks from several people sitting nearby.

"Smooth move." The woman smiled as Brody, his face heating, leaned over to pick up the fork and made the mistake of glancing under the table at her feet. Her white running shoes carried a coating of fine Lincolnshire mud. Jeans and tennis shoes were such an American uniform that an unexpected—and unwelcome—pang of homesickness stabbed Brody in the gut. He hadn't thought about it before, at least not consciously, but he hadn't talked to another American in the seven years he'd been living in England, unless talking to the TV counted. Swineshead didn't exactly qualify as an international tourism destination.

The woman leaned over to peer at him under the table, and Brody sat up abruptly. Since when had he turned into a total idiot? "Can you talk?" she asked, looking back toward Greely, who'd returned to the bar. "Do we need an interpreter?"

"I can talk." And sound pretty damned defensive, apparently. "You'd be looking for me why?"

The woman gave him a tentative smile, and the fact that she looked as uncomfortable as he felt gave Brody a reassuring sense of control. He was being ridiculous; there was no reason to panic. Yet.

"My name's Samantha Crowe, and I was told you had a room I could rent for a month or so."

Brody blinked. He wasn't sure what he'd expected her to say, but it wasn't that. "Who told you I had a room to rent?" It hadn't been Greely; he'd never volunteer personal information about one of his patrons. They weren't good buddies or anything, but he knew Brody well enough to realize he screened his short-term tenants closely and hadn't taken many on since his paintings had begun to sell.

She bit her lip, and Brody's gaze dropped involuntarily from the green eyes to the full lower lip caught between her teeth. He'd been wrong. She wasn't plain at all.

"A man at the local inn told me. The Grain Bin or something like that." She paused, then added, "Their rooms were taken. It's the place a few blocks down, near that gorgeous old church."

The Grainery had a few rooms above the restaurant, and it was rare for all of them to be rented out. Still, it was possible. It didn't make Brody any less suspicious, though, given Cynthie's news night before last.

"Try Boston. There are plenty of places to stay there." He pushed his plate aside, shifting in his seat to leave.

She put a hand on his arm and he stilled, looking back into those green, green eyes. "I really need to stay here in Swineshead. Won't you consider it? I'll pay more than your regular rate."

Samantha Crowe had an almost desperate air about her, and Brody found himself wanting to respond in a way that would bring a smile to her face. He bet it would light up those eyes like a Lincolnshire summer. But the stakes were too high for him to play hero; plus, he was in no position to indulge an attraction to a woman.

He opened his mouth to say no, but what popped out instead was, "Why are you in Swineshead, Samantha?" He needed a good kick in the ass. Engaging her in conversation would simply encourage her.

"Call me Sam. Samantha's too long." She sipped her beer with almost mechanical movements, seeming to choose her words carefully. "I'm a graduate student from the States . . . Well, I guess you could tell that from the accent. Anyway, I'm here for a semester doing research into King John's last trip through Lincolnshire before he died."

"Ah." Brody leaned back. He'd been right about the student part. "We get a bit of that in the summer, especially since all the Robin Hood movies came out. People are always disappointed to find there's nothing left of Swineshead Abbey except some rough earthworks. You can find some medieval reenactments closer to Nottingham and more historical documents in Lincoln. I doubt you'll find much here." And that was the extent of his helpfulness. "Good luck, though."

Greely paused on his way to another table, his arms laden with plates of steak pie. "Did she tell you she was from that place your Waves are footballing on Saturday?"

Brody frowned. "You're from LSU?"

She smiled at Greely, and Brody felt an annoying and completely inappropriate wish that she'd turned that smile on him instead of the flirtatious publican. *No women, remember? Especially one that shows up right after a security breach with your name on it.*

"I'm not a big football fan, but I think it's the Crimson Tide and not the Waves," she said. Brody could have told her Greely only called them the Waves to be annoying. "I'm here doing history research. I know there isn't a lot to see, but I want to examine whatever local records are here," she said, glancing at Brody as if to assure him he was part of the conversation despite his uncanny resemblance to a mute caveman. "I'd like to talk to some of the locals who've had family here for generations and see what old stories have survived, true or not. Maybe even talk to the people who own some of the oldest buildings."

"Then Brody's your man," Greely said. "That old cottage you live in—the one with the spare flat—dates to the thirteenth century? King John probably rode right past there on his way to the abbey."

Brody gave Greely's departing back a scowl. "Seventeenth century," he said. "But I still can't rent you the room. Sorry." He thought fast. What excuse could he give that didn't sound paranoid? He'd like to not come across as such a jerk, but feared it was too late to fix that. "I'm in a big rush to get ready for an art show next month, so I really just don't have time to get the place ready for a tenant."

"But Tom said . . ." She paused and bit her lip.

"Who's Tom?" Thanks to his bachelor status and lack of cooking skills, he knew everyone who worked at the Grainery and its first-floor restaurant by name, and none were named Tom. "Who did you say sent you to find me?"

"I told you, a guy at the—"

"There's no one at the Grainery named Tom." Brody leaned toward her and mimicked her gesture from earlier, placing a hand on her forearm. It felt fragile beneath her sweater. Then again, if she'd been sent to kill him, it didn't take a lot of physical strength to pull a trigger. "Tell me the truth."

"I am telling you the truth." She pulled her arm free but wouldn't meet his gaze. "Maybe Tom's new at the Grainery. Why would I make up something like that?"

For the same reason you won't look me in the eye, you little green-eyed liar.

"Why indeed." Brody stood and stuck a few bills under the edge of his plate. "Good luck finding a place to stay, Ms. Crowe. I'm afraid it can't be with me."

He made his way outside without looking back. Part of him wanted to stay and talk to her, hear about what was going on in the States beyond the little he heard on the BBC. He could listen to that accent that reminded him of his former life. But it wasn't worth risking his life, and she'd just lied to him. No sweet green eyes were worth that risk.

On the way back to the parsonage, he passed the Grainery and thought about stopping to see if its rooms were really full, and if it had a new (and indiscreet) employee named Tom. But it really didn't matter. He'd never see Samantha Crowe again.

Ten minutes later, Brody pulled the little white VW into his drive and killed the engine. As usual, he took a few seconds to scan the house and property visible from behind the house where he parked. Not even a leaf looked out of place. He was getting downright neurotic, though, so he made a mental note to call Cynthie after she got off work to find out if she'd learned anything new about the security breach.

As soon as he got within a few feet of the back door, he saw the red light blinking behind the ivy. Damn it, he'd changed his security code night before last, but the system had been tripped again.

CHAPTER 8

What an absolute jackass. Sam watched Brody Parker walk to the bar and talk to the bartender, then head toward the exit without so much as a backward glance. Good thing she'd officially given up men, because he had STUPID CHOICE stamped all across his broad shoulders. Killer body, tight little butt in worn-out jeans, thick dark hair a little too long, eyes such a dark brown they bordered on ebony. A sexy little cleft in his chin that even a dab of what looked like green paint didn't ruin. He had a bit of a limp, which made her want to take care of him. And he was an absolute, unmitigated jerk.

The perfect ingredients of a disastrous man choice, in other words. Just her MO.

She returned to the bar. "What is his problem?" she asked Greely, who stood with his arms crossed. She'd noticed him watching Brody's and her final exchange with a smile as if he were viewing an entertaining film. Definitely a comedy, and not a romantic one.

"My American friend is beyond my comprehension, love. I suspect you frightened him."

Right, because she was five feet and six towering inches of badass in geek glasses. She'd thrown her contacts in the trash as a first step in her new commitment to a life of celibacy. "Imagine that. And I didn't even have to bring out my machine gun. Why would you think I scared him?"

"Young Mr. Parker is a bit of a loner, but I suppose it's the artist in him. Artistic types aren't good romantic prospects, I'd venture."

Sam huffed out a frustrated breath. She didn't care about Brody Parker's love life. She needed a place to stay, and Psycho's henchman Tom had misled her. Either Tom hadn't made the arrangements with Brody as planned, Brody hadn't gone along with those plans, or this was some kind of challenge or game Psycho had devised to test her resolve.

She might fail at this task—the odds were pretty good that she didn't stand a chance in hell of finding a treasure trove of royal jewels lost eight hundred years ago. She still might well end up fleeing to some remote corner of the globe as her deadline approached, throwing away her own career, praying David would land on his feet, and knowing her mom would get drugs from someone else if not from Psycho. She'd be saving as much of said jerk's money as possible in case she needed to start over with yet another name.

But if and when she failed at this quest, it wouldn't be for lack of trying. Going along with it as long as she could might even help her research in the long run.

"Tell me how to get to Brody's house," she urged Greely. Helpful Tom had only told her it was on the old abbey grounds. "Point me in the right direction, and I'll change his mind."

"Ah, I don't think so, fair Samantha. I'm sorry, but I think Brody was clear on his answer. Boston's only a few miles east and there are plenty of places to stay."

Finding a nice, neutral hotel in Boston was tempting, but she wanted to remain in Psycho's good graces until she had time to figure out a plan or an exit strategy. And his henchman, the very polite, calm henchman, had been very clear: she was to stay in Swineshead, and she was to stay with Brody Parker. Brody just hadn't gotten the memo.

Wheedling the address of Brody's house out of the pub owner would take too long and might make him suspicious enough to warn his friend, so she figured she'd head down the street to the Grainery and ask around there. There couldn't be that many seventeenth-century cottages housing American artists.

The Grainery was a square, three-story red brick building with white cornerstones and a black, steeply pitched roof. The restaurant and inn dominated a prime corner spot on the Swineshead High Street, a grand name for a few charming blocks of small businesses dominated by the majestic old St. Mary's Church.

After parking, Sam walked around the church grounds for a few minutes, formulating a plan. She hadn't eaten, and the beer had made her light-headed when she needed to stay sharp. So the best idea seemed to be eating lunch and hoping for a chatty waiter or waitress.

The dining room of the Grainery was all cream-colored plaster and wainscoting, with a fireplace in the corner that had been lit in recognition of the chilly, damp weather. Unlike the dark confines of the Black Dragon Pub, it was bright and cheerful and warm—or maybe it was the absence of Brody Parker's cold attitude. Maybe if the Brody Parker information-gathering mission didn't pan out, she could take a room here after all.

"What'll you have, duck?" The middle-aged woman who'd handed her a menu smiled at her from above a pencil poised over a pad and pronounced her term of endearment to rhyme with *rook*. "Don't believe I've seen you 'round here before."

"I'm here to do some research for a couple of weeks, on Swineshead Abbey," she told the woman after ordering. "Are there local historians I could talk to? And I was told there was an old cottage near the abbey site that occasionally rented rooms—the owner's supposed to be an artist. Do you know anything about it?"

She was on a bona fide fishing trip; all she needed was a rod and reel.

"Oh, we have a lot of old-timers who love to talk about that bit with King John and the monk that poisoned him." The woman, who'd introduced herself as Betty, handed Sam's order to another passing waitress and took a seat at the table. Sam could've jumped up and hugged her. Betty was a talker.

"Do people here really think the king was poisoned?" Current scholars favored the account that John stopped in Swineshead after he'd contracted a steadily worsening case of dysentery. However, a lot of the old folktales had him being poisoned by a Cistercian monk at the abbey after he'd demanded to have sex with the abbot's wife.

"Oh yes, indeed." Betty nodded with vigor. "There are those who claim to be descendants of people who did business with the monks at the abbey, and they swear the stories passed down to them are true.

"But as for the cottage." Betty glanced at the bar. "You're probably talking about the old Jessop place. It's out past where the abbey used to be. A nice young American man lives there now, a painter." She pointed to a landscape hanging on the wall behind the bar. "He was the great nephew and only heir of the old parson, or something like that. He comes in here and eats dinner a few nights a week."

Nice young man, her ass. Sam had a few other names she could be calling Brody Parker.

"I heard he takes boarders occasionally." *Fish, fish, fish.* "I thought it would be nice to stay closer to the abbey while I was in town."

Betty nodded. "We have rooms here if you need one, but Brody Parker does take on the occasional tenant, mostly during the summer. I don't have his number but can probably ring up someone to get it. My nephew Jet's one of his mates."

Damn small towns. All she needed was Betty calling up her nephew and trying to get information on Brody for an American woman who wanted a room. Brody would know she was coming before she could crank the car. "No, that's okay. I'm driving out that way after I leave here. Is it on the same road as the turnoff to the abbey?"

"It is." Betty got up and settled her chair back in place. "Hard to see from the road, but if you drive on past Abbey House—that's the house built on the site of the old abbey—the Jessop cottage is another half mile or so past that, down a narrow lane on the right. Nothing else out there much besides farmland and cows."

"Thanks." More thanks than Betty could guess, as she bustled off to resume her waitressing. Her departure left Sam to eat her burger and study the painting behind the bar. A small handwritten card had been taped to the wall next to it: "*Fens at Dawn*, Brody Parker, between Swineshead and Fosdyke." It was beautiful, she had to admit, with an eerie, almost medieval feel to its depiction of fog lying over half-submerged bits of land. If Sam's theory about the lost crown jewels was wrong, and the conventional wisdom right, a scene such as the one in Brody's painting was probably what faced the king's baggage train as horses, wagons, jewels, and riders headed for a deadly date with quicksand.

A half hour later, Sam stopped at the market a few doors down and picked up some toiletries she'd been almost out of when Psycho struck. She'd left London in such a hurry she did little other than pack up the few things she owned and load them in the car.

When she'd closed the door of the flat behind her, she'd had an overwhelming sense that she'd never see it again. She had only six weeks left on her fellowship, and four of them were going to be eaten up doing the bidding of the sick freak. The last two might be spent running or trying to salvage her imploding reputation and career prospects.

She drove along Abbey Road, trying to block out the Beatles tunes that had been dancing in her head by cranking up BBC Radio 4, which was playing the audio of a televised miniseries made from an Anthony Trollope novel. At least it was noise, and it wasn't threatening her or demanding that she stalk some guy who didn't want anything to do with her.

Question was, what could she say to Brody Parker to get him to take her on as a tenant—and why did Gary want her staying with this American artist? The only thing she could think of was that the old cottage Brody lived in had some clue or significance to the King John story of which she was unaware. Even if it hadn't been built until the 1600s, it could have been constructed on the ruins of an older site.

Sam slowed at the sign pointing her to Abbey House, a stately two-story manor house with a dormer-windowed attic. In her box of research papers was a sheaf of documents showing how the house had been updated over the centuries since it had been built in the early 1600s atop the ruins of the old Swineshead Abbey, using materials salvaged from the original building.

Abbey House had been sold for well over a million pounds a few years ago, but Sam didn't know whether or not it had current residents, or what kind of problems she might run into if and when she needed to snoop around on the grounds. She'd cross that moat when she got to it.

For better or worse, stealth was among her skill sets.

CHAPTER 9

Damn it. It was virtually impossible to keep paranoia at bay when shit kept happening.

Brody stared at the red blinking light for a couple of seconds, torn between whether he should get back in his car and return to Swineshead, or whether he should just continue inside and hope it was either a malfunction or a commonplace burglar he could beat senseless.

Beating somebody senseless would feel pretty good at this point. After seven years of peace and quiet, he had finally begun to think he could settle in and move on with his life. Now this.

It wasn't likely a burglar. As Cynthie had rightly pointed out, Swineshead wasn't exactly awash in criminals of any sort, a pleasant change from his former life in Miami. Worst-case scenario: someone was inside, knew he was here, and would be waiting on him. In that case, he'd have to find a way to stall until he could maneuver the time and space to retrieve his gun from inside the sofa frame. Or get his ass shot trying, since he'd left his small pistol on his bedroom nightstand.

He took a deep breath, waiting for his pulse to stop pounding so hard it echoed in his eardrums. Turning the knob, he found the door unlocked, so he pushed it open and waited outside. He more than half expected the click of a released safety or the barrel of a gun to come inching around the corner at him again, only without Cynthie on the other end this time.

But all was quiet. A sense of relief washed through him. He needed to give that security system an overhaul, or maybe replace it altogeth—

"Come in, Mr. Parker. We need to talk, and it will be difficult with you standing in the doorway."

Son of a bitch. Back to the worst-case scenario.

Brody turned his head and quickly scanned for a car but didn't see one. Slowly, he walked into the entry hall, his boots sounding like gunshots on the hardwood. He didn't see anyone. "Where are you?"

"Come into the den, if you please."

Awfully damned polite for an assassin or a burglar. Then again, this was England, the land of the stiff upper lip and proper manners. Brody walked toward the den, glancing around him for something to use as a weapon. His gaze landed on a letter opener he kept on the hall table where he threw his unopened bills and junk mail.

Quietly, he scooped it up and slid it up his left sleeve, with the pointed end resting in his palm. It wasn't his first choice of weapon, but he could hurt somebody with it. He took a deep breath and stepped through the big open doorway where dark rustic beams rimmed the white plaster. A dark-suited man rested in old Parson Jessop's rooster chair, his posture on the surface self-consciously casual. There was a coiled tightness beneath it, though.

The guy was in his early forties, maybe a little older, with dark hair going gray. He sat utterly still, and Brody's first impression was that the man had to be either a professional hit man or a cop. Ironically, both of those types seemed to have the same quiet, serious demeanor that spoke of endless patience, pent-up energy, and restrained violence.

Only not quite so restrained, in this case. Grasped in the man's right hand was a big semiautomatic, a .45 caliber from the look of it. True, the gun was resting on the guy's thigh, but he had a finger on the trigger and Brody would bet the Alabama Crimson Tide's whole season that the safety was off. No silencer, however, which tipped the scale more toward cop than hit man.

"Have a seat, Mr. Parker. The sooner we finish our little chat, the sooner I can leave and let you get on with your life—with a few changes, of course."

Of course. The guy had an agenda. "I think I'll stand, thanks. At least until you tell me who you are, how you got here, and why you're sitting in my house with a gun."

"You can call me Tom, and I drove, of course. This is quite a large parcel of land, with plenty of hidden spots for one to park if one doesn't mind a bit of a stroll."

Good thing to know. He could walk around and look for tread marks or clues, assuming he lived through this encounter.

The man waved the weapon toward the sofa. "As for why I'm here, there's something I need you to do for me. But let's sit and chat calmly, please."

Funny how the guy could sound so reasonable and polite while waving around enough firepower to blow a softball-sized hole in Brody's head.

And . . . wait. "Tom? You said your name was Tom?" Not the first time he'd heard that name today. "You're the Tom who sent Samantha Crowe to rent a room from me?"

A look of surprise flitted across Tom's face for only an instant, followed by a flash of a scowl, followed quickly by bland neutrality. Definitely hit man or cop; he recovered too quickly. Unfortunately, Brody had met his share of both, so he had plenty of comparisons and he trusted the reactions he saw.

"If you had answered your phone this morning, you could have saved me this personal visit. I must insist you sit, and please drop whatever makeshift weapon you're holding in your left hand." Tom gestured again toward the sofa, and Brody considered rushing him and planting the letter opener in his throat. He wasn't fast enough to charge before Tom could get off a shot, though.

He dropped the letter opener on the floor and sat on the sofa, on the end farthest from his visitor. The end closest to his gun.

"That'll teach me to ignore my phone. Where are you visiting from?" Brody always turned off his phone when he painted and hadn't gotten around to turning it back on. No one called him except Cynthie, and she knew his habits. "I'd have made some hors d'oeuvres if I'd known guests were coming. Pigs in blankets, maybe." Cop humor, which might or might not translate here.

Tom smiled, and Brody couldn't help but think the man didn't look so much evil or devious as he looked bone-tired. "Where I'm from doesn't matter. What matters is that you do what I ask. First, rent your room to Samantha Crowe. I want her nearby so you can keep an eye on her at all times."

Brody thought his eyes had already been on Samantha Crowe entirely too much. "Why the hell would I want to do that?"

"Because I will leave you no other options, Mr. Parker—or should I say, Mr. Freeman? Should I call you Nathan? Or do you prefer Nate?"

Brody's heart stopped, stuttered, and restarted at a furious pace. The room suddenly felt too small, his scalp tingled as if someone were running fingernails across it, and his lungs struggled to pull in enough air. His mouth went the way of the Sahara.

Damn it. He hadn't had a panic attack in more than five years, but apparently his body hadn't forgotten how to do it. The room began going gray around the edges, and he gulped a deep lungful of air. He'd be damned if he would faint like a girl in front of this asshat.

Brody fisted both hands and dug his nails into his palms hard enough to draw blood. Within seconds, the pain diverted his mind from the panic to his throbbing palms, allowing his breathing to even out and his heart rate to slow down. The adrenaline drain was so fast he felt giddy.

During those long months in the rehab facility, one of his physical therapists had taught him that little trick. It worked really well except for the bloody palms.

"I see I have your attention." Tom's expression remained impassive, his blue eyes steady and his mouth a rigid slash across his face. "Regretful business, I realize."

Regretful business? Anger began pushing the fear out of Brody's mind, and he welcomed it. Anger was easier to channel. "What the fuck do you want?" His voice came out low and rough. "How do you know about Nate Freeman?"

Better, how much did he know? Although the name alone was enough to get him killed.

He eased his left hand between the sofa cushion and arm, pretending to shift his position while he felt for his gun.

"I moved your firearm." Tom's voice held a trace of amusement. "I have to admit I almost didn't find it. The sofa frame was the last place I looked. If you'd hidden it on the other side of the arm, I likely would've missed it."

Great. Lessons in weapon concealment from an extortionist. Wait. He didn't say he'd confiscated it. "What do you mean you moved it?"

"It's on the table beside your bed. Nice security system, by the way, although it needs an update. You might have use of the gun, so I didn't want to leave you defenseless. And I should tell you that if you manage to kill me today, which I don't think is likely, there are individuals who know where I am and, more to the point, know about Nathan Freeman. Should I fail to arrive at my next destination on time, your identity will be released to the press. I believe your American journalists would find it an intriguing story since your death was front-page news and had many repercussions."

Fuck. Brody rubbed his eyes, wishing he could start the day over. The fen was too foggy to get much painting done, he'd shown way too much interest in a woman who was apparently stalking him, and now some lunatic named Tom was sitting in old Parson Jessop's chair and threatening oh-so-politely to blast his world apart if he didn't start stalking the woman in return.

He wished he knew what the hell was going on. "What do you want? Rent Samantha Crowe a room and what else?"

"As I said, keep an eye on her. She's here under the guise of doing university research, but she's actually been contracted to search for a valuable treasure here in Swineshead."

What treasure she could find in Swineshead was beyond him, but Brody felt as tired as Tom looked. "So you want me to help her find this treasure?"

Tom leaned forward in his chair. "On the contrary, Mr. Parker. I want you to make sure she does *not* find it. The man she works for must never get his hands on it. Sabotage her efforts—it will be simpler if she's living here. If by some chance she does find it, you must take it from her before she can give it to her patron. In that event, kill her if you have to, but be discreet about it, of course."

Kill her? The man was a sociopath. Brody propped his elbows on his knees and decided to share that opinion. "You're fucking nuts. I am not killing Samantha Crowe or anyone else, not to get some sort of treasure. You've watched way too many Indiana Jones movies, buddy."

Tom laughed, and the sound sent a chill down Brody's spine. Actually, that hadn't been a joke. "Ironically, this is rather an Indiana Jones type of adventure. Ms. Crowe is looking for the lost crown jewels of King John, you see, and in the unlikely event that she finds them, I do not want them in the hands of the man she's working for. He does not deserve them."

Now Brody knew the man was insane. On the other hand, if he was telling the truth, Brody had nothing to worry about. "Tom, I hate to break the news to you, but people around here have been looking for those crown jewels for almost a thousand years. Every farmer who has plowed a field between here and King's Lynn over the last eight centuries has hoped to unearth a crown or a scepter or at least a fucking silver spoon. But guess what? Those babies are long gone, whether they sank in quicksand or washed out into the North Sea." The king's demise, and the whereabouts of his jewels, were favorite pub topics in these parts—a hundred years ago.

Tom leaned back in his chair again and crossed his legs, picking at a bit of lint on his trousers. "You're quite likely right. In which case, by November fifteenth, if Ms. Crowe fails to find the jewels, she is no longer your concern, but mine. I also will forget everything I've learned about your unfortunate life as Nathan Freeman, and you may go back to your painting. I have no wish to bring any harm to your doorstep if it can be avoided."

"Well, aren't you kind." Brody's sense of impending doom had cooled since the guy obviously wasn't planning to kill him or to expose him—at least not immediately. A bit of snark gave him the illusion that he had some control. "What's the significance of November fifteenth?"

A quick calculation told him that date gave him twenty-eight days to develop a game plan. To find out who this Tom guy was and, above all, stop Samantha Crowe from doing anything stupid. Like finding King John's crown jewels. Then if she faced consequences for her failure, it wasn't any of his business.

This much he knew: he was not starting over again. He'd found a new life that he actually enjoyed. He'd found peace. He'd found a place to call home when he'd thought such a thing was out of his grasp. He was thirty-three years old, and he didn't have it in him to go on the run. Been there, done that, not doing a repeat.

And if he had to work with Tom the Sociopath and stop that little green-eyed gold-digger Samantha Crowe in order to hold on to his life, so be it.

CHAPTER 10

Sam had driven up and down Abbey Road through twenty minutes of Anthony Trollope and fifteen minutes of the BBC Radio 4 shipping forecast before she finally spotted the narrow lane leading into a grove of trees. She must have passed it at least a half-dozen times. If this lane didn't lead to Brody's house, then she would concede defeat for today and return to the Grainery.

Once she'd bumped the little Ford through the trees and reached the clearing beyond it, she caught her first glimpse of the house and it almost took her breath away. It was a historian's dream cottage. Ancient brick, what looked like a courtyard, ivy coating half the walls. What must it be like to live in a place like this, and how lucky to have inherited it. All she would inherit from her mom were ulcers and unpaid bills, if she were lucky.

Sam's apartment throughout college—the cheapest thing she could find in a neighborhood where she was afraid to venture out at night—was almost as spartan as her Bayswater flat. She'd held down two jobs and a full course load to even get that much and still send a little money to her mom each month.

It also looked like the perfect place for an artist to live. Brody's painting had been pretty good, at least to her amateur eye. Even if Brody Parker tossed her out on her backside, she'd enjoy seeing the interior of the place.

She parked behind a muddy white VW sedan that wasn't much bigger than the car she was driving, and took a deep breath before getting out. A detached building constructed with the same vintage brick as the house sat off to the side, probably the space he rented out. This really was an ideal location for her. If she had to do her exploring of the old abbey grounds under cover of night to circumvent the current owners, she didn't have far to travel. Plus, it was just downright cool.

Taking a deep breath, she got out of the car and walked to the closest entrance, which looked like a back door off a small patio or courtyard. She knocked and prepared to wait. She thought about hiding, because if he looked out the window inset into the back door and saw her, Brody might not even answer. He'd struck her as the quintessential temperamental artist.

But he opened the door before she finished knocking, looming in the entrance and taking up more space than she'd expected. He was taller than he'd seemed at the pub, maybe six two or six three, and built more like an athlete than an artist.

He also looked royally pissed off as he looked down at her with thunderclouds in those impossibly dark eyes. He said nothing, which was just awkward.

Time to make her sales pitch. "Hi, Brody. I'm sorry for just showing up like this and I know it's almost dark. But could I please explain why I want to rent a room from you so badly?"

"This should be interesting," he muttered, stepping back and motioning her inside with an exaggerated gesture and pent-up sarcasm that made her want to kick his shins and leave. Damn Tom for not doing his job.

The small foyer inside the door featured thick cream-colored plaster walls with wooden beams. An open doorway led into a room to the left; what looked like a short hallway led straight ahead. To the right, through another open doorway, she saw the gleam of stainless steel, so this was probably a kitchen.

Still silent, Brody led the way through the left-hand opening into a cozy den with exposed brick on two walls, a pair of facing mismatched sofas, one green and one aqua, and an ugly behemoth of an armchair that looked as though it might have been here for centuries. Brody Parker might be an artist, but those artistic skills didn't extend to interior decoration, apparently. She could do wonders with this place, given enough money.

"Take the rooster chair," Brody said, slumping on one of the sofas. "And then let's just cut to the bottom line."

Which meant he didn't plan to change his mind. Well, she wasn't giving up that easily. If getting a room from him was a test, she didn't intend to fail it. "Look, you don't have to like me, but at least hear me out."

Brody shrugged and gestured toward the chair.

Sam sat, took a steadying breath, and realized she was wringing her hands. Not the message she wanted to give, so she tucked them beneath her thighs. "I'm sorry I lied about the Grainery being full earlier today. The real reason I wanted to stay here, once I heard you had a little rental flat avail—"

"Heard it from Tom, right?"

Damn it, he wasn't going to let the Tom thing go. "Right, and the reason I wanted to stay here is because it's so close to Abbey House."

"You won't be able to do much research at the house; it's privately owned." Brody crossed his legs, propping an ankle on his knee, and leaned back. When he stretched his arms along the sofa back, the muscles under his tight-fitting black T-shirt bunched in beautiful peaks and valleys that Sam had an unreasonable urge to touch. Which definitely was not on her agenda.

"Um, sorry. What did you say?" Had he told her to get out?

Brody Parker was a punishment from above, no doubt about it. A beautiful asshole of an unattainable man, just so God could rub in her face the bad choices she'd made before she'd vowed herself to a life of celibacy.

"I'll speak more slowly." One edge of his mouth curved up in an infuriating smirk. "Abbey...House...is...a...private...re-si-dence." He dragged out each word as if talking to someone who couldn't understand a simple declarative sentence. "You can't just wander in with a spade and start digging up their lawn and garden."

Had she mentioned digging? She hadn't mentioned digging because she hadn't thought that far ahead.

"I'm just doing research. I'm sure they'll allow me to walk the grounds. I also have a list of locals with deep family ties to Swineshead, and oral histories—even many generations removed—are always helpful. In fact, maybe there are stories you've heard about this place that could help. I'd love to hear them."

He stared at her a few uncomfortable seconds before speaking, and Sam would've given up half of Gary's blackmail money to know what was going through that mulish brain of his.

"You know, when I first met you today, I was knocked a little flat by talking to another American. You're the first one I've met since moving to Swineshead several years ago. You made me homesick."

Homesick? Was that why he'd been such a jerk? "Where are you from originally?"

He paused a few moments, which was weird. It wasn't the type of question one normally had to think about. "Alabama, which is why Greely, the guy that owns the pub, was so interested in you supposedly being from LSU. How's the weather in New Orleans this time of year?"

Sam badly needed both a soda and either a shield or a suit of armor. Her mouth was dry, and he kept zinging arrows at her, trying to trip her up. But she had neither, and he hadn't offered her one of the sodas he was drinking in front of her. If he was a fan of Alabama football, he knew very well where LSU was located.

"You must have been gone a long time and forgotten a lot," she said. "LSU's in Baton Rouge, not New Orleans, although I grew up in NOLA."

Brody took a sip of his soda. "Right, I'd forgotten." He set the can on the end table and leaned forward. "Here's the deal. Take it or leave it. A hundred pounds a day, with kitchen privileges, but only when I'm here. You will not have a key to the main house." His voice was flat and void of emotion. "You can move in immediately. I'll expect you out of here by November fifteenth at the latest."

A gasp bubbled up in Sam's throat but she swallowed it down, and it wasn't just the outrageous price he was charging. It was that date—her deadline to either turn in the crown jewels or be ruined.

"What's the significance of November fifteenth?" She realized her voice sounded reedy and thin, but that was kind of how she felt. He couldn't have just pulled that specific date out of his nice little butt. Coincidence only went so far.

"Cut the shit." Brody's voice was hard and chillier than the air whipping across the flat landscape outside. "Tom was here. The real Tom, not the fake employee at the Grainery. So I know what you're after and that the person you're gold digging for has given you a deadline."

She had no comeback for that, so she simply nodded.

Two hours later, Sam stood in the middle of the apartment above the garage or outbuilding or whatever it was. She'd peeked in the window to the garage part of the building, and it looked as if Brody used it for tools rather than parking. A few hand tools lay on a small table outside the door.

As for the apartment, the floor plan was simple: one huge bedroom with an antique iron bed so high she thought she might need a stepladder to get on it, and a bathroom half as large as her Bayswater flat. No kitchen, which explained his need to throw in kitchen privileges.

She'd been thrown for a loop by Brody's coldness and then by learning that Tom had been here. Obviously, Brody no longer believed her research story, but when she'd questioned him to learn how much he knew about the other part—Gary or the crown jewels or the blackmail, trying not to give away any details herself—he'd clammed up, speaking in monosyllables and only answering when asked a direct question.

He obviously didn't like her, which on some level hurt her feelings. Which officially made her an idiot. Tom must have said or done something to change Brody's mind. She'd tried to ask enough oblique questions to piece together an answer, but Brody's word quota for the day had obviously been met and she'd grown tired of butting her head against his stubbornness.

Although her knowledge of him was limited, Brody Parker didn't strike her as the kind of man who'd respond to a financial offer. Judging by this place, he had enough money to get by. Not rich, maybe, but not strapped enough to do something for money that he'd been dead set against doing only a few hours earlier.

Sam had to wonder if Brody was in the same position as she was, and Tom or Psycho had gotten to him with some type of threat. There might be some secret in his past, or someone he wanted to protect, that was compelling him to cooperate. Which meant they should be working together to find the jewels.

The other option? He and Tom had some past history and he owed the guy a favor.

But she'd only know the answer if he'd talk to her. Time to try another shot at peacemaking.

CHAPTER 11

When Brody had moved into the old Jessop house, he'd cleaned it top to bottom, ridding it of what seemed like at least a century of accumulated dust and dirt. According to local lore, the parson had been born here, as had his parents and grandparents and maybe even great-grands.

He'd made only one foray into the cottage's attic, which housed many, many boxes of Jessop family history, including a trunk containing a set of thick hardback journals that Brody had dragged down to his bedroom. He'd always intended to go through the rest of the Jessop boxes or at least to turn them over to the Lincolnshire historical society, but he kept putting it off, thinking the parson's things belonged here in this house where they had likely been created or acquired.

His reluctance to revisit the attic had absolutely nothing to do with the large number of spiders he'd encountered on his one attic mission. Armies of them. Hordes.

The journals, at least, seemed spider-free, and he'd always meant to read them. Things got in the way. Life got in the way. Art. The secret desire of his heart to create beauty, which he thought had died at the hands of his practical father. Ironic that it took starting over, dying in some way, for it to be reborn.

Now that Samantha Crowe had her moneygrubbing green eyes set on finding any remaining secrets regarding King John's crown jewels, however, Brody renewed his determination to read the journals. John Jessop had supposedly been quite the local historian. But good Lord, how the man could go on and on about the escalating prices of dry goods and his concern for the daily welfare of the poor and the eternal souls of the wealthy.

After a couple of hours, at least part of which time he spent imagining Sam unpacking in his little bare-bones apartment, and way too much of which he spent thinking of her in his little bare-bones apartment's shower, Brody finally gave up on journal reading for the evening. He returned it to the box with all the others stashed beneath his bed and ambled into the kitchen, restless and dissatisfied.

Guess blackmail had that effect on him. Or the proximity of a woman he found attractive but untrustworthy. And who it had been suggested he might be asked to kill. Never mind about that.

He opened the fridge and cabinets, surveying the paltry options before finally settling on nice, American peanut butter and jelly sandwiches. He'd laid four slices of bread on a plate and had a golf ball–sized dollop of peanut butter teetering on his knife when he heard the back door rattle, followed by a soft knock.

It was too soon for the blackmailer to be back, so odds were good that Sam wanted food. And, annoyingly, he kind of wanted to see her. Maybe he shouldn't have judged her as a money-grubber without knowing her better. It was possible she didn't really know the type of people she was working for, but not likely. Brody needed to be on his guard; she could suck him in with green eyes and a familiar accent.

He settled the knife against the edge of his plate and padded to the door. She'd turned to face the grove of trees between the cottage and the road, and in profile, when he couldn't be distracted by her eyes and the red glasses, he noticed the slightly upturned nose and full lips. Samantha Crowe, as he'd suspected before, was more than the sum of her parts. Not a stunning beauty that was drawing attention from everyone the moment she entered a room, but a woman who grew more attractive the more you saw her.

Then again, other than the blissfully unattainable Cynthie, the only women Brody had spent time with the past seven years were waitresses and well-meaning village matrons who thought it their duty to ply him with baked goods. He never refused a nice baked good.

She turned back to him and smiled; it looked good on her. "Sorry to bother you again so soon, but I thought maybe I could use the kitchen."

Brody caught himself smiling in return and wiped it off his face. She was a gold digger, and he was being blackmailed into babysitting her. "Come on in. I was just making a sandwich myself."

He led the way back to the kitchen, which was really the only updated room in the cottage, with slate floors and countertops that managed to look modern and still fit in with the vintage surroundings. "I don't keep a lot of food in the house, but you can buy whatever you want in town and store it here."

"You eat in the Grainery a lot? I noticed one of your paintings above the bar."

Brody paused in the middle of smearing his peanut butter across the bread. "So you have been in there? I thought that was all made up." Because she sure as hell didn't meet Tom at the local inn.

"Okay." Sam held up her hands in a surrender gesture, made a little less effective by the slices of bread dangling from her fingers. "I was told by Tom that you'd be expecting me, so when I met you in the pub and you clearly had no clue what I was talking about, I improvised."

He couldn't help but smile. "Not your strong suit."

She laughed, a pretty sound that drew his gaze to her mouth. A really pretty mouth.

Not going there. He spooned out enough strawberry jam for a one-inch layer on both sandwiches.

"I'm working on a master's in history; we research stuff to death. So, no, improvisation is not in my skill set. I like to poke and prod and plan. Thinking on my feet usually makes me fall flat on my ass."

Brody constructed his sandwich and opened the fridge for milk. "So you're a grad student? I thought that was a made-up story, too. That you were working for some guy to find King John's lost crown jewels." Some guy that Tom the Blackmailer wanted to thwart and was willing to sacrifice Sam's life to do so. For the first time, Brody realized the implications of that. Tom was playing both sides. He was pretending to help Sam and her employer while at the same time blackmailing Brody to sabotage them.

Quicksand—that was what this whole clusterfuck was. How could he find out who Sam was and whom she was loyal to? Did she know she was being played from both sides?

"You're right, and so am I," she said slowly, focusing far too intently on her own PB and J. "I am looking for King John's crown jewels. But I really am a grad student from LSU. I'm in England on a fellowship, to study my theory that King John didn't send his jewels on that shortcut through the Wash with the rest of his baggage. I've been working at the British Museum in London. Actually coming to Swineshead to look for the jewels is . . ." She paused, thinking. "It's a recent development, you might say."

A recent development because someone offered her money? Or something else? "I think you should back away from it and go back to your museum research." Brody decided against the milk and pulled another soda out of the fridge. When he turned back to the counter, Sam was looking at him with wide eyes, her mouth pursed as if waiting for a kiss. Which is exactly where his mind went.

"But I thought . . ." She bit her lower lip, and Brody wanted to try that so badly his teeth hurt. God, he was a sex-starved idiot and hadn't realized it. He'd just not been around a woman in a long time.

Once he got all this crap out of his life, if he had a life left, he was so going to let Jet or one of his football buddies fix him up with some party girl who wouldn't care if he had sex with his shirt on.

Or he could blindfold her. Yeah, blindfolds were good.

He moved to her side of the counter and handed her a soda. Her mouth was at his Adam's apple level. He could shift his head just a little to the right, lower it a few inches, and be there.

"I thought you were supposed to be helping me find the treasure. I mean, why else would Tom and Psych—I mean, my employer—want me to stay here instead of in Boston or at the Grainery?"

Brody breathed a sigh of relief as his libido gave way to his brain. Close call. "Let's sit down."

He led her into the den, where they sat on the facing sofas with the coffee table between them, giving them a place to rest their plates and sodas. He needed to figure out how much to tell her without jeopardizing himself.

"I was asked to give you a room and was told what you were here for, but helping you never entered the conversation."

True enough. Sabotaging her was another matter. Never mind he'd been ordered to kill her if she succeeded in finding the treasure and didn't hand it over. "Your employer must be offering a lot of money to drop your research and tackle something like this. I mean, what do you think the odds are of actually finding the jewels?"

Sam held her plate in her lap, chewed her sandwich, and looked at the fire. Brody had lit the fireplace as soon as she'd gone up to her room. Tonight was going to be the chilliest so far this year, a reminder that winter this near the fens was cold and wet.

Brody thought she looked frightened, or maybe she was shivering from cold. "You need me to stoke the fire?"

"No." She set her plate back on the coffee table. "I was thinking about your questions. Honest answer? I don't think I have a ghost of a chance of finding the crown jewels, especially without access to the Abbey House grounds and a team of archaeologists. Even if my theories as to where they are prove to be true. I think my . . . employer is crazy."

That much, Brody would tend to agree with. "Then why are you working for him? Why take the job? Well, unless the money's really good."

Again, she waited a long time before answering. "Something like that."

Brody had gone through college, but he'd never had to scrape to get by. As long as he stayed on the career path his father chose for him, at least through college, he'd had all his needs met. His physical needs, anyway. A degree in political science didn't do much for the soul or the spirit. He'd known his share of fellow students desperate for cash, though. They'd sell plasma, do no-brainer odd jobs, even serve as paid guinea pigs in crazy research projects. Why not try to dig for long-lost jewels?

Except for the Tom question. "Sam, do you know much about this guy you're working for, or how Tom fits into the equation?"

She looked surprised. "I assumed Tom was a friend of yours since he was able to change your mind so quickly about letting me stay here."

Brody picked up his dishes and went back into the kitchen. He was dancing on eggshells here. He couldn't exactly say he was being blackmailed, could he? Not when he still wasn't sure who worked for whom, and why.

"Am I wrong?"

Brody started. He hadn't heard Sam follow him into the kitchen, and she stood behind him, too close.

He turned and gave her a nice, vague answer. "My relationship with Tom is . . . complicated."

Her eyes searched his face, and he couldn't stop his fingers from curling along her jaw. She closed her eyes with a little sigh and then stepped back.

"I probably should tell you that I find you really attractive. Oh my God, *really* attractive. But I've taken a vow of celibacy."

Brody didn't know whether to laugh, cry, or strangle her—or all three, in that order. His willingness to give her the benefit of the doubt only went so far, though, and what a shame that she seemed as attracted to him as he was to her. There was some serious chemistry.

Still, he was intrigued. "Let me get this straight. Now you're a history grad student *nun* from LSU? That's a new one."

She gave him an eat-shit-and-die look that tugged at something deep in his gut. Damn it. He liked this woman. He wouldn't kill her; that much was a given. How far could he really go to even sabotage her?

"I'm not a nun, goof nuts. I just have such horrible judgment where men are concerned that I recently came to the conclusion that celibacy is the only possible solution."

He took a step closer, close enough to feel her body heat and give him his first non-self-induced hard-on in longer than he cared to admit. "That's a waste, Samantha Crowe. You could plow the field without buying the farm, you know."

She laughed, and it came out as a snort, which made them both laugh. "Oh, tell me you didn't just say that. Where the hell *did* you grow up?"

He grinned. "Rural Florida. My grandfather owned a citrus farm."

Her smile slowly faded as her gaze dropped to his mouth, and she unconsciously wet her lips. He couldn't possibly kiss a woman he was about to sabotage. He was a bigger man than that. His moral principles were overly developed. He took advantage of no one, and expected . . .

He angled his head and then stopped. This was not happening, even if he had to take cold showers until November 15.

Brody heard Sam's slight intake of breath, then its release as she took a step back.

"I'm really sorry you've taken that vow of celibacy." Brody's voice sounded like it had been scraped across a grater. "But I guess I should tell you I swore off women eight years ago."

Sam's voice was as breathy as his was tight. "Then I guess we're in the same lonely old boat, and I'd better go back to my room before we both get in trouble."

"Guess so." He leaned against the counter and watched her walk out the back door into the courtyard, giving him a mischievous green-eyed smile before turning away.

Yeah, they were in the same boat of frustration, all right. He just wasn't sure how many leaks it had in it, or whose fleet they were sailing for.

One thing was certain. Brody needed to talk to Cynthie as soon as she got to her office in the morning—without losing track of Sam. After thinking a few minutes, he slipped out the door into the little courtyard and grabbed a large red-handled awl he used for journal binding and had left sitting on a table outside the garage. He looked up to make sure he hadn't been spotted. A soft light shone through the curtains of the room above the garage, but no silhouette shone through. He tiptoed to the driveway.

One good stab in the back rear tire and the little black Ford settled into a skewed tilt. That should keep her occupied for the morning, as long as old King John hadn't buried his treasure in a mechanic's shop.

CHAPTER 12

Tom Nelson had slogged his way from Brody's house through the muddy fields, driven through a slow, cold rain all the way back to London, and then sat in endless afternoon traffic. Which is what he got for not taking the bloody train. But train tickets could be traced, and Tom had been careful to drive a rental car from a small, out-of-the-way dealer in order to remain inconspicuous.

Then, to keep his schedule as normal as possible, he'd spent the rest of the afternoon at his office, late into the evening. His team was investigating a case of suspected money laundering, so he'd stared at a computer screen for three solid hours, examining bank records and tracing deposits.

"You decided to live here, old man?" The kid who stuck his head in the door from the next office had joined the unit six months ago fresh from university and had more computer skills than Tom would ever master. Although he'd gotten pretty damn good for an old relic.

"Leaving in a few, junior. See you tomorrow."

"Right then. You're the last one here."

Tom rubbed his eyes and rolled his head from side to side, cracking out the tension built up from the last few days—really, more like two years—of wishing he'd never heard of C7. Or picked up a deck of cards.

He'd just shut down his computer and loosened his tie, ready for the evening commute, when his cell rang. Probably Donna, asking when he'd be home, anxious for more than the cursory report on his trip to Swineshead that he'd been able to give earlier from the road.

"Hello, love." He was anxious to get home to her, the woman who was once again his confidante as well as lover. Ironically, this whole mess had brought them closer. Her resolve gave him strength.

"Aw, sweet. I didn't know you cared, Tommy."

Which would teach him to look at the identification screen on his phone. "Brent, you bastard."

The laughter on the other end of the call—almost a giggle— reminded Tom how very young was this auburn-haired American billionaire. Brent Sullivan was a walking billboard for the old George Bernard Shaw quote about youth being wasted on the young. Why should an immoral overgrown brat like Brent Sullivan have so much?

Tom knew the kid wasn't stupid, however, and he'd do well to stay a step ahead of him. So far, he thought he'd succeeded.

"Funny you should call, Brent. I returned this morning from making sure our young friend Samantha Crowe was settled in Swineshead. I wanted to ensure that she hadn't hopped in that car you provided and driven halfway across Europe."

A half beat of silence followed as Brent digested that news. Good. It meant Tom was indeed a step ahead. "Good, good. So our Samantha is cooperating?"

"She is. In fact, she made some progress today by finding a room to let on a property that was once part of the abbey there in Swineshead. She's quite convinced that's where the treasure will be found."

"Awesome." Brent practically purred into the phone, the arse-wipe. "Did you hire someone locally to keep an eye on her since you have a job in London and can't be there? Don't you think it's needed?"

"Well, let me consider." Tom pretended to think while he finished packing his briefcase of files to take home—everything he'd been able to pull about Brody Parker and Samantha Crowe and their former lives. "I honestly don't believe it's necessary at this point, Brent. It's less than a couple of hours to Swineshead, so it's simpler for me to keep tabs on our young friend without bringing anyone in from outside C7. Plus, it makes me feel as if I'm earning my ten percent. Wouldn't want you to feel you'd wasted your investment."

"Oh, never a waste, Tommy. I've enjoyed the photos you had taken—the ones before that dickhead professor's face was substituted for mine. That photography alone earned your commission."

Immoral bastard. "It was quite a piece of artistry, if I do say so." Like he'd look at such tripe. He'd seen just enough to know the shots were clear.

"This place she's living—who's the owner?"

"A young artist, actually, the great-nephew of an old Lincolnshire family. Has no clue what she's about, of course. He believes she's a student on a research holiday."

Brent huffed into the phone. "I'm not sure I'm comfortable with that. It would be easy for her to confide in him, which is another person we'd have to pay off or eliminate."

How casually he talked of "elimination," but hadn't Tom done the same thing when he issued his orders to Brody Parker? When he'd taken a person that he'd normally consider quite a hero and blackmailed him into cooperating? When he'd told him so blithely that he might need to kill Samantha Crowe?

Tom Nelson wasn't very high on his own list of favorite people right now.

"I'll keep an eye on things, Brent, not to worry. If it looks as if Samantha is confiding in this young man, well, I'll just have to take care of it, won't I?"

Brent laughed again. "Angling for a bigger percentage? We don't pay by the body count, you know. In fact, if we have to resort to murder, I have to pay a penalty to the other C7 members, including you. But I like the way you're thinking."

Didn't Tom already know about the body-count rule too well? It had happened once, and he'd anonymously donated his entire share of the "death penalty" paid by their Italian member to a variety of London charities.

After a few more reassurances from Tom that things were well in hand, Brent rang off and left him sitting alone in his office suite. Everything here seemed to mock him—from the fluorescent buzz of the lights to the faint scent of the industrial cleaner that kept their work space pleasant—all to better do the everyday work of upholding English law.

His own hypocrisy weighed down his shoulders as he gathered the final set of files that he'd planned to take home. He and his wife of almost twenty years would pore over them, looking for more holes through which he might make his escape. Not something he'd ever envisioned them doing back when they were young and he'd tried to imagine what their middle and later years might be like.

Things would get better, though. Tom had sharpened his computer skills quite well when it came to accessing files and interpreting data. After all, it had gotten this gem for him—a thick, heavily documented folder on the business dealings of one Brent Sullivan.

Even billionaires had to have a chink in their armor.

CHAPTER 13

"We have to talk."

Brody hadn't been able to wait until Cynthie got to her office; he called her at 6:00 a.m. after a sleepless night that alternated between thinking about the soft lips of Samantha Crowe and the troubled look in her eyes when he asked questions about her employer.

He punched and abused his pillow as he tossed and turned hour after hour, wondering how much Sam knew about Tom, whom she really worked for, and what the real end game was. She had effectively danced around every attempt he'd made to find out.

Cynthie's voice was still husky with sleep. "You do realize I have the day off, right, Brody? Remember? It's the day Wyl returns from Edinburgh? Our tenth wedding anniversary?"

Brody tried to backpedal. "Sure, I remembered. It's why I wanted to catch you early. You know, before you went off to . . ." What did women do to prepare for an anniversary? Bake? Shop? "To do stuff."

"Uh-huh. Tell me more lies." He winced as he heard the distinct sounds of bedclothes rustling. So much for her being able to sleep late on her day off.

"Sorry to wake you up so early, but there's some weird shit going on here and I wanted to talk to you about it."

"What kind of weird shit?" Her voice lost its sleepy rasp and assumed its Cynthie-the-NCA-agent sharpness.

"Blackmail. Threats. Hit orders. Sabotage. You know, the usual weird shit."

She was silent for a long time. "Where are you?"

Standing in his foyer, looking out the back window to see if Sam was awake and stirring yet. "I'm at home, but I'm alone. I can talk."

"If this is as bad as it sounds, I don't want to entrust it to wireless. I can meet you in King's Lynn in an hour. *Is* it as bad as it sounds, Brody?"

He sighed. "No, it's worse."

"Right then. I'll meet you at seven thirty a.m. at a spot called Bareo's. I'll text you the address. We can talk, and I can pick up sweets for Wyl and make him think I spent the day in the kitchen baking things to tempt his palate."

Cynthie didn't cook any more than Brody did. "Yeah, he'll fall for that one."

"He'll pretend to, which is why I love him. And why you need a woman of your own so you can tell her lies and she'll pretend to believe them."

Yeah, well, he'd gone a lot farther down that road than he'd intended, and his lips had wanted to lead him into further temptation. "Whatever. I'll see you soon."

"Do I need to bring my gun?" Cynthie's voice held warm laughter, but Brody didn't see the humor.

"Might not be a bad idea." He'd take his as well.

He spent the hour-long drive down the foggy A17 to King's Lynn pondering the mystery of Sam Crowe. She looked like a grad student. She talked like a grad student. He had the feeling that if he ever got her started talking about King John and the crown jewels and her theories about their loss, she would go on for days without taking a breath. There was something earnest and almost sweet behind those red glasses—or else he'd been bewitched by the eyes of Lincolnshire green and the gentle curves of her figure.

Which he totally needed to get out of his head because somehow Sam and her figure were mixed up with Tom the Blackmailer. Tom had looked quite sad to be threatening Brody with almost certain death, but he'd also been willing to make that threat without much of a crack in his cop-like demeanor.

She also was mixed up with whomever Tom was trying to double-cross. Was he a good guy, or someone like Tom, or worse?

This whole situation felt as if he were a pawn being moved around the board by master players in a game he didn't understand, and he wasn't sure if Sam was a player or another pawn. Maybe even both, depending on who was backstabbing whom.

After spending most of the past few years in Swineshead, Brody felt like a country rube visiting the big city as he drove into King's Lynn during morning rush hour. Never mind that King's Lynn was less than half the size of Gainesville, Florida, and didn't come close to the population of a single Miami suburb.

Traffic built around him on all sides, creating an unhealthy sense of claustrophobia along with it. Again it hit him how much happier he was now than in his old life. If someone gave him the opportunity to return to the Miami rat race as Nate Freeman and spend the day working for asshole rich guys, navigating rush-hour traffic two or three times a day, he wasn't sure he'd take it. Not anymore.

Being around Sam had made him realize he was lonely, but it hadn't made him nostalgic about his old life.

He used the GPS on his phone to find the address Cynthie had given him and circled the block a few times before snagging a parking spot. She must have flown like a bat trying to escape the flames of hell, because her dark sedan was already parked around the corner.

She'd found a table at the far end, set apart from the others. He saw why she'd picked Bareo's—the rich, comforting scent of coffee permeated the place, along with its favorite companions, sugar and pastry. He picked up a couple of Danish and a coffee before making his way to the back, where Cynthie watched him with brows knitted like those of a worried mother hen, if hens had brows.

"Have a good drive?"

"Sit down." She didn't crack a smile, and her hazel eyes studied his face with a somberness he rarely saw. "You look like hell, Brody. Start at the beginning."

So much for easing into it. He went through his encounter first with Sam and then with Tom, and then again with Sam. He omitted anything pertaining to green eyes, full lips, huggable curves, or impulses that might lead to kissing. He'd admit to being threatened and blackmailed, but confessing to unbridled lust extended beyond agent-client expectations.

Cynthie sat back, staring toward the front of the shop where a couple of teenage girls giggled over an assortment of cupcakes. Brody didn't think she saw the kids; her mental cogs were spinning like a hamster wheel at dinnertime. "Tell me again your impressions about this Tom guy. Not so much what he said—you went over that—but what your gut reaction to him was."

Brody twisted his coffee mug around two or three times, thinking. "My first thought was that he was either an assassin or a cop, so I thought he was there to kill me or had more news about that MI6 security breach. When he didn't shoot me right away, and before he began his blackmail spiel, I'd decided he was a cop or agent. Definitely in some kind of law enforcement."

Cynthie had extracted a pen from her bag and doodled on the back of a napkin. "What made you think cop?"

"He was . . . I don't know . . . restrained." Brody envisioned Tom sitting in old Parson Jessop's armchair, the gun resting on his thigh, his fingers relaxed around the trigger. "He was no stranger to that .45; he was comfortable with it—not waving it around like some female agents I know."

Cynthie's mouth curved up at the edges, but the smile was faint. "Sexist beast. What else?"

"I remember thinking he looked tired and stressed out. And he didn't seem to have much taste for what he was doing to me. I mean, he wasn't enjoying himself like a sociopath would." Brody frowned and fiddled with his napkin. "It was almost like he was doing it because he had to—but that he *would* expose me if I didn't cooperate."

"A reluctant blackmailer." Cynthie chewed absently on a muffin that looked dense and bran-like and kind of gross. "Interesting. Do you think you could sketch him from memory?"

Brody sat upright, his heart rate accelerating to double time. "Maybe. God, I hadn't even thought of that. What an idiot." Maybe because on some level, he still thought of himself as a computer security guy, not an art guy. Would that ever change?

He felt around in his pockets. "Damn it." He stayed covered in paint half the time and had graphite under his nails the other half. And today, he didn't even have an ink pen.

This time, Cynthie did smile—a real one. "I figured as much. You might be an artist, Brody, but you're a guy first. And guys are never prepared for anything."

"I resemble, I mean, resent that." He watched as she pulled a pencil with a nice soft lead for drawing and a nine-by-twelve sketch pad out of her bag. Amazing. "Do you have a change of clothes and a spare pair of Wellies in there, too?"

She laughed. "Nope. I'd actually bought this to see if you'd do a sketch or something for Wyl as an anniversary gift." She shrugged at his raised brow. "I know, I know. Last minute. NCA agents are never prepared either."

"I have something in the car for you that'll probably work— some new pieces, and I'll donate your choice to the cause. In the meantime . . ." He took the pad and pencil, shoved his plate and mug aside to make room in front of him, and closed his eyes. "Give me a few minutes."

In his mind, he fixed the picture of Tom as he'd looked when he'd finally gotten Brody to sit down. His posture had relaxed more, the lines on his face drooped into what would be their natural position. Outlining the basic shape of Tom's face, with its slightly square jaw, firm chin, and narrow features, Brody took the face apart bit by bit in his mind. The nose was very regular, but the creases leading to either side of his mouth had been deep. His hairline hadn't receded, but there were heavy flecks of gray at his temples. He had short side-burns. The mouth was wide, with rather thin lips.

His eyes had been blue, kind of a chambray-denim blue. He couldn't show that in the drawing, but he could show how Tom's left lid had begun to droop a bit as happened with age. It gave him a squinty, harder look than he might otherwise have.

Brody alternated visualizing with his eyes closed and sketching what he remembered. Staring at the drawing, he made a few adjust-ments. Shadows under the eyes, a few crow's-feet.

Finally, he handed it to Cynthie. "I've been wondering about his name." "Tom" was almost too common to be an alias. "If you're going to make up a name, you'd go for something common, but not some-thing so common that it would be suspicious. Like 'Tom.'"

Cynthie had been examining the drawing, but looked up, frowning. "You know, that's a really good point. What I'd like to do is take the drawing and show it to some of my colleagues at MI6 and NCA—the ones I know well enough to trust. I'll also see if I can get my hands on the logbooks for who has come and gone from headquarters about the time those lists were pulled. I'll have to be quiet about it. People in my line of work watch each other's backs, as well they should. But on the outside chance that he's another agent, I don't want to alert Tom that we're looking for him."

The idea caused Brody's Danish to settle in his stomach like a block of concrete—or a pair of cement shoes headed for the River Welland. "Be really sure, Cynthie. I mean really, really sure."

"I know what's at stake, Brody. I don't want you having to pick up and start over again—or worse."

"I won't do it." That was about the only thing in this shitbox of a situation he was sure about. "Rise or fall, I'm staying in Swineshead."

"What about the woman, Samantha?"

Brody stilled, cursing internally at the face that appeared in his mind.

"Oh my God. You like the woman."

"I don't even know the woman." Did he sound defensive? He sounded defensive.

Cynthie shook her head. "Well, well. Doesn't that complicate things. You're supposed to sabotage the first woman you've shown any interest in, to my knowledge, in the seven years I've known you. On the one hand, I'm glad to know you're human. On another hand, couldn't you find a nice English girl who isn't involved in criminal activities?"

Brody opened his mouth to protest, but he was busted. So he shut it again and said, "I'm sabotaging. I punctured her tire last night so she'd be stuck dealing with a mechanic until I got home."

"Uh-huh." Cynthie raised one perfect eyebrow, and Brody didn't much like the smirk on her face. "Did you take her spare? Because most women know how to change a tire, you Neanderthal. It isn't rocket science."

Well, fuck that. He hadn't even considered that she'd have a spare.

Still shaking her head, Cynthie gathered her bag of pastries and her purse and stood. "Come on and show me what I'm giving Wyl for our anniversary. I'm glad you have a future as an artist, because you suck at sabotage."

CHAPTER 14

What were the lines to that old Ray Charles song? "If it wasn't for bad luck, I'd have no luck at all." Sam didn't know the tune, so she made one up as she opened the trunk of the Ford and pulled up the carpeted flap to expose the spare tire. One of those useless little temporaries, but it would do well enough to drive around Swineshead until she got the flattened tire repaired.

She glanced around Brody's driveway but didn't see any telltale nails or building materials lying around. She'd probably picked up a nail between London and Swineshead and the tire had taken this long to go flat. At least it hadn't blown out and left her stranded in the swampy areas closer to the Wash.

This was the day's second unexpected delay. First, she'd overslept, her body probably trying to compensate from the stress of the last few days. She awoke to the unfamiliar sound of nothing. An occasional bird. A total absence of traffic. She could even hear the freaking dry leaves rustling on the tree outside the bedroom window.

Now the flat tire. Brody's car was already gone, but that was no big deal unless he'd seen it was flat and had left anyway. That would be a real jerk thing to do.

No point in getting more paranoid than she already was. Besides, she didn't need help changing a tire, and she was glad he'd left early to do whatever artists did. She didn't want to face the inevitable awkwardness of the Morning-after-the-Almost-Kiss. She'd thought about it way too much anyway, especially since her trust level in him had dipped.

There was too much he wasn't saying. How he and Tom were connected, for one thing. What Tom had done to change Brody's mind so quickly about renting her the room. The fact that not only was he not planning to help her find the crown jewels, but he was trying to talk her out of looking for them at all.

As if she had that option.

She didn't know if Psycho would distribute those photos and the journal pages and her arrest record if she tried to find the crown jewels and failed, but she had no doubt he'd do it if she didn't go through the motions of trying. Never mind about her mom, about whom she worried even though Elaine had never treated her as anything more than a potential source of income. And she'd been the eternal enabler, clear up until her flight left US soil headed for England.

In ten minutes, Sam had the tire changed, the flat in the trunk, and was on the road to Swineshead. She stopped in front of the house that had been built from the ruins of the old abbey centuries ago, before people had an interest in historic preservation.

There were no signs of life around the place, but it was still private property and she didn't relish being hauled in by a local constable for trespassing. She'd explore it by stealth if needed. Besides, she didn't really believe the place to look was on the site of the abbey building itself. In some genealogical research done among families living in the area surrounding the Wash, she'd uncovered some veiled notations regarding Swineshead monks hiding things of value elsewhere on the abbey's vast holdings.

She hadn't shared this with anyone outside her academic colleagues, but her money was on the site of Witcham House, a former moated manor on the abbey grounds. She just had to find it. The old St. Mary's Church dated to the 1300s, but remaining structures from King John's time a century earlier? Not so much.

Which led her, in the absence of a local library or museum, back to the Grainery. A girl had to eat, right? Besides, she'd noticed the all-day breakfast on the menu when she'd been there before and it was 7:00 a.m.

She found the restaurant just opening and a few patrons ahead of her. Spotting Betty on her way in, she waved and sat at the same table.

"Back again, duck?" Betty smiled. "How'd you do on your quest to track down our local artist?"

"Great—thanks for all your help." And all the help to come. "I had some questions about local history. Can you recommend anyone I could talk to who knows where all the bodies are buried?"

"Hang on, then. I'll be right back." Betty hustled off to turn in Sam's breakfast order and returned a few minutes later with a worn book. "There have been a couple of historical books published on the town history. You can borrow this one; just bring it back. We like to keep it for visitors, you know."

Sam nodded, her fingers itching to start thumbing the pages. "What about old-timers who've had families here, who might know some of the really old history? Stories that've just been handed down from generation to generation."

Betty thought for a moment, tapping a pink-painted nail against her chin. Sam didn't see a wedding ring, and Betty's helmet-like hair looked recently curled and sprayed in place. Maybe Friday night was a hot date night in Swineshead just like everywhere else.

"I'm thinking the best person for you to talk to is the professor—old Miles Thornton. His people have been here forever, and he's made it a hobby in his older years since his retirement to dig into people's family stories. Taught for years down at Cambridge."

Sam's foot tapped on the floor with nervous energy. This was exactly the type of person she needed. "Could you give me his name and address? I'd love to talk to him."

Betty frowned. "I don't know about that, duck. It's not my place to—"

Sam swallowed her impatience. "It's okay, I understand. Maybe you could give him a call? I'd be happy to meet him for tea here or wherever he'd like." She pulled a notebook out of her bag, tore off a sheet of paper, and wrote down her name and phone number. "He can call me himself if he'd like to talk."

Betty took the card and stuck it in the pocket of her slacks. "I'll ring him on my break. I'm sure he'll want to talk to you; start that man on local history and he'll go for days."

Perfect. Sam next got directions to a mechanic's shop and a half hour later, stuffed full of sausage and eggs, waddled off to get the tire repaired.

The kid who patched her tire was maybe eighteen, thin, and pasty pale, with yellow hair so spiked with gel it might cut you like a razor blade if you touched it. If not, and you still wanted to be cut, he had a razor blade on a chain around his neck. He also sported an impressive selection of tattoos, quite a few depicting things Sam didn't even recognize. She was used to being the oldest in her college classes—two jobs didn't leave time for a full course load so it had taken her a while to get through school. But this boy made her feel like a very old twenty-eight going on sixty.

"Guess I picked up a nail driving up from London yesterday," she said, watching as he ran soapy water over the tire, looking for air bubbles. "A big nail." The hole looked wide enough to drive a truck through.

"I don't think this was no nail," the boy said, fingering the rubber before lifting the tire and taking it to a machine.

Sam followed him. "What do you mean, it wasn't a nail?"

Once he had the machine running, he motioned her outside where it was less noisy. "I dunno for sure, right, but usually if you run over a nail and it don't stick in the tire, you either have a little slow leak or you have a hole what isn't round."

Which meant . . . what, exactly? "So what do you think caused it?"

The boy shrugged and scratched his head, causing his faux hawk to sway from side to side. It sprang back in place once the itch was scratched. "I'd say from the size of that hole, it weren't done long ago and weren't no accident. Coulda been a screwdriver, ice pick, awl, something like that."

Sam stayed outside while the boy went in to finish what he described as a short-term patch on the tire because the hole was too big for it to hold forever. The longer she waited, the angrier she got.

Brody Parker had a set of awls lying on a table outside the garage. He had tried to discourage her from looking for the jewels, but would he go so far as to try to sabotage her? And if so, was giving her a flat tire the best he could do?

It couldn't be anybody else, and he wasn't getting away with it.

As soon as she got the car back, she drove down High Street and saw Brody's VW parked near the Black Dragon. Good. He'd be busy with lunch, maybe the last meal he would ever eat once she ripped him a new esophagus using his own awl.

First, she'd make sure she wasn't accusing him unjustly. She passed the Dragon and drove straight to the house, parking a little farther from her previous spot just in case there was a nail lying around and the kid was wrong. She didn't even have to break into the garage like she'd done last night, although her old skills at lock picking came in handy more times than she'd like to admit.

No, there on a table next to the garage door, sitting right out in the open beside a pair of muddy running shoes and a couple of stained paintbrushes, was an awl with a red wooden handle. The largest one from the set, she'd guess. That son of a bitch.

Shoving the tool in her bag, she got in the car and drove back to town, parking a couple of spaces down from Brody. She paused, torn between confrontation and revenge.

A buzz from her pocket startled her, with a chaser of fear. Any phone call now could be Tom or, worse, Psycho. At least Tom had his

British manners to keep him in check while he issued threats. But the number was one she didn't know.

"This the girl that wants to know where our bodies are buried?" The high-pitched but still strong male voice helped her decide her course of action. Old Miles Thornton would be happy to talk to her at his home up near the old North End Mill, as long as she could come right away. He was leaving in the morning to spend time in the city with his grandkids.

"I'll be there in ten minutes," she told him.

But first, payback's a bitch, Brody. She stabbed the awl into the right rear tire of his white VW and listened to a satisfying hiss for a few seconds before leaving him to get his own damn tire fixed.

CHAPTER 15

"I think God doesn't like you, my friend." Jet Worthington, walking a few steps ahead of Brody as they made their way through a light rain toward their cars, stopped next to the white VW, looking down.

"Shit. Perfect." A flat tire. Seriously flat. The rubber was pooled below the hubcap like it was made of liquid. "Wonder what I ran over to get that?"

"Nothing." Jet picked something up from beside the tire and held it up. "This was no accident. I think somebody doesn't like you. Probably not God after all, though. He doesn't usually need to resort to hand tools."

"Let me see that." Brody snatched the red-handled awl from Jet and looked at it. It had a deep *X* etched with a knife on the end, so it was definitely his. He'd made the mark so he could find the big awl by feel, without taking his eyes off his bookmaking materials. This was the one he used to make his final binding punches.

That damned woman had punctured his tire.

"You look like you know who did it." Jet was grinning. "Spill it. Was it a woman? You got a secret life I don't know about?"

"Don't you have to get to work?" Brody hadn't planned on lunch with Jet—the guy talked too much—but he'd run into him at the Dragon and didn't have any excuses.

"Yeah, I'm on the fishing boat until Wednesday, so I'm headed for the Boston harbor," he said. "We bashing heads in football on Thursday?"

God only knew what hell would break through with Sam and his friend Tom and her mystery employer by Thursday. "I might have to beg off next week. I'll let you know."

As Jet continued the additional block to his car, Brody looked up at the gray, heavy sky and let the rain wash over his face. Might as well get this done.

Opening the trunk, he removed his spare and jack, making quick work of changing out the flat. On impulse, he pulled the small pistol from beneath its carpeted cover and slid it into the pocket of his jeans. One never knew when it might come in handy. If he'd had it on him the day of Tom's visit, he might not be involved in this mess.

He dropped the tire off at the nearest mechanic's shop, planning to pick it up later. Then he headed for home, where he fully intended to read Sam the riot act. She was going to tell him once and for all what was going on, by God, so he could make a rational choice about how to handle it. His life was on the line, and she was playing silly playground games.

Brody could tell as soon as he'd turned off Abbey Road onto the drive to his house that she wasn't there. Not that he was nervous or anything, but he couldn't resist stopping and making a quiet check of the hidden parking spot, which was empty, and the security light above the back door, which burned a comforting, steady green. Only then did he walk back to his car.

Where might Sam have gone? Brody got in the car, turned it a one eighty in a series of practiced moves, and drove back toward town. He pulled off the narrow road at the entrance to Abbey House, looking for any sign of movement or a suspicious black Ford, but everything was silent in its shroud of gray rain.

He sat for a minute, thinking about where she might have wandered off to. The town didn't have a library, but she might have an interest in looking at the records of the fourteenth-century St. Mary's Church. She'd said she was interested in getting oral histories of old-timers. Where would one be able to get the town gossip and recommendations of people to talk to?

He'd just come from the Black Dragon, and she hadn't been there or Greely would've mentioned it. So he drove toward the other option: the Grainery. It was in the dead center of town and everyone made his or her way there eventually.

The lunch crowd had emptied out, so Brody found an easy parking spot and ran inside, wishing he'd thought to pull on a hoodie. He could practically feel his hair plastering itself to his skull.

The inside was warmth and comfort, as usual. "We haven't seen our famous Swineshead artist here in a while—you here for a late lunch?" A young waitress or hostess or bartender, he wasn't sure which, approached him from behind the bar when he took a seat. Betty, a Grainery waitress who'd been on the baked-goods brigade when he first moved to town, had tried to fix him up with her more than once, and her name was . . . he had no idea.

"No, actually, I was looking for a friend and thought she might've been here earlier. American woman, blond hair, average height, green eyes." Amazing green eyes that flashed when she was angry or laughing or, as he knew from their almost-kiss, aroused.

The waitress's name was either Ashley or Amber, he thought, so he rolled the dice. "You're Amber, right?"

She smiled, her face lighting up at his superb memory, and he kicked himself for the swine he was. "Right. And your friend . . . I think she was here when we first opened today. She was talking to Betty. I'll get her to come round. Do you want a drink, Brody?"

She certainly knew his name. Brody the Swine of Swineshead. "No, sorry. I'm in a bit of a hurry." Yeah, to get out of here before he felt pressured to make a date.

"Right then. I'll find Betty."

Amber left with a shy smile back at him, and Brody returned a halfhearted imitation. While he waited, he studied his painting that hung behind the bar. It was one of the first ones he'd done after coming to Swineshead, at least one of the earliest ones he'd let anyone see. This was the one that had prompted Cynthie to insist on trying to sell his work for him. She'd only gotten him into a couple of minor galleries in London but had been successful in getting his work in just about every gallery in the East Midlands.

He'd even had a couple of shows, one in Lincoln and one in Nottingham. What would his father have thought of that? Brody suspected he'd tell his only son to stop wasting time and find gainful employment in some type of legitimate work. He'd heard that litany enough when he was a kid and then again when he'd parlayed his political-science major and computer-science minor into a security job instead of law school. First, he'd kept his art hidden, but by the time he hit college he'd quit creating it altogether.

"You remember painting that one, duck?"

Brody started, unaware the woman had slid onto the stool beside him. She looked to be in her late forties or early fifties, with a helmet of dark hair streaked with jets of silver he didn't think she'd had when he first arrived in Swineshead.

"I do remember." He glanced up at the painting, then back to the woman. "It's one of the first I ever did out on the fens. Made any more of your famous scones?"

She smiled. "That I have, duck. I might have to drop some round for you again. Amber said you were looking for the American girl that comes in here a bit . . . what was her name?"

Brody wasn't sure if this was a test of his honesty or a fishing-for-information expedition. "Samantha Crowe," he said. "She's renting my guest room."

"Right." Betty nodded, apparently satisfied with the answer.

"I'm looking for her today; she left her phone at the house and I thought she might need it." *Liar, liar.* He seemed to be doing it a lot since Sam came to town. "Amber said she was here earlier today?"

Betty laughed. "Yes, she was asking for people she could talk to about the town's history. I don't think she left her phone, though, duck. She had it with her. I saw it."

"Ah, busted." Brody used to be better at lying. His skills had deteriorated. "I just need to talk to her. Do you know where she went?" It occurred to him for the first time that it might be a good idea for him to have Sam's phone number.

"Maybe." Betty told him that Sam had hoped to talk to Miles Thornton, a retired Cambridge professor who was a Swineshead legend when it came to knowing all the local lore. Brody had met him a couple of times at the Black Dragon. "My guess is that if Miles is in town, she's up at his place near the North End Mill, getting her ears talked clean off her head."

And maybe getting information that would help in her search for the lost crown jewels. "I'll check up there. Thanks."

It took another five minutes to extricate himself from Betty, it being a slow part of the afternoon in the restaurant, but finally Brody escaped. He had been up to the old windmill a couple of times in his years in Swineshead, but he still made a few wrong turns before the top of the red brick structure came into view.

He'd heard it had been built in the nineteenth century, when this area wasn't quite as far inland as now, and had worked until the early 1900s. Someone had bought the property and the derelict windmill a few years ago and restored it. Now, like most of the spots around here of historic significance, the windmill lay in private hands.

A small one-lane road branched off to the east just before the windmill, and it led to Miles Thornton's house, a much more modern affair than one might expect a history buff to own. It was constructed with white wooden siding and black trim and shutters, with a wide porch and a classic bright-red front door.

In front of it sat a late-model black SUV and Sam's little black Ford.

Brody parked at the end of the driveway and thought about what he might say now that he was here. His anger had cooled during the wait at the Grainery, especially over the tire, so he couldn't rightly knock on the door and chastise her for doing exactly what he'd done himself. He deserved to have his tire punctured. She'd simply been letting him know he'd been busted. Any skills he might have at sabotage had rusted along with his ability to lie. The tire episode had been a real school yard effort, and he was done with it.

Maybe, instead of going on the offensive with no moral high ground to stand on, he should wait until she got back to the cottage and then apologize—after he created some plausible reason for him to have punctured her tire in the first place. That settled, he pulled out and headed back into town.

A big dish of humble pie went down better with beer, so Brody stopped at the market and picked up a couple of different locally made brews, along with assorted meats and cheeses. At a bakery down the street, he added some fresh, soft bread and two kinds of pastries.

Overdoing it much, asshole? Yeah, well, he had no believable reason he could give her for starting the whole tire war, so his only hope was to divert her attention.

The driveway leading to his house was already ponding heavily, and he splashed as far to one side of the parking area as he could to give Sam room near the back door. He hoped she'd been better prepared for the rain than he was.

His wet shoes skidded on the slate tiles outside the back door, so he pulled them off and carried them inside. He dropped them in the basket he kept inside the door for that very purpose and made his way to the kitchen, leaving big wet footprints on the floor from his rain-soaked socks.

By the time he got the food put away, he was freezing, and the daylight, which had barely qualified as dim today anyway, had already begun to fade. He looked out the window toward the highway, hoping to see the little black car bouncing through the widening pools of water across the drive.

He shouldn't be worried. She was from Louisiana, for God's sake. The woman must know how to drive in water. Didn't New Orleans go underwater after a half hour of rain?

The inside of the cottage felt damp and aged, but Brody didn't want to start a fire until he'd changed into clothing that wasn't cold and soaking wet itself. Walking into his bedroom, he tugged off his black T-shirt and wrung it out, droplets of water splashing on the floor. He turned on the water in the bathroom, shucking his jeans and briefs and shivering naked in the chill for the eon and a half it took the hot water to reach the shower.

Finally, he was able to step into its warmth and sighed as his muscles relaxed under the pounding. The old cottage had good water pressure but an undersized water heater. Replacing it was on the long list of home-improvement jobs he never seemed to get around to doing. Maybe next summer.

A loud banging noise interrupted his warm-water reverie, and he stepped out of the stream of water, listening. It had come from the front of the house, which meant, as Brody suspected, they were in for a real North Sea storm, the first of the season to roll in. Once it really got started, the winds would batter the windows and howl around the corners like a rabid cat or a crying woman. The rain would slash through the air with none of the gentleness and cleansing of the spring rains. It would be all violence and ferocity.

Brody turned off the water, trying not to worry about Sam being out in this mess. Surely with the weather deteriorating so quickly, she'd stay with Miles Thornton and ride it out. He rattled around that big house by himself anyway, as far as Brody knew.

By morning, it would be colder and the rain would have moved on.

Another banging noise jerked his attention to the bathroom window, panes of frosted, theoretically opaque glass that he'd never worried about anyone seeing through before. The house was too isolated, and crime was virtually nonexistent.

Except that unless he was badly mistaken, that was Samantha Crowe with one hand banging on the window and the other cupped over her eyes, her nose resting against the glass as she looked inside. At him. Who was naked as the day he fought his way out of the womb.

CHAPTER 16

Sam hadn't intended to watch Brody Parker take a shower, only to peek inside to see if he was in the bathroom so he could let her in the house.

But damn, that man was sexy. He was facing her, his head thrown back and eyes closed as the water cascaded over every ridge and muscle and . . . everything. She had to look, right? She might have taken a vow of celibacy, but she hadn't taken a vow of blindness.

You're an absolutely pathetic loser, Sam's inner nag said, and she agreed. Anyone who'd stand in the middle of a monsoon and ogle a man in his shower should have "LOSER" stamped on her forehead.

As soon as Brody stepped out of the water and saw her, his mouth and eyes battling for which could open the widest in shock, she stepped away from the window and splashed her way around the corner, returning to the back door. And yeah, giggled a little, the laughter bubbling up and spilling out before she could get it under control. She hadn't laughed much in the last couple of days, so it felt good even if she knew it was going to be short-lived.

She'd never been quite so wet and cold in her life. The wind had picked up, stabbing horizontal blades of rain into her face as she waited at the back door. For a few seconds, she wondered if he might leave her out here, but then the door opened and he stood there with a white towel slung loosely around his hips, which would have been sexy as hell except for the black T-shirt he'd pulled on. Droplets of water dripped from his black wavy hair onto his shoulders, getting said T-shirt wet.

"Nice fashion statement." She gave him her best lopsided smile as he moved aside to let her in. "You're shy about going without a shirt? You have man boobs, don't you?" Which would be a crime against nature.

"I certainly do not." Looking offended, Brody pulled the T-shirt up, exposing a rock-hard set of damp abs and nice, firm pecs without a trace of man boob. He jerked the shirt back down before she started salivating, which was good, given her celibacy and all.

"Why were you leering in my bathroom window?" He cocked his head. "Are you stalking me? How long had you been watching?"

Not nearly long enough. "Just a few seconds. I knocked on the door earlier and you didn't answer."

He glanced out the door, where the rain almost obscured the garage. "Where's your car?"

"Ah, that's the real story. Do you have a fire lit?"

Brody closed the door, shutting out the hiss of rain hitting the slate courtyard. "Not yet. I was going to do it as soon as I showered. Give me a minute to get dressed." He made no attempt to leave, though, but instead treated her to a head-to-toe visual inspection that she could swear grew a little heated when his gaze landed on where her soaked, thin sweater clung to her breasts.

Her nipples perked up just to make sure he could see them, the traitors. They didn't want her to be celibate. They wanted to be touched and licked and nibbled on, even if the attention came at the lips and tongue and teeth of the man who'd punctured her tire.

"Uh, you were going to get dressed?" This was getting more than a little awkward.

"Right." He shook his head, as if trying to jolt himself out of a daze. "You're wet."

How could he possibly know that?

"Are you locked out of the apartment?"

Oh, rain. That kind of wet. "No, but there's a leak. Over the bed. And my car's stuck, and . . . Maybe you should get dressed." Because her brain wasn't working properly and needed a minute to recover.

"Right." It seemed his go-to word when he didn't know what to say. "I'll be just a minute."

This time, he turned and walked down the short hallway toward what Sam assumed was his bedroom, treating her to an angelic vision of muscled man legs and a tantalizing swish of white towel . . . and what was up with that T-shirt?

None of your business, nag told her. *You know how to start a fire. Make yourself useful.*

The inner nag had been with Sam as long as she could remember, although she seemed to have taken a holiday the night Sam had made the so very wrongheaded decision to accompany Psycho back to his hotel suite. But most of the time, the nag was around. She couldn't blame that practical, no-nonsense presence on her mother's influence, because God knew practicality was not part of Elaine Sonnier's playbook. Sam didn't know who her father was—Elaine had claimed it was a half-dozen different men over the years, depending on what she was trying to force Sam into doing. Or force Carolina into doing; Samantha was beyond her control.

Except that wasn't really true, was it? Sam wadded up some sheets of newsprint and stuffed them beneath the logs she'd piled on the fireplace andirons, then took one of the long matches in the box on the mantel and swiped it across the strike plate.

The irony of her relationship with her mother struck her hard as she sat on the floor with her legs tucked beneath her, watching the fragile paper ignite and crumble to ash even as it sent the flames up to catch on the slow-burning logs. She could pretend Elaine had no hold over her anymore, but it was worry and sorrow over her mom's message just over a week ago that had sent Sam to the pub where she'd met Psycho Gary, or whatever his real name might be.

Maybe the need to deny the type of life she'd come from had made her vulnerable to Gary's smooth flattery. And Elaine had been part of Gary's blackmail trifecta: her juvenile record, her affair with David, and her mom.

"You okay?"

Sam swiveled at the sound of Brody's voice. He'd changed into a pair of dark chinos and a red sweater and carried a pair of dark socks in his hands. He still looked sexy as sin.

"I'm fine. Just trying to dry off a little and get warm."

"What happened? Where's your car?"

"It's floating in one of the lakes that have formed in your drive-way." She'd maneuvered around a couple of them, but this one fooled her. "I underestimated how deep it was."

He sat on the sofa and leaned over to pull on his socks. "Sorry about the leak in the apartment. It's right over the bed?"

She nodded and got up to sit on the sofa, then realized how soaked she was and sat on the wooden straight chair at the desk instead. "I don't think the mattress got too wet. I stripped off the bedding so it would dry out, and put the trash can on the bed to catch the water. It's pretty big and sturdy, so it shouldn't fill up or turn over."

Brody stood up and looked out the window. Instead of slacking, the rain was coming down harder. It wasn't like the Louisiana frog splashers Sam had experienced all her life, where the raindrops grew to the size of dimes and fell heavily enough to hurt when they hit you. But this was a respectable storm nonetheless.

"I can't fix it until the rain stops," he said, turning back to her. "Why don't you go over and get what you need for tonight. You can shower here and stay in my spare bedroom. I store art supplies in there, but it has a bed and is next to the hallway bathroom."

Bad idea, said the nag. *Cold, rainy night. Alone with this bad-news tire saboteur that turns your girl parts to jelly and makes your breasts think they have a mind of their own. Bad, bad idea.*

"Sounds like a good idea," she said. "I can fill you in on what Miles Thornton had to say. Do you know him?"

"I've met him a couple of times but don't really know him," Brody said. "I've heard he's made local history his new life's work since he retired from teaching and moved back up here from Cambridge. Was he able to give you any kind of information that'll help you find King John's crown jewels?"

Did he sound cynical, hopeful, or worried? Sam thought a little of each but didn't want to get into it with him just yet because they seemed to have reach some kind of an uneasy truce for the moment. She wanted to get settled before springing Miles's surprise on him—and her own question. Namely, why he'd punctured her tire this morning. The only reason she could come up with was to keep her here, to prevent her from going out and looking for the crown jewels, the quest from which he'd already tried to discourage her. And why was that?

She had a lot of questions for Mr. Brody Parker, but he was playing nice for the moment, and she was starting to shiver despite the warmth of the fire.

"I'll fill you in on Miles when I get back." She got up and winced at the squish of water between her toes when she took a step. Her best pair of walking shoes might never recover.

Brody stood in the doorway, and she felt his gaze on her as she ran across the courtyard and opened the entrance to the steep, narrow stairwell that led to the apartment.

Once upstairs, she decided to take the few clothes she'd need in her messenger bag instead of lugging her whole suitcase down the stairs, only to bring it back up tomorrow. The bag still contained the thick manila envelope from Psycho, though. She hadn't known what to do with it and didn't want to risk anyone seeing it, so she'd kept it with her, always within reach.

She didn't want to take that envelope of nastiness into Brody's house, however, so she slid it under the mattress, careful not to upend the trash can still collecting the water that dripped from the ceiling. She didn't think Brody was the type to be prying in her suitcase, but then again, she also hadn't thought he'd puncture her tire. Better to hide it than leave it in the suitcase for him to find. Just in case.

On second thought, the mattress was a bad idea, too. What if Brody needed to pull it off the bed to let it dry in the sun—the best thing to keep it from molding? She pulled the envelope out and stuck it under the bed instead. Judging by the number of dust balls keeping her secrets company, that bed hadn't been moved in years.

But wait. He might need to move the bed in order to repair the leak. Paranoia was taking hold again. She looked around at the few hiding options remaining. Finally, she stuck it on the shelf of the small closet, wedged beside a couple of shoe boxes that looked as if they had been there since the parson's youth.

Gathering her stuff, she headed for the stairs and bypassed the jacket hanging on the back of the little desk chair. No point in putting it on now; she'd just get the inside of it wet.

Sam splashed back across the courtyard, and Brody met her at the door, holding a couple of folded white towels.

"The bathroom's in the hallway? I'm freezing." Her teeth were chattering again.

"Yep, follow me." He led the way into the short hallway off the foyer, taking a turn to the left about halfway down. "Bedroom's in here if you want to leave your bag." He flipped on the light, and over his shoulder Sam glimpsed piles of stuff and boxes of more stuff. It looked more like a warehouse than a bedroom. "Bathroom's next door."

He set the towels on the edge of the small, old-fashioned pedestal sink. "Water pressure is good, but give the hot water about a day and a half to get to you."

She laughed. "Sounds like the house I grew up in."

The wait was more like two minutes, and as soon as she could stick a hand under the faucet stream and feel warm water, Sam stripped off her wet clothes and climbed in—literally climbed. The tub was narrow and deep and, she thought, made of iron. Also like the one she'd grown up with.

The warm water of the shower heated her skin and chased away the last of the chill. At least she hoped it was the water temperature and not the image of Brody in his own shower. She might dream about that image tonight, unless he pissed her off too much about the tires or didn't react well to one of Miles's theories that this house might sit on a possible resting site for the jewels.

She honestly didn't think that theory was a strong one. Maybe it was even the weakest one she'd heard. But it was interesting, anyway, as were some of the things the professor had told her about the former owner and Brody's far-removed uncle, Parson Jessop.

She dressed quickly, mimicking Brody's style with simple jeans and a light sweater, and ran a brush through her wet hair. Why hadn't she brought her makeup bag and hair dryer over here?

Because this is not a date, nag said. *It's an interrogation.*

Damn straight. Time to find out why her landlord, host, and lust object had attacked her Goodyears with an awl.

CHAPTER 17

Brody kept himself busy while Sam showered, getting out the food and preparing a diversionary feast.

Before long, the smell of warm toasted bread filled the kitchen. Brody sliced locally produced sausage and roast, then began cutting rich yellow hunks of cheese to pile alongside the meat.

"Something smells like heaven." Sam crossed the entry hall into the kitchen, looking pretty heavenly herself. Her wet hair was drying in soft waves that he'd like nothing better than to weave his fingers through.

"Have a beer." He nodded toward the fridge. "I picked up a couple of local brews I thought you might be interested in trying. Or there's wine if you'd rather have that." Mr. Sincere and Accommodating, that was him. He sure wasn't going to mention the tire incident until she did.

"Beer's good." Sam opened the fridge and pulled out a bottle of amber. The opener lay on the counter next to the fridge, so she opened the bottle, tossed the cap in the trash, and took a tentative sip while Brody watched.

She smiled. "The beer *is* good."

"Glad you like it. I think so, too. You remember Greely, the pub owner?" When Sam nodded, he continued. "He's part owner of this brewery along with a cousin of Betty's, a woman who works at the

Grainery. The business is in Boston. I think the amber's their best, but the dark's pretty good, too—well, for dark. I still don't have much taste for it."

"Me either. I think it's because we don't see stout much in the States unless it's a bar that sells Guinness." Sam gestured to the spread of food. "What's the occasion? I know this stuff wasn't here last night when we were feasting on PB and J."

Here it came. Brody had spent the whole time he was preparing the food trying to come up with a plausible excuse he could give for sabotaging her job, or mission, or quest, or whatever it was. He hoped his plan worked, because he still wasn't sure where she and her mystery employer fit into the whole scenario with the two-faced Tom. Only that the stakes had to be high, and she was in more danger than she knew. Brody wouldn't kill Sam to get the crown jewels if she found them, but Tom might.

Brody stopped slicing and laid the knife beside the plate. He looked down at it a moment before lifting his gaze to hers, searching her face for a clue to her state of mind. Was she angry? Disappointed? Confused? He saw only a mild, calm pair of beautiful green eyes, daring him through her red-framed glasses to lie to her again.

"It's a peace offering and an apology. I was massively stupid about the tire."

Sam's breath seemed to catch; he'd surprised her, judging by the widened eyes and the slight parting of those soft pink lips. Then the eyes narrowed.

"Then I'm sorry I did the same right back at you. Maybe. It depends." She picked up a crumble of roast beef from the edge of the plate and stuck it in her mouth. "Why did you do it?"

"Let's fix a plate and then we'll talk." Because he kind of liked the vibe they'd had between them ever since he opened the door to find her like some half-drowned orphan waif. Make that a half-drowned orphan waif who'd gotten shamelessly turned on watching him shower. How pitiful was it that he found that sexy? Did it make him some kind of exhibitionist?

She didn't argue about delaying the serious talk. "Fine with me. My lunch at the Grainery is long gone, and that bread smells amazing."

They both piled the simple white plates full and moved to the living room with the beer and dinner.

"We can eat here." Brody cleaned a couple of painting magazines and a London newspaper off the coffee table, piled them on the desk in the corner, and tossed a couple of throw pillows on the floor.

Once they were settled in and Sam had tried each of the meats and cheeses and breads—all local products with which Brody was familiar so he could tell her their histories, he finally sat back and stared at the fire a few moments. Time for his performance.

"I punctured your tire because I didn't want you to go looking for the crown jewels," he said. "I had an early meeting to go to in King's Lynn, and I thought if you got up and found the flat tire, you'd spend most of the day trying to get it fixed and wouldn't have time to search."

She'd been nodding slowly and now arched a brow. "Because girls can't change tires, right?"

Yeah, Cynthie had nailed that one. He was a sexist idiot. "Well, you obviously proved me wrong. How did you know it was me and not just a random flat?"

She paused a moment, looking into the fire herself and raising a bit of cheese to her mouth, chewing absentmindedly and looking sexy as hell. "I noticed some tools sitting outside the garage, including that set of awls with the red handles, so when the little tattooed mechanic guy in the village said the hole had to be made with something big like an ice pick or awl . . ." She shrugged.

Which would teach Brody to leave his tools lying around, although his career as a saboteur was over.

"What do artists use awls for anyway?"

Changing the subject, was she? He reached behind him on the sofa and picked up a sketchbook, one of his simpler ones. A couple dozen nine-by-twelve pages of heavy cold-press paper with a rigid, embossed leather cover, all bound together with an intricate weave of leather cord.

"I make my own sketchbooks and journals." He handed her the book and realized as she ran her fingertips along the embossing that he'd never before shown anyone his raw journals. Even Cynthie didn't see his pieces until they were finished, much less the messy process of getting to the point of actually creating a painting.

Yet he liked watching Sam's face as she flipped through the pages. The flickering light of the fire played in shadows across her features, and he found himself leaning over to see which sketches were making her smile.

"These are beautiful. Different from the painting I saw, though. More playful, more personal. It's like looking into your soul or seeing the world through your eyes." She shook her head. "It must be amazing to be able to create something from your own thoughts like that. Where I look at something and see a blank page, you see a whole world. You went to art school?"

Brody laughed at the very idea. "Oh, no. I drew a lot as a kid but then quit until a few years ago. Until I moved to Swineshead, in fact. Art was a hobby, not anything that real men should pursue as a career option."

"Ah." Sam leaned against the sofa and clasped the sketchbook against her chest, putting Brody in the odd position of being jealous of his own sketches. "That sounds like a parent talking."

He hadn't intended to open up that much. She had the unconscious ability to put him at ease, and that was a dangerous place for him to visit. "Something like that."

She stared at him a few awkward seconds, then shrugged. "It's okay. I sure don't want to talk about my mom either."

He wasn't the only one opening the door into the past, or at least letting it crack open a sliver. "What about your dad?"

Sam laughed, but it held no humor. "I have no idea who my father is, and if my mother knows—which I doubt—she isn't saying."

Brody wasn't sure how to respond to that, so he didn't. He tried to relate Sam's childhood with his own. She'd apparently grown up with a single mother in a not-so-great neighborhood of New Orleans while he'd had all the physical comforts he needed in his upper-middle-class small-town Florida neighborhood an hour outside Tampa. All his physical needs had been met, but none of his emotional needs. He wasn't sure which was worse. Sounded like she hadn't had either one.

"That was a great distraction, but you still haven't told me why you don't want me to find the crown jewels. Or even to look for them." Sam set the sketchbook aside and shifted to face him, curling her legs beneath her. "Make me understand."

Time to test out his excuse. "It's because of Swineshead. I don't want to see it change."

Sam's eyebrows lowered, creating a little crease between them. "I don't get it. What do you mean?"

"It's selfish, I guess." He took a moment to organize his argument. It helped that he believed it was true. "If you find the crown jewels, or even *one* jewel or a cup or anything people thought belonged to King John, Swineshead would become like a medieval Disneyland. There's some of that in Nottingham already."

He leaned forward. "I don't want to ruin this job you're probably getting well paid for, but think about it, Sam. Every treasure hunter on earth would come in here with a metal detector and a shovel. Most of the old abbey lands are privately owned now, so people's lives would be uprooted, their homes and property damaged. The government would have to step in and regulate everything. The whole town would change."

About halfway through his speech, Sam had looked down at Parson Jessop's old worn area rug and begun picking at it. He waited for the arguments. That it would revive the economy of a town that was far from prosperous. That it would restore a great piece of British history. That it would make her an academic star before the ink was dry on her diploma.

But when she looked up, her eyes shone with tears. "I understand what you're saying, and you're right. I hadn't even thought about it that way. But you don't understand. I have to do this, Brody. I have to. My life depends on it."

CHAPTER 18

Sam wanted to cry. She felt Brody's passion for this town. She didn't know what had brought him here, but he genuinely loved it. That much was clear.

But how could she explain her lack of options without knowing how he'd really gotten brought into this and how he and Tom were connected?

"Look, I understand your career is important to you." Brody reached out and took her hand. God, he thought she was doing this out of selfishness. It was true that she'd wanted to find support for her theory that the crown jewels were here in Swineshead, but it had never even occurred to her to actually try to find them. She was no archaeologist. He must think her insensitive and careless of what something like this could do to the village he loved.

"You don't understand, Brody."

"Sure I do. I really do. This would be a huge thing even for a seasoned academic to find, much less someone just starting out. But think about the cost, Sam."

The cost. He had no idea. She looked at their hands, fingers twined together, and for the first time since that morning in Starbucks before Tom had shown up, she thought about running. Saying to hell with it all, taking the money she had left, and hopping the next northbound train.

But if she took that step, it was both irrevocable and permanent. She'd never be able to go back to Louisiana without looking over her shoulder for a fire-breathing Gary whoever-he-was to come swooping in on his private jet to kill her. At the very least, she had no doubt that Psycho would follow through with his threats to humiliate and discredit her and ruin David's career in the process.

Even if she'd be able to live with those consequences, what about her mom? Maybe Elaine didn't deserve better than to fall deeper into addiction with Gary's help. Hell, she might even welcome a new source of drugs. But she was still Sam's mother and Sam couldn't live with it. She wasn't sure she loved her mother, but she didn't want to be the cause of her being more miserable. Or worse.

If she only knew where Brody stood. "Tell me about Tom. How did he convince you to rent that room to me?" She watched his face and knew the second a veil dropped over his gaze and he clammed up like some primitive organism on the edge of the Wash, protecting itself from the coming high tide.

"He just asked, that's all." He shrugged with a casual rise and fall of his shoulders. "I can always use the extra income."

Sam didn't think so, but until he could convince her that he wasn't in league with Tom, she couldn't come clean with him about the blackmail. For all she knew, he was in on it. She didn't think so, but it was possible.

"Well, let's just agree to disagree." She finished off the last of her beer. "The chances of me finding so much as a royal spoon are pretty slim. As you say, most of the land is privately owned. I can't exactly start digging up every lawn that lies on the former abbey grounds, even if I knew the proper way to conduct an archaeological investigation." Something Psycho Jerk had obviously not considered.

Brody's shoulders relaxed, and he leaned against the sofa again. "Look, I really am sorry about the tire. I can't promise to help you in your search, but I promise not to try and sabotage you again. If you find something, well, then we'll figure it out."

He looked sincere. He sounded sincere. But as Sam's inner nag would be quick to point out, her judgment when it came to trusting men was suspect. Still, he was offering a truce and she should take it—and then keep her eyes and ears open.

Brody got up and moved to the sofa, so Sam did the same. The floor had gotten pretty hard.

"What else did the professor have to say?"

Should she even tell him? Not all of it, not tonight. She was too exhausted. But she could share parts of it. "From all the local stories he's put together over the years, and there have been a lot of them, the professor thinks it likely that the historians have at least part of it right. The locals like to believe the most colorful story."

Brody laughed. "The murderous monk story? I think I've heard it. Wasn't there a frog involved?"

"Exactly. Shakespeare's play follows this version of the story." Sam smiled at the memory of the professor's animation as he recounted the far-fetched tale. "King John supposedly came riding into Swineshead Abbey to visit, sending his baggage train with the crown jewels on a shortcut across the Wash, where they all sank in the quicksand. Meanwhile, the horny old king demanded a conjugal visit from the abbot's wife, and a monk named Timothy slipped him some wine poisoned with toad spittle, or something like that. He died a few days later."

"Hold that thought." Brody went to the kitchen and brought them back a couple of fresh beers, apparently thankful that they'd moved away from the subject of Tom and sabotage. Frog spittle was safer. "So what else did old Miles have to say? Did he have a theory about where to look?"

Was he interested in the answer because he wanted to stop her from going there? She'd try to give him the benefit of the doubt. "He had a couple of ideas. He really thinks a place called Witcham House is the strongest possibility. Do you know where that is?"

Brody frowned and shook his head. "I don't think I've ever heard of it. It's near here?"

She wasn't sure either. She'd written down the directions, but by the time she left the professor's house, the deluge had started in earnest, and it didn't seem like a good time to be taking a leisurely drive through the outskirts of Swineshead. "I think it's behind your property, maybe a quarter mile back, but I'd have to look at the professor's directions."

"Nothing but farmland back there. I don't remember seeing any old buildings around here—well, other than this house and a couple of abandoned farmhouses."

"The building's not there anymore," Sam said. "It was a house built in medieval times—not a castle, I don't think, but Miles said it had a moat. The moat was filled in, and now there are two farmhouses on the site. Maybe those are the abandoned places you're talking about. He says there are some earthworks on the property."

Where she needed to go on a little, judicious scouting mission. Maybe even dig. She couldn't forget that her one-month deadline was getting closer to three weeks.

Brody continued to pepper her with questions about her visit with Miles and she continued to answer, but her mind raced ahead to bedtime. Namely, his. As soon as he was asleep, she planned to do a little sleuthing at the professor's other most interesting site—here. Parson Jessop, Miles had said, was quite the chronicler of local history. Miles had badgered him to have his writings published, but the parson always refused. His work was nothing but memories and stories and half-remembered histories, he'd said. No one would be interested in the ramblings of an old man.

Sam was very interested in his ramblings. She just didn't trust Brody enough to ask him outright if he had found any of the parson's writings or would let her look through his attic. She'd spotted an attic door in the ceiling of the hallway, and as soon as Brody was asleep, she planned to investigate.

Only he seemed to be wide-awake. Finally, she feigned a yawn instead. "I'm sorry. It's been a long day. Started out with some manual labor, you know." She smiled. "Changing a tire."

Brody laughed. "Touché. Come on, let me get some clean sheets for the guest bedroom and we'll get you set up."

She followed him into the room, waiting while he opened a cabinet in the hallway and pulled out a set of sheets. "I can do that." She held her arms out and he handed them to her. "Just let me know if there are things I shouldn't touch."

"Nothing much of interest in here. This is basically my supply room, but there is a trail leading to the bed."

When she'd first arrived, Sam had set her bag inside the door but hadn't fully appreciated the sheer amount of stuff in here. She didn't know what half of it was used for. She opened a box filled with big plastic jars and lifted one out. "What's gesso?"

"It's pronounced with a *J* sound, like juniper." He picked up a couple of boxes and hefted them to make enough room around the bed to change the sheets. "It's a thick paste that you spread on canvas or paper to make it take the paint better. Makes the paint go farther."

Who knew art required so much stuff? She thought of the artist as a solitary, tortured, slightly mad Van Gogh type, sitting in a field of poppies with a brush, an easel, a canvas, and a palette.

"Here, I'll help you get the sheets on. Give me the end of the fitted sheet."

Sam shook out the slightly wrinkled riot of purple and teal flowers. "I hadn't pictured you for the floral type." She turned her head to the side to study a white blob with wings. "Make that flowers and birds."

"It came with the house." He laughed. "You wouldn't believe what old Parson Jessop had stuffed in this house."

She was counting on it being quite a lot. "And exactly how did you end up here?"

Brody hesitated, which made Sam's inner nag sit up and notice. That was a pretty straightforward question; why would he have to think about his answer?

"I inherited it, actually." Brody stretched the elastic corner of the sheet around one end of the mattress and stretched the sheet toward the foot of the bed. She mimicked his movements on the other side. She'd heard he inherited the house, but that didn't really explain why he decided to live in it. "I didn't even know I was related to the man. He was like a three-times great uncle twice removed, or something like that."

"And you just picked up and moved here from the States?" There was more to that story, she'd bet.

"I was ready for a change, and it seemed like a chance to start over." Brody nodded at the other sheet, which Sam had piled on top of a box. She unfolded it and shook it across the bed.

"I'm sure it was a definite change."

"It was." He walked around the bed, took the pillowcases out of her hands, and tossed them on the bed. "For what it's worth, I'm glad you're here tonight."

Again, he'd surprised her. This time, though, she didn't see any secrets in his eyes, just that dark liquid brown that she could drown in if circumstances were different. "I'm glad, too."

And she meant it. If she had to be in this screwed-up mess, at least she was with someone whose company she enjoyed—except for the lying and sabotage part. At least the lust was good.

As if thinking the same thing, Brody slipped his hands around her waist and pulled her to him. He was warm and solid and smelled like wood smoke and spices.

Inner nag poked her head up again. *Are you really going to kiss the man who might have apologized for the tire thing but evaded every other question you asked him?*

No, but she was going to kiss the man who'd made her dinner.

He angled his head and caught her lower lip between his teeth, then pressed his lips softly against hers, testing. Nag popped her head up to remind Sam of the celibacy thing, but Sam batted her away. She wasn't sleeping with the guy; she was kissing him.

His soft little groan when she opened her mouth to his told Sam he felt the electricity between them as much as she did. His hands stroked her back, and she reached up to circle his neck with her arms . . . and he jumped as if she'd poked him with a cattle prod.

"What?" She searched his face, looking for a clue as to what she'd done that startled him. "Did I do something wrong?"

"No." Brody's face reddened, and he almost stumbled as he backed away from her like he couldn't get out of there fast enough. "Sorry. I didn't mean to take advantage of you like that. Let me know if you need anything else. Sleep well."

He practically ran out the door.

Brody thought he'd taken advantage of her? Not likely. He'd gotten spooked—that was the only word Sam could think of to describe the near panic on his face when she'd put her arms around him. Earlier, he'd answered the door in a towel and that stupid T-shirt. What was with Brody Parker and his body issues?

Because it was a damn fine body.

CHAPTER 19

Brody threw off his blanket for at least the twentieth time and glanced at the bedside clock. It was after 3:00 a.m., and he hadn't slept for a nanosecond.

First, he'd tossed and turned in humiliation at the look on Sam's face when he ran from her kiss like a scalded cat—or a man with a scarred back that her fingers were in danger of touching.

After he'd finally made peace with the fact that he'd made a complete fool of himself, his mind had spun with wild, improbable stories of medieval Swineshead, a time when the village, which now was located so far inland, had sat close enough to the Wash for the river to flow right up to High Street during high tide.

Sam had shared more of Miles Thornton's personal opinions on King John, including the fact that he had agreed with Sam's theory on the location of the crown jewels. King John had been experiencing such a downward spiral in his fortunes, she believed he wouldn't have let the crown jewels out of his sight. The barons had made him sign the Magna Carta the year before, and half were still in league with the French, believing it would be better for England to fall under French rule than to let John continue his monarchy.

The man was understandably paranoid, something Brody knew way too much about.

He rolled out of bed and turned on the lamp. Might as well get up and do something productive.

Halfway to the door, he stumbled when the lamp blinked a couple of times and went out. Along with the clock and the small air cleaner he ran all the time to help keep the air cleared of noxious paint fumes.

With the electricity off, the storm outside no longer sounded cozy and comforting; it sounded creepy and violent. The rain hit the windows in sheets, setting up their own eerie rhythm.

He felt his way along the bedroom wall, opened the door, and took cautious steps down the hallway. Finally, he reached the living room, where enough embers remained in the fireplace for him to see the desk and retrieve his flashlight.

Settling into Parson Jessop's old chair, he wondered if Sam had been able to go to sleep in the middle of his towering piles of supplies. Whenever he went to Boston or to London, he'd stock up on art boards and canvases, acrylics and inks, gessos and other mediums, brushes and sponges, and whatever struck his fancy. It all went into the room. The only reason Sam could get in there at all was that he'd cleaned it out a little so Cynthie could spend the night after telling him about the security breach at MI6.

He hoped she'd had a good anniversary with Wyl, and then he hoped she'd make some headway on finding out Tom's identity. He'd give her until Monday before bugging her. Besides, he needed some time in the small room off his bedroom he called Security Central, digging around online to see if he could find anything himself. But finding someone named Tom who might or might not be in law enforcement in London, a city of eight million people? Talk about a proverbial needle-haystack situation.

There was nothing he could do until the power came back on, though. Brody sat back, thinking again about all the trouble old King John was causing eight hundred years after he died. The old bastard would probably love it.

The king had been ill when he made his five-day visit to Swineshead Abbey in October of 1216, Sam had said—historians thought he had a severe case of dysentery, while the locals were going with the poison-by-monk story. Both she and, it turns out, the professor believed one of two things happened. Either some or all of the jewels were stolen by the monks or the abbey staff and stashed on the grounds, and the king was too ill to realize his personal fortune was gone. Or King John, sick and paranoid as his monarchy fell to ruin, had hidden the jewels somewhere on the abbey grounds himself so they wouldn't fall into the hands of the French or his rebellious barons, perhaps intending to retrieve them when things settled down.

Since King John died only four days later, he never got the chance to retrieve them, and rumors took the place of documentation in a time when even the monks had stopped writing of contemporary events. Which is how mysteries were made.

Whatever else she might be—gold digger, glory seeker, or just ambitious—Sam really loved her work. That had been clear. As she talked about her conversation with the professor, her face had lit up, her eyes bright and cheeks flushed. What she told him had been fascinating but not nearly as enticing as Sam herself. Had he really thought she was plain when he first met her? He hadn't looked beyond the red-framed glasses, which she claimed she wore all the time now that she'd taken her so-called vow of celibacy.

A vow he really wanted to challenge. But that couldn't happen. She was attracted to him, he knew that. They practically sizzled when they touched. But she hadn't seen the scars he carried, and even if he was willing for her to see them, which he wasn't, he couldn't explain them. Better to live on the dreams of what being with her might be like than to be ripped apart by reality. Reality was one ugly son of a bitch.

He slumped in his chair and closed his eyes, thinking about that kiss and how sweet it had been before he went into freak-out mode. Even with the lies and distrust, he'd enjoyed this night more than any he'd spent since all the shit went down in Miami. Even before then. With a jolt, Brody realized something that must have been obvious to Cynthie and the matrons of Swineshead who wanted to feed him and play matchmaker: he was lonely. Sam had reached in and knocked away some of the barriers he'd built around himself, and he found that he didn't want to rebuild them.

When she left, as she had to do in about three weeks if Tom's deadline of November 15 held true, it was going to hit him hard.

With a slight buzz, the electricity kicked back on and Brody started at the sound of a thump overhead. He watched the ceiling as if its plastered white expanse and dark wood beams might give him a clue to the source of the noise. All was quiet for a few moments, so he relaxed. He had enough worries without hearing the ghost of King John in his attic.

Another thump brought him out of the chair. Something more solid than a ghost was up there. He had visions of big rats or gophers or whatever ran wild in the Lincolnshire countryside, rampaging through his attic, feasting on Parson Jessop's family treasures, and breeding to create a giant rodent army. He'd put rat traps up there after a mouse invasion a couple of years ago but hadn't given it another thought.

Something above his head shifted again, followed by the sound of an object rolling across the attic floor so clearly that Brody could envision exactly where it started and stopped. It had come to rest somewhere over the desk.

The lights were on and he was awake, so he might as well check it out. He had some extra traps in the pantry off the kitchen, so he retrieved them, baited them with a couple of cheese cubes left from dinner, went to the center of the hallway, and pulled down the attic ladder as quietly as he could. No point in waking Sam if she'd been lucky enough to sleep through this miserable night. And no point in alerting the rats that he was coming.

Not that the rats were his greatest fear. There were spiders up there.

Trying to keep the image of giant, eight-legged hairy beasts out of his mind, Brody climbed the stairs, sticking his head through the attic opening and reaching up for the light switch tucked behind a support beam. Thank God his faux relative Parson Jessop had updated the cottage when he was well into his eighties so he didn't have to brave spiders with only a flashlight or candle.

As soon as he flipped the switch, the attic lit up with a soft yellow glow, followed immediately by a shriek.

Brody turned toward the sound with a jolt and slipped, banging his bad knee on ladder rungs on his way down and catching a foot so it flipped him upside down. He landed shoulder first, followed by his head hitting the floor with a teeth-jarring crack.

Flopping onto his back, afraid to move farther in case something was broken, he opened his eyes and stared up at the gaping square of the attic opening above him. Framed in the center, looking down at him in shock, were two Lincolnshire green eyes behind a pair of red-framed glasses.

CHAPTER 20

Ten years of the straight life had definitely eroded her skills. Sam stared down the attic opening at Brody, her pulse racing but her body frozen in place. It seemed like forever before he opened his eyes and looked at her. He finally did, but his dark eyes definitely looked dazed. She wasn't sure his brain had reengaged.

At least he was alive. "Don't move. I'm coming right down."

"Uh-huh."

And he could speak. Well, more like a grunt. It was a start.

She climbed down the ladder, cursing herself for turning into a girl. Once in the attic, she'd used the flashlight she kept in her bag to maneuver the land mines of trunks and old furniture, moving carefully to make sure she didn't trip over anything and wake Brody. Then the freaking batteries died and she'd been left in the dark.

Her game plan had been to wait until daylight sent enough illumination through the small attic dormer window to find her way back to the entry, let the ladder back down, and hope Brody wasn't such an early riser that he caught her. In which case she'd have to start making excuses.

No, instead, he'd sneaked up the ladder and flipped on the lights, scaring the crap out of her.

By the time she reached the bottom, he was struggling to sit up, although without much success. "Wait, Brody, let me help."

She prayed he didn't have any kind of spinal injury, then slid her arms beneath his shoulders and helped him sit. He wore a pair of loose black running pants with a drawstring at the waist and a gray T-shirt. Make that a gray T-shirt with a bloom of red spreading on his left shoulder. He was bleeding.

"Do you think anything's broken? Should I call an ambulance?" Did Swineshead even have a hospital? She thought she'd spotted a medical center somewhere in her wandering.

"No ambulance." Brody's words slurred. What if he had a concussion? "Help . . . up."

"Okay, let's take it slow." She pulled one of his arms around her shoulders and hoisted while he pushed off the floor with his other arm. They teetered southward a couple of steps, but they finally got him upright and somewhat steady.

"Come on. Your bedroom's closest." She started him toward his bedroom door and, after the first couple of steps, was relieved to feel him carrying more of his own weight, his steps surer. He was coming around.

She helped him sit on the edge of his bed, which looked like a couple of gators had rolled around in it. The duvet was crumpled into a fluffy mess and hung halfway onto the floor, and the sheets looked like he'd tried to tie them into a rope ladder.

"What the hell were you doing in the attic?"

Oh yeah, he was coming around all right.

"I was—wait, you're bleeding. I need to look at that." The shoulder of his gray T-shirt was a wet, solid red now. "Take off your T-shirt so I can look at it. Do you have a first-aid kit?"

"No. Get out of here." His voice was sharp. Okay, he was angry. He had a right to be. But he was nuts if he thought she was going to leave him bleeding and with a possible concussion.

"Stop being stupid." She reached behind him, grasped the bottom of the T-shirt, and tugged it over his head before he could react.

He snatched it out of her hands. "Get out of here, Sam. I'm fine."

"No, you're not. Your shoulder—" As she talked she'd climbed onto the bed beside him, standing on her knees to get a look at his wound. But it was his back that drew her attention. The top third of it, from below his neck to the bottom of his shoulder blades, was covered in scars. Not just a scar or two, but a shiny field of solid skin that looked almost like pale flesh-colored wax had been poured over it. The edges were red ropes of scar tissue.

They stayed frozen in place for what seemed like an eternity before Brody spoke, softly this time. "Sam, just go. Please."

The image of him answering the door in a towel and a T-shirt, and then pulling away from her when she touched his neck, suddenly became clear. He hadn't wanted her to see this; probably hid it from everyone. Whatever she did now would set the tone for the future. Not that they had a future beyond three weeks, but Sam realized she didn't want him to push her away. Damn it, despite his lies and evasiveness, she liked Brody Parker.

"No, Brody. The only place I'm going is to the bathroom to get a wet washcloth and see how bad your shoulder's banged up. I think there are splinters in it."

He didn't answer, so she looked around the room. There were three doors leading off of it besides the closet, one for each wall except where the head of the bed rested. One door was closed, one led to the hallway, and the third stood open. Bingo—she could see the edge of a sink through door number three, plus it was the right location to have the window she'd been looking through earlier.

Sam half expected Brody to be gone when she returned with a cloth she'd finally found in a cabinet over the toilet and soaked with warm water after a long wait for the water heater to do its job. She'd also found a first-aid kit in the cabinet. Nothing fancy, but it should have bandages and alcohol.

Brody hadn't moved, however, and didn't look up at her when she climbed on the bed next to him. He stiffened when she laid the warm cloth over his shoulder, but gradually relaxed as she washed off the blood with gentle pressure. "It's not deep. I think it's just the hard-wood floor equivalent of rug burn, with a few splinters thrown in."

She dabbed it with alcohol, earning a hiss from him, then covered it with bandages and taped them down.

After securing the last strip of tape, Sam trailed her fingers lower, onto the smooth skin of the scar.

This time, he did move. "Stop."

"Brody, we all have scars. Yours are just more visible than most."

He glared up at her briefly before returning his gaze solidly to the vicinity of the floor. "Get out of here."

How could she push through that wall he'd built up around himself and show him it didn't matter? Just saying the words wouldn't cut it, because he was scarred inside as well.

"You might as well shut up about that and accept that I'm not going anywhere. You can tell me what happened to you, or you don't have to. You know what? It doesn't matter. I'll apologize for snooping around in your attic, but I won't apologize for not being afraid of you or grossed out or filled with pity or whatever it is you think I should feel after seeing your back."

Harsh, but she had a feeling that was the only way she'd be able to pull a chink out of the wall.

Again he didn't answer for a while, but this time when she reached out and touched his back with her fingertips, then with her whole hand, he didn't try to pull away.

"It was a fire. An explosion, technically." His voice was soft, as if coming from another room. Or maybe another lifetime. Was that why he needed a new start and jumped at the chance to move to rural England?

"I can't imagine the pain." God, it hurt like crazy when you burned a finger on the edge of a cookie sheet. What would it be like to have your whole back stripped down to muscle and tissue?

"I was facedown, flat on my stomach, for months." He paused, as if unsure whether or not he wanted to continue. Sam moved behind him on the bed and wrapped her arms around his waist so he could feel her support without feeling her watching him. It worked.

"There were, God, I don't know, something like forty operations. They kept telling me how lucky I was because it was only my back and not my face or hands, and it didn't extend far into the muscle."

"Was that when you hurt your knee as well?"

Brody had placed his hands over hers but instead of pushing her away and releasing himself from the circle of her arms, he held her arms around him more tightly. "Yeah, they probably could've reconstructed the knee better if they could've done it immediately, but the burns had to come first." His fingers stroked across the backs of her hands. "And it was complicated by—it was complicated."

Okay, there was a definite story to be told, but Sam had pushed enough for now. "Why don't you lie down for a while. I can get you something to drink."

"Stay with me." His fingers, which had been steadily stroking the backs of her hands, stilled. His voice was barely more than a whisper, hardly audible over the storm. "Or you don't have to."

"I want to."

She moved so that he could lie on his back, and waited for a cue from him as to where he wanted her—close, or just in the general neighborhood. With his left arm, he pulled her down to nestle against him like a lover. Or a friend, even with all the lies they'd told each other and continued to tell. What could they have been to each other, had they been in a different situation?

In a different situation, I'd never have met him. Funny how flashes of good shone through even the greatest horrors. Life took, and then it gave.

She needed to tell him the truth, or at least that she was being blackmailed into looking for the jewels. If Brody were working with Tom, he probably already knew at least the basics. If Tom hadn't told him anything at all and they had some other kind of relationship, maybe her coming clean would convince him to help her—or help her find a way out.

"Brody, we have to talk."

When he didn't answer she lifted her head so she could see his face, relaxed now in sleep. Once he woke up, though, they would clear the air. He'd been forced to trust her tonight, at least a little. It was time for her to do the same.

CHAPTER 21

Brody woke with a start, his kneecap tapping a painful cadence that vibrated all the way down his leg, his head pounding, his shoulder—actually, the things that didn't hurt would constitute a shorter list.

Sam slept next to him. They'd pulled apart sometime during the last few hours, no longer wrapped up in each other but still touching back-to-back.

His scarred back to her smooth one. But his scarred psyche to one that maybe was equally scarred. From the few hints she'd dropped, her life had not been an easy one. Maybe wounded spirits recognized each other and could accept even the deepest scars.

Of course, he hadn't told her more than the surface of the truth, but he'd never seen the things in her eyes that he'd most feared about being with a woman again. He'd seen concern, but not repulsion. Compassion, but not pity.

In gratitude for that, he would let her slide on the subject of plundering his attic in the middle of the night. Maybe.

He got to his feet, careful not to wake her and standing in place a few seconds to make sure his knee would support him. The dizziness he'd felt after the fall had moved on. Someone should give the man a medal; he could walk without assistance.

He grabbed his clothes and hobbled into the hallway bathroom to dress. Then he made his way to the kitchen and went through his usual routine of pulling out a coffee filter, measuring the dark grounds, filling the coffeemaker, and setting it to brew. Once it was done and the rich, sensual smell of dark roast had filled the room, he poured a cup and went outside with a makeshift sandwich from last night's leftovers.

He had to dump water out of his favorite courtyard chair and then cover the seat with a couple of towels from the kitchen, but he wanted to enjoy the crisp fall air, fresh and invigorating after last night's storm. The driveway had drained except for craters of mud, and now that it was clear, he could see Sam's car sitting about halfway between the house and the main road.

What had she been looking for in his attic in the middle of the night? And why be secretive about it?

His best guess was that the professor had said something to send her searching. Miles knew about old John Jessop's writings because he'd mentioned them on both the brief occasions when he and Brody had crossed paths. Maybe he'd mentioned the journals to Sam, and Sam was on the hunt for them, thinking they might illuminate more about the fate of the crown jewels.

Which they might very well do. If Brody had read them as he'd intended, he would know that answer.

He'd find that out when she woke up. Hell, he'd let her read the journals if she wanted, and then maybe he'd give them to the professor. He'd always thought the parson's writings deserved to stay in the parson's house, but that had been wrongheaded. They could contain important information, and if the past few days had taught him anything, it was that this life could be snatched away from him at any moment.

In the meantime, he could stretch out his sore muscles by assessing the water damage to the garage suite. He wasn't up to climbing on the still-wet roof, but he could at least make it habitable again.

Not that he didn't like the idea of Sam in his bed, but he had to be realistic. Maybe she hadn't been grossed out at the sight of his burns, at least not visibly, but they still had a hell of a lot of secrets they hadn't shared.

He got the extra room key from the kitchen drawer and made his way up the narrow stairwell. He took it slowly, lifting himself up each step with his left knee to minimize how much he had to flex his right.

The scent he'd come to associate with Sam—light, floral, and sweet—hit him as soon as he left the landing and entered the main room of the apartment. The feel of her arms around his waist came back to him as an almost physical sensation, along with that sweet scent that had enveloped him. He wanted to be in that place again.

But not yet, because he also smelled wet plaster, which wasn't nearly as pleasant. The trash can Sam had set on the bed had done its job and was about half full of water. Once he'd dumped it in the tub to drain, he came back to survey the ceiling.

A big dark stain bloomed out from a dark crack about six or eight inches long. Brody had lived in this old house long enough to know that the whole thing would have to come down. The wet plaster would sag around that crack until it eventually collapsed under its own weight. But it would hold until mid-November, when . . . well, he didn't know what would happen then.

For now, he could do a patch job. Make that another patch job. This was a new leak, but it was far from being the first. The building needed a new roof. He limped back down the stairs, glanced out for any signs that Sam was awake and moving about, then unlocked the garage. He found the tub of plaster compound beneath a stack of leather sheets he kept for making journals and took it and the stepladder back up.

Next job: moving the bed. Even if he could get to the cracked ceiling without moving the whole thing, he didn't want it underneath the patch job in case it didn't hold during the next rainstorm. It wasn't like the room had that much furniture in it. He could just shift it to a different wall.

Shifting it didn't prove that easy, between the sore shoulder and the screwed-up knee, but he eventually budged the heavy iron piece of furniture far enough to get the ladder under the ceiling crack.

He opened the closet door and reached up for the toolbox on the top shelf, wedged next to a couple of old shoe boxes full of receipts and photos that had come with the house. The edge of a thick envelope stuck out between the wall and the boxes, though, and that was something Brody hadn't seen before.

He tried to remember the last people who'd rented the place. He thought it was an older Danish couple on their own historical pilgrimage last spring; they'd come to see the area where a premedieval Danish settlement had been located just outside Swineshead.

He reached up and grasped the envelope. If it was some of the couple's genealogy stuff, he could always mail it to them.

He opened the clasp and pulled out a thick sheet of papers and a stack of photos of—holy shit. Pornography? He didn't think he'd be mailing this to the old Danish couple; he was pretty sure it was illegal to mail porn between countries. Then again, he'd never had the need to ask anyone. They really hadn't looked the type.

He glanced at a couple but then set them aside. Having sex was awesome. Looking at other people having sex? Not so much.

Time froze when he studied the top sheet of the next set of paper-clipped items. A woman's face looked back at him from what was clearly a police mug shot—no, a girl's face. Although she was a lot younger, he was pretty sure it was Sam's face. The name on the police report was Carolina Sonnier, and it was dated twelve years earlier. Sam's sister, maybe? A cousin?

The girl had been arrested for burglary at a New Orleans residence and had been caught when she tried to sell the stolen items at a pawnshop in Kenner, Louisiana. A handwritten notation on the side of the page read "third—juvenile." Brody remembered when Florida had adopted the habitual-offender three strikes law, and he seemed to recall that Louisiana had done it even earlier. So this Carolina Sonnier had her third conviction, but had skated by as a juvenile.

As he scanned the pages, he began putting the picture together. Since she'd been eighteen at the time of the third arrest, Carolina Sonnier had been tried as an adult and served six months in a state facility located in St. Gabriel, Louisiana.

A sheet attached to the back was a copy of application for a legal name change.

From Carolina Sonnier to Samantha Crowe.

Brody's breakfast sandwich turned to lead in his stomach. No wonder she'd been so adept at rifling through his garage, although she'd screwed up by making so much noise in the attic. Then again, she'd been caught three times, all on burglary charges, so she didn't seem to be that good at it.

But the photos. His throat dry, Brody reached for the stack again, flipping through them until he found one showing her face. Sam's. Carolina's. Whoever she was.

The air had been sucked out of the room and what had been a cool almost-winter morning turned stifling.

He wanted to throw it all back in the envelope, move the bed back into place, and to hell with the ceiling.

His hands kept moving, though, setting the photos aside again and continuing their invasion of Sam's privacy. Next came a couple of handwritten photocopies of what looked like journal pages, but the few lines he read didn't make sense, so he shuffled them aside and picked up the final page, a typewritten note.

Dear Carolina, it began. *Thank you for sharing ad nauseam your research and theories on the whereabouts of the crown jewels that England's King John had the misfortune to lose back in 1216. Now it's time—*

"What are you doing?"

Sam stood in the doorway from the landing holding her bag, her voice shaking, her gaze riveted on the files in his hand. Brody climbed to his feet as quickly as his injuries would allow, and one of the photographs slipped from his hand, fluttering to the floor to rest faceup between them. It was a particularly graphic one.

"Oh God, no." Her voice was no more than a soft, anguished groan, and Brody threw the files down and started toward her. She'd already begun backing onto the landing with short, halting steps. "No. I can't. God."

She turned and raced down the stairs, with Brody following. Halfway down, his bum knee gave out on him and he fell.

"Sam, wait!" Goddamn knee. He struggled to his feet, using his hands on the steps to push himself up. By the time he limped into the courtyard, she'd raced down the drive and had almost reached the black Ford. She stopped and looked back as she rummaged in her bag, then turned and got in the car.

Don't start. Please God, don't let the car start. He had to talk to her. He continued to hobble toward her, but a snail could've outrun him.

The little Ford's engine turned and sputtered but never caught. Thank God. Brody walked faster, as fast as his knee would allow, but stopped when she got out of the car again, clutching her bag against her stomach.

Even from this distance, he could tell she was crying. "Sam, it's okay. Come back!" He started toward her again. He had to let her know he understood now—or at least understood some of it. And that none of it mattered.

But she ran. She took off toward Swineshead, angling across the muddy, uneven ground with sure, quick steps. By the time Brody got to her car, she was out of sight.

CHAPTER 22

Sam didn't think about where she was running—just that she had to escape. But that wide-eyed, incredulous look on Brody's face when she'd walked in and realized what he held in his hands? She couldn't outrun that. It had been seared into her brain as surely as if it had been burned with a branding iron.

She ran until she was winded and thought she'd almost gotten to the turnoff into the village. She ducked behind an abandoned farmhouse with weeds higher than the bottom of the front windows and collapsed on the half-rotten wood of the back steps. Her breath came in gasps, and her heart was beating hard and erratically and not just from running. What the hell was she going to do?

Go back and tell Brody the story from your side of things, inner nag told her. *It's the only way you can salvage this total screwup.*

She knew the nag was right, but God, he'd seen those photographs. Why hadn't she burned them? Ripped them up and flushed them down the toilet, piece by piece? She couldn't face him again. Ever.

She had to run and call Gary Smith's bluff. Sorry, David. Sorry, Mom. She was sorry for so many things.

The first thing she needed to do was to figure out what resources she had with her. Thank God she'd grabbed her messenger bag before walking back to the garage suite. She'd planned to transfer everything back to her suitcase except what she'd need for the day. At least for the day she had planned at the time—finding Witcham House and seeing whether or not she could explore there without overt trespassing.

Change of plans. She conducted a quick inventory. The most important thing was that she had her oversized travel wallet with her. Tucked in the back was all of Psycho's remaining cash, as well as her passport. How far was Gary Smith's reach, and how vengeful would he be once he found she'd left his little task unfinished?

The greatest threat she posed to him was exposure if he were anywhere near as wealthy and powerful as he'd implied. A big "if." He might have lied about everything. Plus, she had no idea who he really was or how to find out. Unless he wanted to make a preemptive strike and shut her up before she could learn anything, she should be able to travel freely.

Sam's research files and maps were in her suitcase, so she dug out her cell phone, grateful she'd sprung for global service before leaving Baton Rouge. She looked up information for rail service to Swineshead and, after getting referred to three or four different sites, saw the next train left for Boston at 4:30 p.m. Once in Boston, at a larger station, she'd have a choice of places to go.

Next she looked to see where the train station was located and was disappointed that it wasn't in Swineshead proper but a couple of miles north of the village. More walking. At least the rain had stopped.

Sticking close to the house, she looked around both corners for any signs of traffic before venturing on toward the village. It was a Saturday at not quite midday, so probably any people who were out would be running errands. She needed to avoid St. Mary's anyway; it was around the corner from the Grainery, and she didn't want to be recognized. The restaurant and inn would be one of the first places Brody would look.

If he was looking, she didn't want him to find her. It could be a big "if." If he were smart, he would already have said good riddance to bad tenants and be on the phone to Tom, reporting her truancy. After he'd seen those files, she doubted he was out scouring the town and looking for her.

She slowed her pace, following the road but walking far enough off the pavement that she could hide quickly if she needed to. Every vehicle was suspect. If Tom or, God forbid, Gary himself came for her, they could be driving anything.

An approaching truck sent her scurrying behind a tree, watching with her heart in her throat as an elderly couple drove past. A black sedan almost took her by surprise on a tight, winding curve; she was able to press her body into the vines growing along a wall to camouflage herself.

Sam got to the outskirts of the high street before she heard another car approaching from behind and scurried to crouch behind a couple of parked vehicles. Brody's white Volkswagen drove slowly past, and she could see him inside, scanning one side of the road and then the other. He turned at the next corner, so she veered in the opposite direction for a couple of blocks before resuming her northward course.

Call out to him, nag urged her. *He's looking for you. Trust him not to screw you over.*

Nag must be losing her touch; she was usually telling Sam *not* to trust anyone. Still, the sight of Brody looking for her tugged at her heart and made the tears threaten again. What horrible things he must think of her. Not just the photos, but the arrest record, the pathetic whinings of her journal. All of it.

He'd probably check the usual places first—the Grainery, of course, and the Black Dragon. It was almost lunchtime, so maybe he'd stop to eat.

Keeping her pace brisk, but not so fast as to attract attention, Sam walked a couple more blocks before coming across a small market with an "Open" sign, speaking of eating. She had planned this morning to find Brody and suggest taking him out for breakfast, but, again, plans had changed.

Looking around, she assessed the neighborhood. It wasn't an area she'd visited before, and she didn't know that many people in the village anyway. This market would probably be as good as any for stocking up on food.

She picked up some bread and cheese, a box of crackers that would fit in her bag, and a couple bottles of water. She was standing on the candy aisle, surveying the choices, when a familiar voice rang out behind her.

"Hello, duck. Doing a bit of shopping this morning, are you?"

Oh God. Betty. Next to Brody himself, Betty was the last person she wanted to see.

"Hi, Betty." She turned and faked a sunny smile. "Yes, I'm just picking up a few basics."

"Myself as well. It's my day off." Betty gestured to her clothes—a brightly flowered long tunic, jeans, and white running shoes—as if to prove she wasn't supposed to be waiting tables at the Grainery. Didn't the woman go to church?

"Did your friend Brody find you yesterday, dear? Such a nice young man; you should hang on to that one."

Oh yeah, he found her all right. "He did, thank you." She grabbed a couple of chocolate bars and stuffed them in her basket. "And now I have to run to meet him for lunch. Nice seeing you."

Sam paid for her food and escaped as quickly as possible, cramming it all in her bag and resuming her brisk pace northward. So much for her bright idea of getting a rest; she'd hoped to eat at one of the tables in the corner of the little market. Now she'd settle for a shady spot under a tree, not visible from the road.

A block from the market, she glanced back and saw Betty loading bags into a small silver minicar of some kind. The woman must have Sam radar because she looked up, saw her, and waved.

Lord love a "dook." Sam returned the wave and changed directions at the end of the block, slipping in the shadows between two buildings when she spotted Brody's car approaching. He was still looking for her, but this time nag didn't tell her to flag him down. Maybe she'd given up.

Sam traveled more carefully now—those calls had been too close. She had plenty of time, and although she was no athlete, even she could walk two miles in four and a half hours.

Just north of the village, she found a public park roughly the size of a postage stamp and edged around it to a grassy spot farthest from the road. It felt good to sit awhile and munch on half a cheese sandwich. She went easy on the water since she probably wouldn't find a restroom until she got to the train station, if there. Squatting in somebody's bare brown field would be a last resort.

Get used to it, babe. This is how it's gonna be the rest of your life.

Shut up, nag. She'd carve out a life for herself somehow. Brody had clearly started over, although he'd inherited a ready-made new hometown. She didn't think she was likely to inherit anything, anywhere. But she'd rebuilt her life once and could do it again.

Ironic how insignificant all her academic aspirations had become now that survival had become her main concern. She'd thought taking a new name, finishing school, working like a hound dog to put herself through LSU, getting the fellowship—she'd thought all those things were steps toward proving that she'd left the Eighth Ward behind, once and for all. She'd left behind her mom, the drugs, the days of stealing stuff she could pawn to make rent money or buy groceries. She'd left behind the addicts and drifters she'd called her friends.

She'd left it all, only to find it trotting along behind her like an orphaned puppy trying to catch up with her—all because she'd fallen for the wrong man and made one boneheaded choice after another. And now that orphaned puppy had caught her.

Enough with the self-pity. The situation was what it was. Time to move, if for no other reason than rain was threatening again.

She walked and she walked. Then she walked some more. She crossed fields and made her way over a bridge.

Finally, with more than an hour to spare, cold and soaked from the slow heavy drizzle that had been falling for the last forty-five minutes, Sam came within sight of Swineshead Railway Station. It was a pair of aging two-story red brick buildings with a wide set of tracks running in front of them and stretching out of sight in either direction along the flat Lincolnshire landscape. And it was deserted.

Crap. She tried the door and found it unlocked, so she went inside and read the informational sign: "There Are No Retail Facilities at This Station. Please Purchase Your Tickets Onboard the Train. No Weekend Service."

No weekend service. Something she'd overlooked on the train schedule. She studied the posted times and discovered the next scheduled departure was the Monday morning train to Nottingham. So she'd take that one and enjoy the irony. The old Robin Hood legends held that the hero outlaw earned his fame by defying the sheriff of Nottingham, who was seen as a puppet of King John. She had been the old king's puppet in her own way. She should've known never to pin her future on the man seen by most as England's worst king ever. There had never been another king named John in all the years since and for a good reason. The guy was, by all accounts, an asshole. She was starting to hate him herself.

In the meantime, she had a roof over her head, access to a restroom, and nowhere else to go. She had food in her bag, a cell phone with a flashlight app in case the station wasn't lit, and a book on life in medieval England. Things could be worse. At least she didn't have to be too concerned about being raped and robbed. She sure wouldn't feel safe spending the night in a deserted New Orleans or Baton Rouge train station.

A half hour later, just as darkness fell outside, the lights came on and Sam took it as a sign that things were looking up. Because how much further down could they get?

She picked the most inconspicuous corner of the station and settled on the floor, half hidden by a rusty old bicycle that looked like it had been left here several decades ago. From her vantage point, she could see through the spokes and take in the room in case anyone else showed up.

She tried reading but found herself struggling through a paragraph on bawdy medieval humor for at least the third time and finally gave up. Apparently medieval folks enjoyed jokes dealing with bodily functions and anything that contained the word "fuck." Not much had changed in the world.

She twirled the rubber pedals of the bicycle and thought about Brody. What kind of strength he must have to be able to survive not only the fire or explosion and whatever caused it, but also the months and months of surgeries and rehab it took to recover. The amount of physical and emotional pain he'd had to endure—and continued to endure, judging by his reaction when she saw his back—had to be enormous.

She'd seen that pain in his posture and in his eyes when she'd stripped off that T-shirt. In one of their first conversations, after she'd prattled on about her vow of celibacy, he said he'd sworn off women eight years ago. She had a feeling he hadn't so much sworn off women as sworn off letting a woman, or anyone else, see his scars.

Too bad she'd never get a chance to really prove to him they didn't matter. He was beautiful, and he should have someone tell him that until he believed it. But it wouldn't be her . . .

Sam woke with a start, unsure what she'd heard. A car door, maybe? She looked at her watch and saw it was almost midnight. She'd slept for more than four hours.

Footsteps sounded outside. Someone was walking around the front of the station. The doors of the adjacent brick building opened, followed by silence, then they opened and closed again. This time, the footsteps moved closer.

Sam swallowed hard and hunched farther into her corner, watching the station door through the spokes of the bicycle, glad she'd chosen a dark and relatively sheltered area.

She held her breath as she tracked the sounds of someone walking across the sidewalk in front of the building. The footsteps stopped at the door and it seemed like an eternity, although it couldn't have been than a few seconds, before the door slowly opened.

Brody stepped inside and crossed to the middle of the wide, cavernous room, glancing at the rows of unoccupied wooden benches. Sam couldn't breathe, couldn't move.

He slowly turned around the room, and she felt an almost physical brush as his gaze passed over her and kept going. He hadn't seen her.

Brody turned to leave, walking with a pronounced limp that broke her heart.

Don't be an idiot, the nag said. *Trust him.*

Sam struggled to her feet.

CHAPTER 23

Brody had almost reached the door when he heard a scraping sound and he turned, ready to hightail it outside if he was charged by a rampaging, bloodthirsty badger.

He closed his eyes in relief when, instead, he saw Sam standing in the far corner. She'd been crouched behind a bicycle. He'd been so afraid the image of her standing beside her car and crying would be the last one he'd ever have.

Seeing her now, he was so goddamn angry he wanted to kill someone. She just had to tell him who to kill.

He crossed the room in four long strides that sent razor blades into the muscles above and below his knee, but he didn't give a damn. He stopped a couple of feet from her, searching her face for a clue of what he could give her that would make things better. Her eyes shone with tears, making them brighter and greener. Her lower lip was quivering until she swallowed hard and took a deep, steadying breath. Did she have any idea how strong she was?

"Come here." He took the last step and pulled her against him, stroking her hair, rocking her a little, and letting her cry. God knows how long she'd been holding it in. None of the trash in that envelope had been date stamped so he didn't know if they'd been blackmailing her for days or weeks or months. "It's going to be okay, Sam. We're going to get you out of this."

"H-how? And I don't want you involved any more than you already are. You and Tom . . ." She stepped back. Her voice was stronger, the tears drying, but she still wouldn't look him in the eye.

"There is no 'me and Tom.' I think we need to talk and we need to talk now."

Finally, she looked up at him with a spark in her eyes that might have been a desperate kind of hope. "Here?"

He glanced around. "It's midnight in a deserted train station in the middle of nowhere, which one might think would be safe enough. But we're dealing with some crazy-ass, fucked-up people. We're halfway to Boston; let's get a hotel room where we can talk. Get some rest. Figure out what we're going to do."

She hesitated just long enough for him to see the flicker of worry cross her features. He reached out, cupped her face in his hands, and forced her gaze upward. "You can trust me, Sam. We are on the same side; it's just that we were both too afraid to open up. Now it's time."

"You're right. Past time." She went to the corner and pulled out her bag. "Lead the way."

They walked back to his car and drove in silence along the highway that headed east toward Boston. The quiet got to her first.

"So is there any connection between this Boston and the one in Massachusetts?"

Safe, neutral chitchat. He could handle that. "Yeah, I think it was emigrants from this Boston who gave our Boston its name. It's a port city, not huge but a lot bigger than Swineshead."

Sam laughed. It didn't sound exactly heartfelt, but it at least lightened the mood. "That wouldn't take too much."

"True enough."

He talked about the history of Boston, the landmarks, and anything else he could come up with to fill the time and space, and Sam did her part by pretending to be interested. What they weren't saying hung over their heads so heavily it seemed to weigh the car down, making the fifteen-minute drive into Boston seem to take hours.

He slowed down at signs for a few of the guesthouses and small hotels along the way but didn't stop. He wanted something big and anonymous and full of people, the better to hide in.

Sam seemed to be thinking along the same lines. "Best Western," she said, pointing to a lit sign as they approached the downtown area. "Think they'll rent us a room in the middle of the night?"

"Sure, who turns down money?"

Sam opened her bag and began rummaging. "Speaking of which." She took out her wallet and extracted a stack of bills. "Maybe we should pay cash for the room. I like the idea of telling you all about my encounter with my 'employer,' as you call him, and doing it in a room paid for with his dirty money."

"Gary Smith?"

She laid the cash on the gearbox between them. "Or whatever his real name is."

Ironic. Brody had no doubt that Gary Smith had a real name that contained neither "Gary" nor "Smith." A "Tom," who might or might not be a real Tom. A "Samantha" who used to be Carolina. And then there was Brody Parker, the fake Jessop heir who once went by the name of Nathan Freeman. It was enough to make you dizzy.

They parked at the hotel and walked into the lobby. "Well, you know what this looks like." He smiled at Sam. "A couple checks into the hotel at one a.m. with no luggage?"

This time she really did laugh, and that sound made him think maybe they could find a way out of this, working together for a change instead of against each other.

To give the night clerk credit, he didn't raise an eyebrow at the time or lack of luggage, but he wouldn't rent them a room without a credit card. Brody registered under his name and had them scan the nice card obtained courtesy of the US government. Then he paid with the blackmail money anyway. Sam was right; there was a delicious irony in it.

The hotel was nicer than Brody had expected, housed in a historic three-story white brick building without an elevator and containing rooms that were gargantuan by European standards. He didn't expect they'd be enjoying the flat screen TV, though. They had a lot of years and secrets to catch up on.

Sam had followed him into the room, set her bag on the floor beside the bed, and taken a seat on the red-and-gold-patterned sofa. Now she sat looking straight ahead at something a million miles away, her hands perfectly still and resting in her lap. She reminded Brody of a kid who'd been called into the principal's office—or maybe a police station interrogation room.

"Will it be easier if I go first?" He sat next to her on the sofa and tracked her body language as she fought the impulse to move away from him. He'd already decided he had to tell her everything and trust her, just the way he was asking her to trust him. The only way they could get through this was to start over and keep no secrets.

She shook her head. "This is all my fault. I started it by being stupid, so just let me go ahead and tell it." She took a deep breath, then let it out with a whoosh. "I don't know where to start. At the beginning, I guess, so you'll see how it all happened. You saw the arrest reports."

"You were just a kid."

"Yeah, well." Sam got up, went to the TV stand, and took one of the bottles of overpriced water, screwing off the cap and taking a sip. "It was just my mom and me when I was growing up. She was an alcoholic—*is* an alcoholic—who likes to dabble in drugs when she can find enough money to afford them. Usually she got drug money by picking up guys who'd share a little something as long as they got a little something in return, if you know what I mean. Other than that, siphoning money off our government checks was pretty much her recreational income."

What a way to grow up. And here Brody whined because his daddy didn't understand him. He'd had it easy. "That had to be an awful way to live. A scary way to live."

"It could've been worse." Sam paced to the window and pulled the curtains back to look at the sparse lights of downtown Boston. "I wasn't raped, and she never tried to pimp me out. That happens more than you'd think where I come from. But we never had rent money or money for food or clothes."

"So you stole what you needed to survive." How could anybody blame her? He tried to imagine a life like that and couldn't say what he'd have done in the same circumstances. Maybe worse.

"Don't be too nice to me, Brody." Her voice was harsh. "I wasn't stupid. Well, I was, but I did realize there were other viable options. I could've gotten a job and worked after school to get money. I could've gone to a teacher or a counselor for help instead of pretending I was too damn cool to care. Heck, I could've gone to the police for help and I knew it.

"But I was a product of the neighborhood, and I handled it in the way of the neighborhood. It was the wrong way. Then I got caught. Amazing what six months in a women's prison can do for your perspective."

"That's when you changed your name?"

She nodded. "I became Samantha with the help of a teacher at my high school who, God knows how, saw something in me. She helped me change my name legally, get my GED, and get admitted into LSU. I worked my way through, which is why I'm the oldest grad student in the department. And then I almost screwed it all up."

She told him about the affair with her adviser, and the guy's attempt to buy her off with the fellowship recommendation. He'd like to strangle the son of a bitch. "That wasn't your fault, Sam. The guy was in a position of power and he abused it."

She came and sat beside him again, turning sideways to face him. "Look, I'm not saying all this so you'll feel sorry for me or to make excuses. I've made some mistakes and just plain lamebrained decisions that left me vulnerable to somebody like Gary Smith." She laughed. "I hate to call him that. In my head I call him Psycho. I wonder if I'll ever find out what his real name is."

They were sure going to try to find out. Somehow, Gary Smith was going to pay for what he'd done. "Tell me about him. Where'd you meet him?"

"At a pub in London." She got up to pace again. "I'd gotten a text from my mom telling me to send her rent money. I could tell from the tone of it she was drunk, or high, or both. I was upset and feeling sorry for myself, so I went down the block to the local pub for a drink. I'd never even been in there before. And there he was."

If she'd gone to the pub on the spur of the moment, that meant Gary Smith hadn't stalked her. It had been a chance meeting.

"So you went home with him?"

"Give me a little credit." Sam threw her bottle cap at his head and tossed the empty bottle in the trash can. "No, we just talked. He . . . God, this sounds pitiful. He seemed interested in me and told me I was pretty. Haven't heard that one a lot."

She should have. She should hear it every day. But if he told her that now, he'd sound too much like the monster she was describing. "What next?"

"We went out every night for the next week. Just dinner, drinks, long talks, walks through different parts of London. The last night I saw him, we went to a fancy dinner. And then things got out of control, really fast."

CHAPTER 24

Brody hadn't run yet. He hadn't even let a single judgmental look cross his face. And he hadn't called Tom—at least not as far as she knew—to let him know she'd tried to bolt. But he'd hinted that his relationship with Tom might not be what she thought, and on the basis of that, Sam kept talking. Brody had been right about at least one thing. It was time for both of them to get everything out and take a leap of faith.

She had to trust him or give up and run. She was choosing trust, and, so far, the inner nag hadn't said a word.

If only she'd listened to the nag on that last night with Gary.

"Go through that night," Brody told her, sounding almost as much the businessman as Gary—a comparison she regretted as soon as she'd thought it. They were nothing alike. "This is important, Sam. Tell me everything he said. It might be a clue that helps us figure out who he is."

Which meant either Tom didn't know or Tom hadn't told Brody. She was anxious to hear that story, but not until she got her own out of the way.

"He said it was a special night. He'd closed some kind of business deal that day, and he wanted to celebrate. We went to a fancy restaurant in central London." He'd been excited, a genuine emotion instead of the cool reserve he'd shown most of the week. A cool reserve she'd credited to him being wealthy and well traveled when, really, she now suspected he'd been plotting what he'd do to her.

She shook her head. "When he asked me to go back to his hotel room, I knocked over my wine glass." She looked up at Brody and gave him a wan smile. "Red, of course."

He smiled back. "Of course."

The streak of red wine had dripped off the edge of the pristine white tablecloth and pooled on the floor like drops of blood. She'd been mortified and had seriously considered running out of the restaurant. If only she had.

"So what did Gary do?"

She shrugged. "Just gave his usual smirk, snapped his fingers for the waiter, who had everything changed out in less than a minute."

"Wait a minute." Brody walked to the little hotel desk and rummaged around until he found a sheet of stationery and a pen. "Describe Gary to me. What shape was his face? Long and thin? Angular? Round?"

Sam closed her eyes and remembered that lousy excuse for a man as clearly as she could. "Long and thin, but normal proportions."

Brody began sketching as he asked questions. How Gary's hair had been cut, the color, the shape of his eyes, whether his ears were more pointed or round, whether his neck was thick like an athlete's or thin.

After each stroke of the pen, he'd hold up the drawing and Sam would either nod or add an adjustment. It was kind of a mess when he finished, because he'd had to use pen instead of a pencil and eraser, but it was a close-enough likeness to make Sam queasy.

How had she ever thought him attractive? His hair was a pretty shade of auburn, and he had eyes the color of blueberries at the height of summer, but in the stark black-and-white of the pen-and-ink drawing, she could see that he had the face of a weasel. Easy to say that in hindsight, now that she knew he had the personality of a weasel. And that was being unkind to weasels.

"What happened after you spilled the wine?" Brody lay the pad on the table, facedown. Thank God. She didn't want to look at it. Talking about him was bad enough.

"He dished out a lot of horse crap about how fascinating my research was. Of course now we know why he found it so fascinating. We had another glass of wine, and he asked again if I'd go back to his hotel with him. When I hesitated . . ."

She hated to admit how stupid she'd been.

"What, Sam? What did he do when you hesitated?"

"He said he was glad I had only a month left on my stipend because he'd be back in New York and we'd be on the same continent. He could fly to see me in his private jet, and I remember thinking what a bad idea that would be." Not just from the having-sex-with-a-guy-you-barely-know standpoint, but because, deep down, she didn't like him. She liked that he was attentive and wanted her. Again, pathetic.

"Do you think he really was from New York like he claimed?"

Sam looked at Brody and chewed on her lower lip, which always helped her think. "You know, I'm not sure. I remember thinking when he said it that earlier he'd made me think he was from California. He'd mentioned Silicon Valley a couple of times."

Brody grabbed the pad again and wrote "SF–NYC." "So then you went back to his hotel?"

Sam nodded. "The Bridestall, Suite 202. The weirdest thing there was that when we got to the room, a silver bucket of champagne was already waiting for us. He was so damned sure I'd say yes he ordered it ahead of time."

The nag had begun ringing the alarm bells at the sight of that champagne bucket, but Sam had ignored her.

Brody took his pad and wrote "Bridestall 202." "So you drank champagne?"

"It all gets kind of fuzzy after that. But I do remember drinking a glass and him refilling it. Seemed like it was always full."

Brody frowned and set the pad back on the table. "Was Gary drinking once you got back to the hotel room? Do you remember?"

Sam thought back over the details, which got very sketchy very fast. "I don't think so, or not much anyway. But really, the rest of the evening is a blur. Until I woke up the next morning to an empty room."

Brody got up and walked to the window this time, flexing his knee, which sent a pang of guilt through Sam. "Um, I guess I never apologized for breaking into your attic and then causing you to fall down the ladder."

He looked around and smiled, but it seemed forced. "Sam, do you usually get drunk easily, or forget what happens when you drink? Or did you drink more than usual?"

What was he getting at? "Not really. I usually handle it pretty well. You know, with my mom being an addict, I know my limits."

"I'm wondering if he drugged you. Slipped something into the champagne." Brody returned to sit next to her while her brain spun, trying to consider if there was any way that could be true. "Think about it. He poured the champagne, right? And did it hit you fast once you got back to the room?"

"Oh my God. That sick psycho freak." It made sense now. She had been a little tipsy when they went back to the room, but one little glass of champagne and everything got fuzzy. "But"—and it killed her to say this—"you saw those damned photos. I wasn't exactly unconscious."

Her face burned as if someone had doused it in gasoline and lit a match. She couldn't look at him.

"I don't know a lot about those date rape drugs one hears so much about, but I don't think they necessarily knock you out," he said slowly. "I think some of them just make everything fuzzy. Really lower your inhibitions, and, Sam, look at me."

She really didn't want to look at him. She wanted to fling herself out the second-story window of the Best Western. But he took her hand and she looked up.

"I'm going to say this once, and you're going to listen, right?" He spoke slowly, as if she might not understand him.

Seriously? "Who are you, my daddy?"

He quirked a crooked smile at her. "For the moment, let's say yes. You were the victim here. Yeah, maybe you made some not-so-smart choices, but the asshole is to blame. Not you."

On some level, she knew that to be true, but she'd spent her life being blamed for things she'd done and casting self-blame for things she hadn't. It was a hard habit to ditch. "Gotcha, Dad."

He squeezed her hand. "Keep working on it. You might even believe it one of these days."

It didn't take long to wrap up the rest of the Gary experience: waking up alone in the hotel room, getting the envelope, realizing that he—or someone working for him—had been in her flat and copied her journal.

"Then, before I drove up to Swineshead, I got the car key and that pile of cash in my mailbox that morning. Not long after that, I was at Starbucks trying to look at maps, and I was joined by good old Tom."

"Ah, my buddy Tom." Brody shifted on the sofa until they were facing each other. "Tell me everything about your conversation with him."

She went through it all. "The main thing I took away from him, other than instructions to rent the room from you, was that he worked for Gary, and it was his job to keep tabs on me and make sure I recovered the crown jewels."

Brody's smile looked grim. "Which is not what he told me. Not by a long shot."

CHAPTER 25

Brody made short work of describing his meeting with Tom, including the fact that not only was he to rent Sam the room over his garage, but he also was to sabotage her search for King John's crown jewels.

"I was telling the truth about worrying that the jewels' discovery would change Swineshead in a bad way, but the real reason I wanted you to stop looking was because of Tom and what he said. The rest of what he said."

He paused before adding the last bit. Not only because it would scare Sam, but because it scared him to even say it. "Sam, these guys are serious. Tom told me not only to stop you from finding the jewels, but if by chance you found them, I was to take them from you."

Sam had been eyeing him with increasingly wide-eyed incredulity since he'd begun talking. "And do what with them? And what made him think I'd give them to you if I found the damned things?"

Good, she was more angry than scared. Anger was a much more useful emotion, Brody had learned. "I was supposed to give them to him, I guess. He made it clear he didn't want Gary—your employer, as he called the man—to get them." He took a deep breath.

"He didn't tell me to ask you for them, Sam. He told me to take them and, if you put up a fight, to kill you. And he didn't mean it rhetorically."

Silence, thick and heavy, filled the hotel room as Sam digested that little bombshell. "Holy shit," she finally said. Her face was the color of a bleached sheet.

"Exactly." He waited to see if she was going to ask the question. When she didn't, he answered it anyway. "I never had any intention of killing you, Sam. In fact, the tire thing was the only time I even tried to slow you down."

"Because you're just that nice a guy or because you don't think I have a snowball's chance of finding the treasure?"

Brody shrugged. As long as he was being honest . . . "A little of both. I think the chances of finding it are pretty much nonexistent. But even if you did, I couldn't kill you. I've seen enough violence in my life that I didn't think I could kill anyone unless it was in self-defense, at least not until I heard what Psycho, as you call him, had done to you. That guy, I might be able to knock off."

At that, she smiled. She'd been sitting in the desk chair since finishing her own story but now she moved to sit next to him on the sofa. Outside, the sky had already begun to lighten, and Brody was tired all the way down to his bones. He was getting too damned old to stay up more than forty-eight hours, during which time he'd also fallen down a ladder and chased a woman across most of Lincolnshire.

"There's one big missing piece of this," Sam said, and he nodded. She didn't need to ask.

"You want to know what Tom had on me that got me to agree so fast."

"Does it have something to do with the fire?"

Oh yeah, but that was toward the end of his story, not the beginning. "I told you my dad was dead set against my doing anything with art, right?"

She nodded and curled up on the sofa, watching him intently with those amazing green eyes.

"So I went to the University of Florida—Alabama's just a cover—and got a degree in political science and computing." At her grimace, he chuckled. "Yeah, talk about a one eighty. But I wasn't willing to let him win. He had a law career all planned out for me, so when I graduated, instead of applying to law school I moved from Gainesville to Miami and took a job at a security firm. We designed and installed systems for corporations, and that was fun for a while. We were around a lot of money and got paid well for working with big-time wheelers and dealers."

"Were you good at it?"

Brody laughed. "Not nearly as good as I thought. Mostly, I was young and ambitious, and when a big corporate client came to me on the side and wanted me to handle their cybersecurity on an exclusive basis for three times my salary, I jumped at it."

Sam's eyebrows took a hike. "My inner nag would tell you that sounded too good to be true."

"I wish she'd been there to tell me that. Man, I thought I was hot stuff." What an idiot. All he remembered thinking at the time was that finally his dad would be proud of him. That was the first phone call he'd made after he'd decided to take the offer, and the old man had been so pleased.

"I opened up my own company, hung out my shingle, so to speak, and had a client of one."

He'd also acquired an overpriced luxury condo, a high-maintenance girlfriend, an expensive car, and a big credit card limit.

"What went wrong? Because so far, it sounds pretty sweet."

Brody agreed. "What went wrong was that I started seeing irregularities when the secure financial network I set up was accessed. I thought someone was trying to hack in, so I started quietly watching all the activity on the network. I began to see weird patterns in the international transactions."

"Weird like money laundering?"

"Worse." He remembered the moment everything had fallen into place, the gnawing burn of fear that had set up in his gut and stayed until long after he'd settled into the cottage in Swineshead. The burn that had reappeared in the past few days.

"Not to put a nice spin on it, they were using my security system to launder money coming in from drug operations and imports of illegal weapons. Mostly drugs, and lots of them. I'd thought my job was to keep the bad guys out. Turns out, it was to keep the good guys from discovering what they were up to."

"Oh my God." Sam leaned forward. "You blew the whistle on them. I remember this case. You took down a bunch of hard-core, old-time organized crime bosses in Miami." Her brows formed a chevron over her nose. "But the whistle-blower died, so I must be confusing it with another case. They blew up his house and—" Her eyes widened as understanding dawned. "The explosion . . . They just thought you died."

"You remember right." It was Brody's turn to pace the room. "My real name is Nathan Freeman, and according to all the official records, I was killed when a bomb tied to the Gianovo family blew up my apartment and also injured two of my neighbors. One's still in a wheelchair, as near as I've been able to find out."

But the FBI agent handling his case, the one who'd been arranging for him to go into witness protection, had gotten a tip. Not fast enough to warn him, but fast enough to get him out alive—or at least technically alive.

"I woke up facedown in a private hospital somewhere in the desert Southwest with a new name, identity papers, and history. My nose had been broken so while they were at it, the doctors gave me a new one altogether. Amazing how different a face looks when you replace the nose."

It was all such a blur he didn't remember much of the first few months except for pain, and now, even the pain was mostly theoretical. "When John Jessop, the old bachelor parson of Swineshead, England, died nine months later, about the time I was finally able to live on my own again, I also received a new family tree, British citizenship papers, and a house."

Sam was quiet a long time, staring down at her nails and then at the view of Boston becoming visible outside. "So the FBI worked it out with whatever the British equivalent of it is—the NCA?"

He nodded. "Now. At the time, it was done through MI5 but everything got reorganized a couple of years ago."

"So they worked out this deal, got you citizenship, settled you in. But there's a file on you that somehow got into Tom's hands. Do you think he's in the NCA?"

Exactly his thoughts. "I thought at the time he might be a cop or detective or agent—something. He had that stillness about him."

"Like he was always masking his thoughts and was good at it." Sam nodded. "I thought the same thing."

Brody took her hand. "So that's where we are. We're both getting squeezed from different directions. It definitely sounds like Gary thinks Tom is working for him, but Tom's double-crossing him, or trying."

Sam puffed out a breath of frustration. "So which one's going to be easiest to find?"

"We have a head start on Tom." Brody filled her in on his meeting with Cynthie. "I did a sketch of him, sort of like the one I just did of Gary. Cynthie's going to try to match it to someone at MI6 or at the NCA, maybe someone named Tom."

"And what do we do with him if we find him?"

That much, Brody had figured out. "We're going to play him and Gary against each other until one of them breaks. And that will be our way out."

CHAPTER 26

Sam couldn't remember when she'd been more tired, physically and emotionally. Brody didn't look much better. He kept rubbing his knee, although she was pretty sure he was doing it unconsciously.

She stifled a yawn and looked with longing at the queen-size bed. She wasn't even sure she had the energy to walk to it. How far had she traveled on foot today? Not to mention how many psychic miles she'd gone. She'd awakened in Brody's bed, lighthearted. She'd found him with the blackmail files. Run north with plans of going to Nottingham like a modern-day Maid Marian. Ended up in a portside Best Western spilling her guts and plotting the downfall of a madman.

Made her tired just to think about it.

"What do you think about staying here another day, just to get some rest." Brody didn't ask it as a question; it was more a statement of fact.

"You think it's safe?"

"Don't see why not. You could be doing research here, and I could be trying to stop you. Unless our friends have someone watching all of Lincolnshire, they'll never know we spent the day scheming and sleeping."

She laughed. "Can we sleep before we scheme? I'm wiped out."

"Tell me about it. We'll flip for who gets the shower first." He paused. "You got a coin?"

She dug a good old American quarter out of her bag, called heads, and God bless President George Washington, she won. When she looked back before closing the bathroom door, Brody was staring at the coin, turning it over and over in his palm. She couldn't read his expression, but she suddenly thought of a bunch of questions she wanted to ask him—about whether he missed his family, whether England felt like home now, whether he'd ever want to go back if he could.

For now, though, she left him alone with his quarter and his thoughts. She wanted to scrub the grime of Lincolnshire mud off her body.

The hot water finished off what fatigue had left in terms of turning her muscles to half-melted putty. By the time she crawled out of the shower, she barely had the energy to rinse out her underwear and hang it as inconspicuously as she could from the towel bar.

Knowing Brody had seen her in those awful photos was one thing. Walking into a hotel room with one bed while wearing only a towel was another matter. Sam took a few deep breaths and blew them out before opening the door, like an Olympic diver getting ready to jump into the deep water.

When she walked into the bedroom, he stood with his back to her, in the process of hanging up the phone. "I was telling the front desk to add Sunday night to the room ticket and we'd check out on . . . Monday." He turned and raked a heated gaze across her that woke Sam up just as surely as if she'd been zapped with a cattle prod, not that she knew how that felt. But she was tingling in all the right places.

"You still holding on to that vow of celibacy?" Brody's voice had turned low and had a little touch of a growl to it. Sam fought to keep her toes from curling.

"Well, I should. You have to admit, my track record has been pretty dismal."

He walked toward her. No, stalked. Maybe prowled. She wasn't sure whether to back up and create more distance between them, or to go on the offensive and jump him.

"You gave up women eight years ago, right?"

He stopped close enough for her to feel the heat radiating off his body. "I did." He ran a finger lightly along the side of her neck, down and across her shoulder, and Sam shivered, waiting for the nag to show up. The bitch was silent.

He leaned in and whispered, "But I'm rethinking it."

Then he walked into the bathroom and closed the door.

Damn him.

Thank God.

She did not trust her shaky vow in a bed with Brody Parker—because that was who he was now, just like she was now Samantha—while wearing only a towel. Especially when he might be wearing . . .

She couldn't even go there.

Her imagination didn't have long to work overtime. She'd paced awhile, then had barely crawled in bed, rearranged her towel, and pulled the covers up to her neck when he came out. Also wearing a towel, but without a T-shirt this time.

She watched him walk toward the bed, half afraid of him. Not just him, but afraid of how much she wanted him. And she knew he wanted her, although she wasn't sure why. That crazy chemistry.

"Do you want me to sleep on the sofa?"

She glanced at the bright fabric and tried to imagine him folding his long frame into a pretzel to fit onto it, bad knee and all. "That wouldn't be very practical."

Good Lord, woman, could you possibly get any geekier? The nag had finally made an appearance.

He cocked his head. "Was that a no?"

"No." She pulled back the covers next to where she lay, careful to keep her towel in place.

He slid under the covers, and it seemed to Sam that the bed had suddenly shrunk by way more than half. He turned toward her, rustled beneath the duvet, and whipped out his towel, holding it over the edge of the bed and dropping it with an evil little smile that made something deep in her belly do a somersault.

"You do realize that your death grip on that towel's going to loosen when you fall asleep." He propped on one elbow, and she noticed his floor-burned shoulder had already scabbed over. If he had a concussion, he sure wasn't acting like it.

What should I do? She addressed the nag first, which she'd never done before. The answer was immediate: *Take off the damned towel, idiot woman.*

Right. She feigned a coy smile, knowing her heart was pounding so hard her lips were probably quivering, and unfastened her towel, shifting toward him slightly so she could pull it out.

He snatched it out of her hand and pressed his face against it. "I love the way you smell. It reminds me of the fields around Swineshead in the summer, all bright and sweet."

"Ah . . . it's the shampoo." God, there she went again with the geekdom.

He leaned toward her and kissed her lips lightly, a slight pressure that made her hold her breath, wanting more. But he tilted his head and ran openmouthed kisses down the side of her neck, his breath hot as fire along her skin. "You didn't have the shampoo tonight," he whispered. "And you still smell sweet, so I win."

This time, he kissed her as if he'd consume her, leaving her breathless and tingling in more places than she realized she could tingle, his hands leaving a trail of fire wherever they touched. And they were on the move, across her back, snaking around the back of her thighs and pulling her against him.

She gasped at the heat and the hardness of him as he rolled her on her back and settled between her thighs in one smooth motion. She was so out of her league. Her disastrous man choices had been just about her only experience except for a couple of rough, forgettable teenage rut-sessions. Being the underdog had never felt so good.

"Show me what you like," she said, stroking her hands across his shoulders, avoiding the scrapes, and running them lightly along his upper back. He stiffened when her fingers reached the scars, but she caught his gaze with hers. "Let me touch you."

"First this." He slid off her red glasses and set them on the nightstand. "Your eyes were the first thing I noticed about you. They're my favorite color of green."

"Was that before or after you tossed your fork on the floor of the Black Dragon? You know, I really thought you hated me."

"I was paranoid. I got over it."

She smiled. "I noticed."

He relaxed into her arms, nibbling and sucking along her neck while she ran her fingers along the hard muscles of his back. They flexed beneath the smooth skin in the middle of the scars, and when she stroked the rough, almost corded skin of the edges, Brody shuddered under her touch.

"Does that hurt?" She stilled her hands.

"No, it . . ." he shuddered as another spasm went through him. "It's like it amps up the feeling when something touches that spot. It's a good thing."

Well, in that case, she'd do it some more. She used her left hand to caress the aftereffect of so much pain while she reached her right hand between them to touch him, wrap her fingers around him. It was a heady feeling that was new to her, the power of being able to use a simple touch to make him breathe harder, drive him to groan into her ear a plea to keep touching him, prompt him to pull the hard, sensitive peak of one breast into his mouth so fiercely she thought it might come off.

He pulled away, propping on his elbows, his breathing ragged. "Are you sure you want this? I don't have a condom, but . . . you know."

She grinned. "Eight years, right?"

"Technically. Maybe even eight and a half if I get really detailed."

She stroked his back again, getting a shiver and a smile that lit up his dark, dark eyes in return. "I think you're okay, and I'm on the pill."

He kissed her silly, then whispered. "You never were really committed to this celibacy thing, were you?"

Apparently not, because she ached to have him inside her. She reached down and squeezed him again, stroking this time until he moaned. "You're killing me."

"Then do something about it." She squeezed harder. "Now."

He thrust into her, hard and deep, and almost sent her over the edge with a single stroke that filled her almost to the point of pain. Almost.

He slowed his movements, teasing her, changing the angle of his movements so the rhythm of his pelvis ground against her clit with each deliberate thrust.

"God, Brody, please." She didn't recognize her own voice, it was so rough and needy.

"Please what, Sam?" Another long, slow withdrawal, and an equally long, achingly slow entry.

"Don't hold back. Hard and fast. Please." She was sure she'd be embarrassed at begging tomorrow, but right now, she needed that driving, pounding friction.

"Hang on." His voice was hoarse as his body drove into hers, relentless and powerful as all the sensation in her body flowed to that one place, that one moment that took her breath away. She arched her body against his as if they could somehow meld into one and made him call her name.

CHAPTER 27

Brody woke with a start, unsure where he was for a few moments until he saw the woman who lay nestled against him. Her blond hair spread in a curled tangle over part of his chest, and he liked the look. He could get used to it.

But first, they had to figure out a plan.

As if sensing his thoughts had turned back to the dark side, Sam opened sleepy green eyes and yawned. "What time is it?"

"No idea."

He reached for his cell phone on the bedside table. "It's already twelve thirty. But it was after five before we went to bed."

She stretched up to kiss him. "It was after five when we went to bed. It was later than that when we went to sleep."

He hoped his grin didn't look as goofy as it felt from his end of things. "This is true."

She snuggled against him and stretched an arm across his midsection. "What's on the agenda today?"

He'd been going over that since he woke. "I want to call Cynthie and see if she's made any headway with the Tom search, although it's only Sunday, so I'm not hopeful. Maybe she can find something out tomorrow morning."

"Maybe you could take a phone photo of that drawing you did of Psycho and send it to her as well. You never know who might recognize it."

"Good idea."

Sam rolled away from him, grabbed her glasses off the nightstand, and padded toward the bathroom, the sway of her hips reminding him that if they got their plans made today, he'd have another night to explore that body.

But work first, play later.

"Lose something?" From the bathroom, Sam laughed, and a pair of pants came flying out the door—his pants. They were followed by the rest of the clothes he'd left on the bathroom floor last night. Guess that was his cue to get dressed.

By the time Sam came out of the bathroom, back in her jeans and sweater, he'd dressed as well.

"Breakfast?" He was starving and the assortment of Swineshead market food in her bag wasn't going to cut it.

She laughed. "I think it's lunchtime for the rest of the world. I noticed a restaurant downstairs. Do you think we're presentable enough?"

"Money talks."

"And bullshit walks," she said, grabbing her bag and extricating her wallet. "Let's use the bullshitter's money while we've got it." She handed him half of what looked like a good quarter of an inch of bills still left in the envelope tucked in the back of her wallet.

Brody hadn't spent much time in Boston, but he'd made a few exploratory trips after first moving to Lincolnshire. So he knew that the tall gothic-looking tower they could see out the eatery window was St. Botolph's, a monstrosity of a church with one of the tallest towers in England.

They waited until their sandwiches of locally made cheese and sausages arrived and munched on them a few minutes before Brody finally started the inevitable conversation.

"I think we should do our best to find the crown jewels." He kept his voice just loud enough for Sam to hear but, he hoped, not loud enough for anyone else to eavesdrop. Not that he was paranoid or anything.

"I'd been thinking the same thing." Sam pushed her plate aside and pulled her mug of coffee in front of her. "They give us more leverage if we do happen to find them."

"And in the meantime, it lets you put up a convincing front that you're doing all you can to meet Psycho's demands." Brody waited while the server removed his plate and brought coffee.

As soon as they were alone again, Sam asked, "What about Tom?"

"I'll make up all the stuff I'm doing to keep you from succeeding. If Gary contacts you, you can assure him you're working hard. Just don't mention me or Tom. We don't know what Psycho knows, except I'm pretty sure he has no idea his representative is engineering the failure of his big quest."

Sam stared out the window at the church tower as if it might provide some answers to all their questions. "I wish we knew how to get in touch with them, or when they planned to contact one of us again. It's like we're always waiting for something bad to happen."

"Which is why I think you should move into the cottage with me. I don't like you isolated out there over the garage." He leaned over the table, motioning her to move closer. "Just let me know the next time you want to go rummaging through the attic, 'kay?"

"Screw you," she said, laughing. But she blushed a pretty tint of pink.

"What were you looking for up there, anyway? Did Miles Thornton tell you about all the journals old Parson Jessop wrote?"

Sam looked surprised. "You know about them?"

Yeah, and he wished he could say he'd read them. "I brought them down from the attic a few years ago. They're in a box under my bed."

That light came back into Sam's eyes, the one that showed up when she talked about her research or the life and times of bad King John. "Have you read them? What's in them?"

Brody held up a hand. "No, sorry. I kept meaning to read them but never succeeded. I'm afraid I don't have the passion for historical minutiae that you do. But there's a bunch of them. We can start going through them when we get back."

"Your cottage was on the original abbey grounds, and Miles thought maybe your property had held one of the abbey's outbuildings." Sam drummed her fingers in a cadence on the rim of her mug. "Have you ever found anything around there? Any kind of earthworks or signs of former habitation?"

Brody laughed at the idea he might be digging in the parson's old rose garden and come up with a ruby-encrusted crown or dagger. "The most interesting things I found have been odd old tools the parson liked to collect and then throw in the garage. It took me months to clean that thing out."

Partly, of course, because he hadn't finished healing from the burns. The first year in Swineshead, he'd moved painfully, slowly. It was one reason he'd started lifting weights and taking long walks on the fens as soon as he was able. He'd never been a jock—this was probably the best shape he'd ever been in—but he didn't like the way his muscles had withered in that year plus of rehab.

Sam reached out and touched his arm. "Hey, where'd you go?"

"Woolgathering. Just thinking back to the first year I was in Swineshead. God, I was such a mess."

She tilted her head to the side, her hand still on his arm. "Do you miss it? Your family? The States? I saw you looking at the quarter last night."

That coin had surprised him. He'd even kept it, and now pulled it from his pocket and held it up. "It just surprised me—how seeing old George here took me right back to Florida for an instant and, yeah, I missed it for a few minutes."

The bigger surprise was that the homesickness that had tormented him the first few years in England didn't return. "I miss parts of it, but it's safer for my family to think I'm dead. To be honest, we weren't that close." Something he always would regret. "And I realized last night when I was looking at that coin that I don't think I'd move back. I like it here."

She smiled. "You like being able to be who you really are. Names are just names; who we are is inside. Now you can be an artist."

He hoped so. And it really pissed him off that his future was in the hands of two guys who appeared to have more money than morals.

He finished his coffee and counted out the cash to pay the check. "You ready to continue our scoffing in the face of Psycho?"

A slow smile bloomed on her face. "How might we do that?"

He pointed out to the street, and the row of shops that stretched all the way to the church tower. "We are going shopping, courtesy of Gary Smith."

They searched around the big-box Maplin store until they found a metal detector. After stashing it in the VW's trunk, they returned to the waterfront area and bought a change of clothes and, getting more in the shopping spirit, wandered for an hour around Oldrids department store.

Sam held up two sets of sheets—one striped and one solid. "Which one? The parson's big flowers are going in the trash if I'm sleeping in that room."

Frankly, Brody didn't care—he'd gotten past the shopping-enjoyment stage as soon as the novelty wore off, which was at least forty-five minutes ago. Plus, she was sleeping with him, not in the storage room. "Solids go with everything," he said, assuming an expression he hoped conveyed sincerity and not boredom.

Before heading back to the hotel, they walked awhile along the waterfront of the River Witham. The day had turned colder, and the wind coming off the waterway brought chill bumps to Brody's skin, a reminder that winter was about to arrive.

"There's one thing we haven't talked about," Sam said, tugging her new jacket out of her shopping bag and pulling it on with Brody's help. "And that's what we do when November fifteenth rolls around and we haven't found King John's crown jewels. Because that's our most likely scenario."

They stopped on the bridge over the river and watched the greenish water flow on its way to join the other East Midlands rivers to form the Wash and empty into the square bay off the North Sea. "Okay, here's what I was thinking. You don't have to answer now, but consider it. We have a little time."

Very little. The sand dripping from Psycho's hourglass seemed to be speeding up.

"Okay, I'm not sure I like the sound of that, but let's hear it." Sam crossed her arms against the wind, and they started walking back toward the hotel.

"I think if we get to within four or five days of the deadline and we don't have any solid leads to make us think we can succeed"— he paused and said words he never thought he'd consider saying again—"we should start over. Cynthie can contact my FBI guy in the States, tell him I've been compromised through MI6, along with a friend, and we get new names, new backgrounds, new everything. We reinvent ourselves."

Sam stared at him as if he'd grown horns. "They'd do that?"

He gave a small shrug. "They take care of whistle-blowers; otherwise, nobody would blow the whistle."

CHAPTER 28

Brent Sullivan was getting impatient. The voice on the line was full of bullshit and heavily accented. Felix Grummond had never set foot outside England and it showed.

"Mr. Sullivan, I have the information you asked for and always appreciate your business, of course."

"Talk to me." Brent took the phone to the worktable in the corner of his office, swiveling the chair around so he could look out over the brightly lit San Francisco skyline. From this vantage point, he could see the dramatic red- and golden-lit spans of the Golden Gate creating a glowing silhouette across the blue-black sky.

"I lost track of your girl for a while but found her in Boston—it's a little port town east of Swineshead, it is. Looks like she went on a little personal holiday with the man who owns the place she's staying at. Tall, good-looking bloke, although I prefer the ladies, of course."

If Samantha Crowe was gallivanting around the English countryside, she better be conducting the research that would help find the crown jewels for him, or rather, for "Gary Smith." What she definitely did not need to be doing was taking a personal holiday. "Exactly what was she doing?"

Felix, a private detective from a seedy London suburb, charged by the hour, was far from cheap, and would talk the ears off a donkey. But Brent had used him before and knew he always gave good value—in other words, the bastard had a talent for snooping, didn't mind getting his hands bloody, and knew to keep his mouth shut and cover his tracks. No job was too big or too messy, as long as the money kept flowing his way.

Felix snorted into the phone. "She was shopping, she was. And, if I had my guess, fucking."

"Shopping." Brent stilled, and his voice reflected the controlled, coiled anger that roiled through his gut. "Tell me I didn't hear you right."

"Oh yes, sir, you heard me. I finally tracked them down when the guy, Brody Parker, used his credit card to rent a hotel room in Boston. Nice little town, Boston, and it wasn't a cheap hotel either. One room, one bed. It was pretty easy to trail them after that. They ate, walked around, saw the sights, shopped in a local department store what has some fine merchandise, then holed up in the hotel again. Looked pretty cozy. And in case you're interested"—Brent heard sheets of paper rattling—"they bought clothes and bedsheets and a metal detector. Mostly, though, they stayed in their room. Probably fucking."

Damn it. He should've heard about this from Tom Nelson, who obviously wasn't keeping tabs on Samantha Crowe. Or, more accurately, what he should have heard from Tom was the story of how he stopped them from wasting time and got Brent's pawn back on task.

After Tom had failed to report in for three consecutive days, Brent had decided to invest in his own surveillance. Good thing. Now Tom had some questions to answer.

First, though, he'd set a few wheels in motion. "More work for you, Felix. See what you can find on Brody Parker. Dig deep. And get back to me ASAP on this private line. I'll expect a full report by tomorrow."

He swung his chair around to face the table and opened his laptop. A quick public search for the name Brody Parker yielded only a couple of teenagers on Facebook and YouTube, so the guy didn't have a website or do anything on social media. The only references to a guy by that name in Lincolnshire were on websites for a half-dozen UK art galleries that listed artist Brody Parker's work among their many beautiful offerings. Nothing earlier than seven years ago, so he must be pretty new. Young.

Fuckable.

Damn it. Samantha Crowe could pursue her miserable love life on her own time, what little of it she had left, and she'd done this guy no favors by spreading her legs for him.

He placed a call to Tom Nelson's private line and cursed when an oh-so-polite recording asked him to please leave a name and number and the urgency of his business. "Tom, call me back right now, you bastard."

He didn't leave a name. There shouldn't be any doubt as to where the call originated.

He paced his office with his phone, looking at his schedule for the next few days. There was no way in hell he could rearrange enough things to make possible even a quick there-and-back trip to England. He had a couple of big business deals that needed delicate, personal negotiations. They'd make him a small fortune, which would help him do things like play games with C7.

Felix could do some local work, but he needed Tom in the game. Another slip like this and the son of a bitch could kiss his 10 percent good-bye.

Actually, another slip like this and he could kiss his *ass* good-bye. C7 jobs had to run like clockwork or the cost would be way more than money to all of them, and Tom knew it. Which brought up a couple of interesting questions.

He had to consider the possibility that Tom was being willfully negligent—he had gotten a bit priggish about photographing the sexual encounter and wasn't going to like that he'd already offered his Colombian contact, Andres Moreno, a membership in C7. Who the hell cared how the guy earned his money? Selling drugs or shoveling shit. It didn't matter. He had a lot of it.

So if Tom was getting squeamish about C7 jobs, he'd first try a good scolding. Maybe a threat. A reminder of what they all had to lose.

The other thing he had to consider was the possibility that Tom had flipped sides. He'd seen no signs of it, unless the search on this artist came up with a connection.

Brent didn't give too much thought to that scenario. Tom Nelson didn't have the balls to double-cross him. And even if he had, he wasn't that stupid.

An hour later, his phone buzzed, and Tom's number showed in the window. About damned time.

He didn't bother with pleasantries. "When's the last time you made contact with Samantha Crowe?"

"Good evening to you, too, Brent. Do you have a clue what time it is here? I'll tell you. It's five bloody o'clock in the morning." The man could sound infuriatingly pompous, even from five thousand miles away. "I checked in with her three days ago and things were progressing nicely. She had some good leads. I'd planned to speak with her later today."

"Yeah, well, one of her good leads appears to have taken her straight to Brody Parker's bed. They've been in fucking Boston having a little vacation trip and shopping for sheets. How much do you know about this guy? Did you do a background check on him?"

He didn't know how to interpret the silence that followed. Maybe Tom was surprised that Brent remembered Brody Parker's name. Maybe he was surprised because he didn't know their two pawns had bonded and Brent did. Maybe he was pissed off that Brent didn't entirely trust him. But he wasn't paying the man 10 percent of a potential fortune to be surprised by anything, and he didn't get where he was in life by trusting anyone.

"What the hell does it matter if she's screwing Parker?" Tom's voice didn't sound surprised. It sounded constrained and full of rage. Good. Brent would rather him be angry than clueless. He didn't tolerate cluelessness.

"Haven't you ever heard of pillow talk, Tom? You're a married man. Don't you and your wife tell each other secrets in the dark after she sucks you off? Or are you too old for that sort of thing?" Brent gave a grim smile, waiting for the outburst.

"You're a bloody cretin, that's all you are. And being unusually thick. There are shameful things in that girl's dossier. Even if she is banging the guy, she isn't likely to share that she's being blackmailed. I met her just before she left for Swineshead, and believe me, she's humiliated by what you've done to her. The blackmail. The threats to expose her secrets to her university and the press. The threats to her mother, for God's sake. She's scared, and that's without knowing you threatened to have her killed once this is done."

"Oh, that's no idle threat." The knot in Brent's belly relaxed. Tom was right. Samantha Crowe had too much to lose to be running her mouth, even with a lover. So what if she told Brody Parker she was hunting for the lost crown jewels? It fit in with her academic research. In fact, if she got close enough to the guy and started caring for him, it gave Brent more leverage over her. Another way to squeeze her if she didn't start performing.

"You're probably right, but don't let the situation in Swineshead get away from you again; I won't tolerate it." Brent felt more in control of things now. He didn't like the idea that things were spinning away from him without his knowledge. It made him feel helpless, and he'd had enough of that in his early life. Helpless when his father beat his mother. Helpless when his mother beat him. Nobody got away with making him feel helpless now.

"I want daily reports from here on out," he told Tom. "Daily. We're down to three weeks. Every evening, I want to hear the dulcet tones of your voice."

"Shall I sing my reports for you then? And who else do you have checking up on the goings-on in Swineshead? Either I'm doing this job or I'm not."

"Do your job and I won't feel the need to have someone clean up behind you."

Brent ended the call and swiveled his chair again to survey his kingdom, all bright and sparkling in the dark night, seemingly unaware of the bank of heavy fog rising up from the water and the depths of the hillsides. From this height, he could see it creeping, thick and gray, spreading like molasses. Before long, it would overtake the ground floors of the buildings. Eventually, he'd look out and see nothing but a mass of gray with vague lights twinkling through intermittently. Unusual for this time of year.

Brent suspected more than ever that Tom Nelson, even if he delivered daily reports in a perfect baritone, wouldn't have the stomach to wrap up the loose ends. Especially now that he had not one loose end to tie up with Samantha Crowe, but two. Brody Parker would have to be eliminated as well.

Fortunately, Felix didn't share Tom's misplaced sense of what constituted moral high ground. He just wanted to be paid.

CHAPTER 29

"What a bloody useless day."

Tom's day had started out like a typical Monday. A bad Monday at that. Two new high-profile cases had been assigned to his team, and he had a sixty gigabyte flash drive of files to review by Thursday.

Brent bloody Sullivan was an out-of-control control freak who wanted daily reports—daily!—on that poor hapless girl in Swineshead who, face it, didn't have a chance in hell of finding King John's long-lost jewels. And now his own pawn in the game had mucked up everything by getting his hands in her pants.

Youth really was wasted on the young.

He threw the flash drive on his desk and closed the door to his office, taking a few deep breaths to lower his blood pressure and tossing two more antacids in his mouth. If he didn't have a bloody stroke before all this business was done, it would be a miracle.

When he was done talking to Brent Sullivan early this morning, after making the spoiled brat wait more than an hour to punish him for calling at 4:00 a.m., Tom had talked to Donna and decided a quick drive up to Swineshead was in order, mostly to reinforce his position with Brody Parker.

The new caseload had wrenched that up pretty nicely, though, so he'd run out between meetings and picked up a prepaid phone. He'd have to do his work by wireless this morning. As for Brent and his daily reports, well, Tom could tell him just about anything, couldn't he? Although he found it worrisome that Brent obviously had someone else in place who might not only be keeping up with the two pawns but keeping tabs on Tom himself.

He thought about who it might be. There was a small handful of London detectives who were little more than mercenaries, even a couple he had himself referred for C7 work. Brent could have dealings with any one of them on his own.

From his shirt pocket, he extracted the small square of paper upon which he'd written the phone numbers of both Brody Parker and Samantha Crowe.

He'd try Parker first and hope he had better luck reaching him than the first time. Apparently, when the man was out mucking about in the fields with a paintbrush, he considered himself above answering a telephone.

Damn it all to hell: voice mail. "Mr. Parker, it's your friend Tom. I've received—"

"I'm here, Tom. What do you want?"

Screening his calls, was he? "I hear you and Ms. Crowe are getting along quite famously now. Had a little holiday in Boston? Did a bit of shopping, did you? Bought some fucking sheets?"

Silence from the other end told Tom it was all true. Whoever had been feeding information to Brent Sullivan knew what he was doing. "You said to sabotage her," Brody said, his voice controlled and careful. "So that's what I'm doing. If we enjoy ourselves along the way, what's the harm?"

Tom smiled. Just as he hoped. "Good for you, then. Just be careful what you tell her. She has no idea you're trying to stop her from finding the crown jewels?"

Brody laughed. "Not a clue. And believe me, I can keep her too hot and bothered to even look for them."

"Keep it up, then." He paused before ringing off and laughed. "No pun intended." Maybe that wasted youth could come in handy. He didn't begrudge Brody Parker a bit of a fling.

With one pawn taken care of, Tom prepared to call the other. This one needed a bit more finesse.

His day was definitely on the uptick; Samantha Crowe answered her phone on the first ring. "Is this Gary?"

Interesting. "This is Gary's associate, Tom. Were you expecting a call from our mutual friend?" Here's where things could get dicey. He couldn't be sure that Sullivan wouldn't take a notion to call the girl himself. So whatever he told her had to sound on the up-and-up.

"No, I just didn't know this number. I've been expecting him to contact me and ask how things were going."

Plausible enough. "That's what I'm here for. How was your shopping holiday? Bought bedsheets, did you?"

She paused but didn't sound as shocked as he had expected. He wasn't sure if her nerves were good or she'd been tipped off. Unless they were together, though, Brody Parker hadn't had time to tell her anything. "Fine, but I'd think you'd find the metal detector more interesting. I couldn't get one in Swineshead, so I had to go to Boston. I also wanted to look at a few things at the archives there." She was silent for a second, then, "How did you know? Are you staying somewhere in Lincolnshire?"

"Our friend Gary and I have ways of keeping track. It's best you don't forget that. Are you and Brody Parker having a go at it?"

No answer this time.

"The reason I ask is to tell you I honestly don't care who you show your naughty bits to, or what you do with them. As long as you understand that if you tell him about me or about our mutual friend, his life is as endangered as your own. Do you understand?"

He had to strain to hear her whispered yes.

"Right then. Tell me of your progress with finding the crown jewels."

Ten minutes later, he had enough material to feed Brent daily updates for a week. To her credit, the girl had made strides, talking to locals and locating a parson's writings that had never been made public. He still greatly doubted she'd be able to find anything. After all, the whole of Lincolnshire had been raked for centuries without a single bit of bounty that could be traced to the king. But the important thing for his purposes was that she try.

When she failed, well, that was Brent Sullivan's problem to deal with.

While he was thinking of it, Tom connected his phone to his computer via a USB cable and transferred the phone conversation with Brent to his rapidly expanding file on the pompous little Yank. He especially liked the bit where Brent confirmed that he'd threatened Samantha Crowe's life.

When the girl turned up dead, Tom would have everything he needed to neutralize Brent Sullivan and extricate himself from C7 once and for all. As long as he could convince Brent that everything would go public the second Tom or anyone in his family so much as got a hangnail, they'd be safe. For sacrificing that poor girl's life in order to ensure his own safety, Tom would have to ask penance for the rest of his life.

At least Brody Parker would be safe as long as he stayed ignorant of the blackmail scheme and didn't learn Tom's identity.

Now, time for some real work. Tom popped the flash drive into his computer and waited for the files to transfer, then began going through the first case. A bit of nasty business involving the sale of young girls on an underground black market. This was the kind of case Tom wanted to do, the kind that would make a real difference. This was the real Tom Nelson, distant descendant of His Lord Admiral, not that anxious, indigestion-riddled wreck who'd gotten himself caught in a pact with a group of devils.

Each time an e-mail came in, a small alert flashed in the upper-right hand corner of his computer monitor, and he'd dart his glance in that direction long enough to ensure it wasn't urgent. He'd gotten so practiced at it that he rarely even stopped typing or lost the train of thought over what he was reading.

Until an e-mail showed up that caused him to stop mid-keystroke, his hands poised above the keyboard as if preparing to perform at a grand piano. This particular alert was color-coded red.

Red was not good.

When Tom had set up his new computer, he'd installed an application that he'd been able to get customized so that he'd get a red alert if his personnel files were accessed. He'd know when, and by whom.

The alert had only shown up a handful of times, either at the time of his unit's annual performance evaluations or when he was being considered for transfer. It wasn't time for annual raises to be decided, and since he'd just gotten two new cases, he didn't think he was up for transfer.

Bloody hell, what now?

He clicked on his e-mail program and then on the alert notification. He stared at the information for a few seconds, trying to make sense of it. An agent from MI5, the domestic intelligence organization from which NCA had been carved, had pulled his file a few minutes ago. Unfortunately, an app for mind reading had yet to be developed, so what he *didn't* know was why it had been pulled.

Calling up the interagency directory, he found the number for this agent, Kettler, and rang him up. The call went to voice mail, so he left a message. Just a friendly query to see if Kettler was looking for anything in particular so Tom could help. They were fellow agents, after all.

He might come across as a bit paranoid, but Tom firmly believed paranoia had its benefits.

It took almost an hour for Kettler to return his call, and the man got right to the point. "How'd you know I accessed your file? I just wanted you to know I didn't pull the personal file, only the public one."

Tom let out a breath he hadn't even been aware of holding. His nerves were going to kill him if he didn't drop stone-cold dead of a stroke first. "Glad to hear that. I have alerts pop up whenever my file is pulled. I know that sounds bloody suspicious, right? But I've been bounced around from Scotland Yard to MI5 so many times, and now to NCA, that I always want a heads-up if I'm about to be shuffled again."

Kettler laughed. "Good strategy. I might do that myself. I got moved from MI6 a couple months ago and didn't see it coming."

Which explained why Tom hadn't recognized the name. They'd not crossed paths at MI5. "So why did you pull it? Anything I can help with?"

"No." Kettler paused, and Tom heard the sound of liquid pouring. Teatime, maybe. "In fact, it might be something good for you. One of the NCA agents in another division that I've worked with on a couple of fraud cases called to get your contact information because she heard you were available for a few moonlighting jobs. I was doing her a favor, and you, too, if it brings you some extra income. What kind of extra work are you taking on?"

Tom's head spun. He didn't take private clients and never had. "Must be some kind of misunderstanding, mate. I barely get my own cases handled, without taking on any extra work." Especially with Brent Sullivan breathing down his neck.

"Ah well, she just got some bad information, I guess. You can just tell her that when she calls. Sorry to have inconvenienced you."

A woman, then. Tom shrugged. "No harm done. What's her name so I'll know what she's about when she calls?"

"Cynthia Reid. Handles mostly special interagency cases and a few private clients as well. She said she has more work than she can handle right now and was looking for someone reliable to help."

"Right then, perhaps I can think of someone else to refer her to."

Tom ended the call and looked thoughtfully at the phone. The name Cynthia Reid sounded familiar, but he couldn't place it.

Oh well, he had files to review before he could go home to Donna, share the latest outrages from Brent Sullivan, and relax. He'd been having a few heart palpitations, and she wanted him to see a doctor. But it was stress, pure and simple. Get rid of the stress and everything would be back to normal. Better than normal, because he'd be out from under the thumb of C7.

He was on his third file, the third horrendous case of abduction and slavery, when he remembered who Cynthia Reid was. It popped into his mind from his subconscious, unbidden.

Sweat broke out on the back of his neck as he turned to dig his personal key ring out of his open briefcase.

God, let me be wrong. His hands shook so badly he had to stop and take a couple of deep breaths before he could slip the small key into the locked bottom drawer and pull it open. The original files he'd pulled on the C7 case were at home, but he'd made a copy to lock away here in case he needed access to them during office hours.

He fumbled through the stack of folders, finally pulling out the bottom one and placing it on his desk.

Tom dragged sweaty palms down his thighs, the fabric of his pants drying his skin but doing nothing to relieve the sour taste that had taken residence in the back of his throat. He flipped open the folder and scanned the first page, his focus freezing on the name "Cynthia Reid."

She was the NCA contact for Brody Parker.

CHAPTER 30

Brody took the phone from Sam's hands and laid it aside. From the time she'd ended the call with Tom, she'd been sitting motionless in Parson Jessop's old chair and staring at the worn area rug.

"What did he say that has you so rattled?" He took her hand and pulled her to the couch, where she curled against him and fisted her hand in his flannel shirt as if to hold him in place. But he wasn't going anywhere. "Tell me."

"He threatened you, threatened both of us if I told you about the blackmail or about him."

Good. "That's exactly what I wanted to hear."

Sam pulled away and looked at him, head cocked, eyes worried. "Explain it to me, then, because he scared the hell out of me."

"It means I was right about Tom. It confirms that he's playing both sides. I didn't have a chance to tell you before he called, but he approved of us being together. Told me he didn't care, at least not as long as I continue to undermine your attempts to find the crown jewels and don't tell you that he's made contact with me."

"I guess." Sam wrapped her arms around her middle and rocked back and forth in her seat. "But he knew we were in Boston. Oh my God, Brody, he knew we bought flipping sheets! How?"

He had no clue, but for the first time—and he could kick himself because he hadn't thought about it before—he wondered if Tom had bugged his landline phone. Or bugged the whole cottage. Some security whiz he was.

Tom struck him as old school, but there was no point in being stupid. "Let's take a walk and try out the metal detector."

"What?" Sam shook her head. "No. It's too late. We want to take it to Witcham House."

Brody grabbed one of his sketchbooks and wrote "BUG" on a blank sheet.

Sam's mouth formed a perfectly silent "oh shit."

They walked outside and sat on the far end of the courtyard. "You think he bugged the house while he was here?" Sam asked, pulling her sweater around her more tightly. "I bet he didn't bug the garage or apartment."

"Probably not." Then again, he knew Sam would be staying there. "I doubt he bugged the house, but we need to be careful what we say until I have a chance to sweep it. I should be slapped for not thinking about it earlier."

Sam raised her hand and propelled it toward his cheek, ending in a laugh and a caress. "Well, for now, let's assume he has somebody watching us, so there's a third person we don't know about."

Brody nodded. "It's probably someone local, so you need to be as public as you can in looking for the treasure, and I need to look like I'm at least trying to distract you." His short-lived days of outright sabotage had begun and ended with the great awl caper. Since he didn't know if the new watcher was loyal to Gary or to Tom, he had to play it somewhere in the middle.

Damn it. "It was the credit card," he said. "At the hotel in Boston. That would be fairly easy information to get. I bet that's how our mystery spy knew where we were."

"What would happen if you went ahead and had Cynthie call your FBI contact?" Sam got up and walked to the edge of the court-yard, and Brody could see her gaze combing the countryside and the road, probably trying to determine if they were being watched even now.

"Does that mean you'd consider my idea?" When he'd proposed it as the last-ditch option, he'd told her not to comment until she'd had time to think about it.

"I think we have to consider it. I don't want to die, and it would kill me if anything happened to you."

He'd give anything to see her face right now, but her back was to him, still looking out over the flat gray vista. Had he really only known this woman a little over a week?

"I feel the same way." Damn, he hated talking about emotional crap, especially since he couldn't offer her good times and roses. "I don't know how much of us, uh, you know . . ."

She turned back to him and smiled. "Us. Yeah, I know. How much is real and how much is chemistry and how much is because we're both lonely and vulnerable and thrown together in this crappy situation?"

Brody didn't know why women could just say stuff like that and have it come out right, where men blithered like idiots. "Yeah, what you said."

"What do you think the answer is?" She laughed. "I wish you could see your expression. Do the words 'deer' and 'headlights' mean anything to you?"

Brody scrubbed a palm across his jaw. Easy for her to say. "I think if we'd met under other circumstances, it would've taken us longer but we might still get there." He remembered his reaction to those eyes when he'd first met her at the Dragon, and he hadn't known anything about her.

She smiled again. "I think so, too. So I'll ask you again. What if we just went ahead and talked to Cynthie about a relocation?"

Brody had thought about it. "I think they could pull us out within twenty-four hours. We'd most likely be sent to a safe house somewhere until permanent arrangements could be made."

Sam walked back to sit beside him. "You mean until another old bachelor with no relatives dies?"

"Something like that." The situation wasn't easy. "I think we need to play this out as long as we can, though. There's your career to consider. We could still save it. And there's your mom."

She winced. "So it's all about me? What about you? Admit it; you don't want to give up your life here."

"Busted." He cleared his throat, unsure whether to be embarrassed or pleased that she saw through him that easily. "The totally selfish reason is that no, I don't want to start over again, find a new place to fit in, give up this little art career that I've found and that's given me so much satisfaction." The more he thought about it, the angrier he got. "We shouldn't have to be the ones to lose everything."

"Except each other." Her gaze was soft and solemn.

"Which would be the one thing that makes starting over bearable." He pulled her into his lap. "We'd be doing it together."

"Brody, there's something I need to say to you, now that we've gotten everything in the open. I should've said it before."

He waited, and it was a while before she spoke again. "I want to tell you I'm sorry."

"Hey." He pulled her around for a kiss, inhaling her scent, still amazed at the softness of her lips. "You're the victim here, remember?"

"Yes, but it's still my fault you got pulled into this at all, and I'd give anything if that hadn't happened."

He ran his fingertips along her cheekbones, her jaw, her lips, as if memorizing the contours of her face with his touch. "I don't like the position we're in, but I gotta be honest. I don't regret meeting you."

A glimpse of shiny tears appeared before she turned to nestle against him. "Me too." She cleared her throat. "So what's next?"

"It's cold and already late to be heading out on a field trip to find the site of Witcham House, so I'm thinking we go inside and start reading the parson's journals tonight. I'll do a sweep of the cottage and see if there are any bugs. And I want to call Cynthie Reid and see if she's had a chance to find out anything about our friend Tom."

As expected, he didn't get Cynthie—the woman rarely actually sat at a desk and answered a phone. But she would return his call.

In the meantime, they could stay busy with the parson and his abundance of words.

"I'll make us something to eat while you get the journals." Sam got up and started toward the kitchen. "Anything I need to know before I start plundering through the cabinets?"

Brody gave her a bemused smile. "Since when did you ask permission to plunder?" She'd not shown herself very adept at plundering, and he had the lumps, scratches, and aching knee to prove it.

"It's part of my new antiplundering vow. I had to have something to replace the vow of celibacy that you ruined."

He wanted to charge across the room and ruin it again, maybe on the kitchen counter. She seemed to sense this and held up a warning finger. "Sweep first. This floor is filthy."

He nodded. "Off to sweep. You're no fun." He started down the hall but called over his shoulder, "As for the kitchen, plunder away."

He spent the next hour combing every square inch of the cottage, something he hadn't done in a while. Within a few minutes, the rhythm came back to him, and he moved methodically from room to room, sweeping his fingertips along the underside of every surface, behind every painting, under every freaking box of art supplies. He needed to have a good housecleaning.

Finally, he declared the cottage clean. If Tom had hidden a bug, he'd done it so expertly that Brody couldn't find it. They'd have to take their chances.

Unfortunately, by the time he finished the sweep and got around to pulling the box of journals from under the bed, Brody's knee had already begun to protest the unexpected workout. He tried to convince himself that sitting on the floor would be conducive to healing, but the knee collapsed on him halfway down and he sat with his eyes closed a few seconds, waiting for the pain to recede.

He'd really pulled or torn something in there this time, but he didn't want to tell Sam. She felt guilty enough about his tumble off the ladder—and then down the stairwell by the garage—without adding to it. Surgery was going to be in his future, whether here or in Timbuktu with a new identity. Assuming Timbuktu had orthopedic surgeons.

The idea of Timbuktu, with Sam at his side, didn't bother him nearly as much as it should.

He maneuvered his head under the bed and tugged on the wide, heavy box. There had to be thirty or forty of the damned journals, all filled with cramped writing that made heavy use of loops and swirls. Maybe Sam would be better at reading it than he was.

He'd struggled halfway to his feet when his phone vibrated in his pocket, which he used as an excuse to collapse on the bed and stretch out his leg. Whatever food Sam managed to rustle up, it was going down with a chaser of Nurofen.

He recognized Cynthie's number. "Hey, Cyn, I have news."

She spoke in her agent-at-work voice. "So do I. We need to discuss some things. Preferably in person."

Brody sat up. "You found him?"

"I did. Your instincts were right."

That meant cop, because she probably didn't have a line on hit men. "Who is the son of a bitch?"

Someone who had sworn to uphold the law and did what Tom was doing needed to be strung up by the balls. Naked. In a public square. In a hailstorm.

"I don't want to talk on the phone. It's too late to drive up tonight, and I don't want Wyl involved. I'll drive up first thing in the morning."

Damn it, he didn't like waiting, but he didn't want Wyland Reid involved either. The man's wife might be an NCA Agent, but he likely had no idea the type of people they were dealing with. Dangerous people. Desperate people.

"Want me to meet you in King's Lynn again?"

Cynthie hesitated, and Brody heard a voice in the background. She was still at her office, then. "Sorry. No, this is going to take a while. We'll need to figure out what we want to do, how we want to handle it. I've cleared my schedule. I'll be there about ten in the morning."

"We'll be here."

She paused. "We? Is whatever news you have something I need to know before tomorrow morning?"

He thought about it, but what he had to say would be more meaningful once he knew whom they were dealing with. "No, it can wait. See you in the morning. Be careful."

"Back at you, Brody."

The surge of hope that rushed through his chest made him realize how hopeless he'd been feeling, despite his big words about fighting back. For the first time, if they had Tom's identity, he thought they might have a real chance. There was still a lot that had to go right, and there were certainly a lot of questions that remained unanswered, but hope had reared its head. For now, that was enough.

CHAPTER 31

Tom sat at a corner window table in a small Cheapside Street café in London's central business district, drinking a cup of tea—chamomile, which he hoped would soothe his nerves. For the past half hour, he'd been watching the door of a small building near Paternoster Square.

He wasn't sure what he was looking for, or what he planned to do, only that the woman whose office lay inside that narrow doorway held his entire future in her hands.

Cynthia Reid had done well for herself. Only in her thirties and she'd already managed to become one of NCA's senior agents handling international witness protection cases. She had three active clients, the most prominent of which was Brody Parker. He knew, because he'd spent the last two hours digging into everything he could find on her. He'd also cut through channels to put a trace on her phone, fabricating enough out of his new case file to link her to his child-slavery case. Nothing that would hold up in court, of course, but enough to tap her lines.

He didn't even know who he was anymore.

"You look a million miles away." Donna pulled out the chair across from him, shrugged off her jacket, and ran fingers through her hair. "It's gotten quite windy out."

"Thanks for coming." He shouldn't have called her, regretted it almost immediately, and had even called back to cancel. She was having none of it. *You aren't shutting me out again,* she'd told him. *If it affects you, it affects me.*

Now that she was here, he didn't know how to tell her what had happened. Didn't know *what* to tell her.

"Thanks for coming? That's the kind of greeting one gives a complete stranger. Tom, you're frightening me. Just tell me what it is and we'll fix it. It can't be that bad."

He wet his lips and glanced back out the window. "I've been found out."

Donna didn't answer, so he finally hazarded a glance at her face, grown pale and suddenly looking older than her forty-five years. It was like looking into a crystal ball at the woman she'd be in her sixties. A fine web of lines stretched from the outside of her eyes to her hairline, and others formed creases on either side of her mouth.

Some of those lines were caused by too much time in the sun; they'd all thought suntans were healthy things when they were young, and like most redheads, she had very fair skin that burned easily and tended to freckle. She'd hated the freckles, but he'd thought they were sexy.

Some of the lines came from sorrow over their inability to have children and eventual regrets that they'd never adopted.

But some of them were due to him, and he was about to add a few more.

"What happened?" Donna's voice, usually so strong and determined, shook as badly as the hands he had wrapped around his cup to hold them steady.

"I'm not sure how it happened, but it has. I got a notification today that someone had accessed my personnel file, at least part of it. When I tracked it down, the trail led back to an agent who claimed to want my contact information in order to hire me for a private job."

Donna twisted her wedding ring as she listened, round and round and round. Maybe she regretted ever letting him put it on her finger. "That doesn't mean—"

"One of this agent's witness protection assignments is handling Brody Parker." He looked back out the window. "Her office is over there."

Donna moved her fidgeting from her ring to her necklace, a simple gold chain with a guardian angel charm on it. Tom didn't know if guardian angels existed, but if they did, his had been on holiday lately.

"Maybe it's just a coincidence. Did she ever call you about this private job?"

Tom shook his head. She was grasping at the same straws he'd already squeezed to death. "I did some background work on her after I found out. She handles mostly international protection cases. That kind of agent would never have an outside job needing a detective; everything's too secretive. Parker's one of three cases she has, and the other two live outside England. She asked for me by name, Don. I tell you, she knows."

"But how?" Donna leaned across the table to avoid being overheard. "How would she even know where to begin? You didn't tell Brody Parker your name." She paused, her gaze raking across his face like broken glass. "You didn't, did you?"

His credibility with his wife had really taken a beating if she thought he was capable of being that careless. "I just gave him the name of 'Tom.' No last name. There must be a half-million Toms in London alone, much less all of England." No doubt, in hindsight, he should have chosen "Bob" or "John"—or "Gary."

Donna started at the sound of a kitchen mishap, the crash of a serving tray hitting the floor, a plate or glass breaking. "Well, there's nothing to be done about it now. Do you think she's told him? Told anyone else?"

"No way to know, is there?" A couple at the next table held hands, laughing, feeding each other bits of food with their fingers, and Tom couldn't help but feel jealous at the simplicity of their lives.

Then he chastised himself for being so maudlin. He needed to crawl from underneath this blanket of self-pity that threatened to suffocate him. He just didn't know how.

"Well, let's assume the best." Donna took a deep breath, and when Tom wrenched his gaze from the happy couple, she even managed a small smile. "Let's assume she hasn't told anyone yet."

"I got a tracer on her office line so I'll know when she calls and where—it takes longer to get the cellular trace." He was pretty sure that when he talked to Brody Parker a few hours ago, the man hadn't known anything. But a few hours was an eternity, and in the interim without the cell phone trace there was no way to be sure. "If she hadn't told anyone so far, it's only a matter of hours at most."

"Is there still time for us to do something about it?" The expression on Donna's face startled him—not the fear he expected, but a fierce anger.

"Still time for us to do what, exactly?" He was almost afraid to hear her answer if it was anywhere near as feral as her expression.

"To make sure she never tells anyone. Ever."

Tom stared at her, unable to speak.

"Oh, snap out of it, Tom. Call one of those unsavory detectives you always complain about. The ones with no scruples who'll do anything for money. It doesn't matter what it costs. Have her taken care of."

Who was this woman? "Donna, do you know what you're saying? She's a fellow agent. It would negate everything good I've ever done."

"You're right, I guess." The signs of shock reappeared, and she was again a tired, stressed-out woman heading toward the wrong side of middle age. That sight worried him more than her anger. "Should we make a run for it?"

"Run?" The reality of their situation hit him full force and almost stole his breath. Where could they run to, where Brent Sullivan's money and influence couldn't reach? Or any of the C7, for that matter. They wouldn't rest until he was dead, and Donna alongside him.

Unless Cynthia Reid could be stopped before she told anyone.

He blinked back the tears of fear and rage and frustration that threatened. "God help us both, Donna."

It was her turn to look frightened. "What do you mean?"

"If you'd told me even a day ago that I'd be considering murder, I wouldn't have believed you. I always believed there were lines I wouldn't cross, that I couldn't cross."

She reached out and twined her fingers through his. "Sometimes, it's the only way to survive, Tommy."

CHAPTER 32

Sam wasn't sure what woke her, but her first thought was that it was thundering. Then she felt Brody stir behind her and remembered where they were. England wasn't like Louisiana; Lincolnshire didn't get thunderstorms, or at least not very often.

The bedside clock read 7:00 a.m. She and Brody had stayed up until well after two, going through Parson Jessop's writings, making notes, and plotting strategy about how they could really find King John's crown jewels. The old parson had not only been thorough in his theories and descriptions; he'd drawn stylized maps, including one where he thought the ruins of Witcham House lay buried.

According to Parson Jessop, he'd often looked for evidence of any significant structures on the site of this house but hadn't found any. Sam was kind of disappointed but guessed that would've been too easy.

From one of the local histories, she'd also found the typical lay-out of a medieval manor house. Using the parson's map, they might be able to find where the cornerstones would have been laid. Maybe they could dig a little, try out the small metal detector. Sam had to admit that neither of them quite knew what to do other than walk around the site and hope a crown or piece of pottery or something popped up and invited them to start an excavation.

"What, exactly, do crown jewels consist of?" Brody had asked. "Does each king or queen have different crown jewels?"

Sam had consulted her notes. "Each one did, and they're all cataloged in London, so we know a fair amount of detail about what was lost, especially since he died four days later. Here, let me read part of it to you: 'King John, the youngest son of Henry the Second, had the crown, scepter, and personal treasure that had belonged to his grandmother, the Empress of Germany.'"

She shifted the notes to catch more light. "'There were also goblets made of gold, a golden wand, coins—even the sword of Sir Tristram.' The guy liked his jewels and coins. It's thought the lost treasure would be worth about one hundred million dollars today just in monetary value. If you add the historic significance . . .'"

As the credit card ads said: "Priceless."

Once Brody and Sam had admitted they weren't archaeologists and didn't have much clue how to become overnight dig experts, that left kissing. Lots and lots of kissing. They'd ended up making love in front of the fire . . . twice. At least. All Sam knew was that when they finally moved it to the bedroom, she'd felt satisfied and used up in the best kind of way.

But as good as that was, this was even better. She'd never even imagined being able to wake up next to a man who knew her secrets and still wanted to be with her, and who trusted her with secrets of his own. Truth was heady and powerful and sexy.

Nag tossed in her own opinion: *Not to mention he's really hot.*

Couldn't argue with that. Sam glanced back at Brody when a knock sounded on the back door, then what sounded like someone trying the lock. He was sound asleep.

She slipped out of bed and pulled on one of his T-shirts. No point in waking him until she knew what was going on. It might just be that Cynthie had arrived earlier than expected. Still, she picked up the small pistol from the nightstand, just in case it was Gary or Tom or whoever they had spying for them now, in which case she'd find out how much she remembered from the handgun and firearms classes she'd taken in Baton Rouge.

"Oh, holy Mary mother of God. You scared the shit out of me."

A petite brunette with a ponytail and dark-rimmed, no-nonsense glasses stood in the entry hall in a shooter's stance, the back door wide open behind her. She held her own pistol, a lot bigger than the one Sam carried. "I have a key. Really."

Sam grinned. "You must be Cynthie, the one who shot the hole in Brody's foyer wall."

"Only because he tackled me like an American footballer. And you must be Samantha." She looked pointedly at Sam's bare legs and oversized shirt. "Whose relationship with my friend Mr. Parker has progressed beyond the tire-sabotage stage, apparently. Good for you. Keep him in line."

Brody had told Sam that she would like Cynthia Reid, and he was right. She knew Brody hadn't had a chance to tell Cynthie her whole sordid story, though. The woman seemed to approve of Sam in theory right now. She'd likely change her mind once she knew everything.

"I'll wake up Brody. Help yourself to whatever you can find in the kitchen, which I'll warn you isn't much."

"I can find my way around. Sorry to be so early but I had a feeling we should all talk sooner rather than later." She laughed. "I'm one who always criticizes people who get *feelings*. Get Brody moving, and we'll have a proper chat. I'll make coffee."

Twenty minutes later, with both Sam and Brody in jeans and sweaters, they all sat in the living room with coffee and pastries Cynthie had brought from London. The small talk had started out easy but quickly became stilted and tense. They were all avoiding the hard subjects.

Finally, Brody sat his plate aside. "Who goes first?"

"Why don't you start?" Cynthie leaned back with her coffee cup, listening intently as Brody started with Sam's date with the so-called Gary Smith. When he got to the blackmail portion, he faltered.

"He had some incriminating pics, uh, stuff from Sam's past that, uh—"

Oh, holy cow. The woman was in this mess; she might as well hear the truth. "He had set up cameras for our night together, dug up some dirt on an affair I had with my thesis adviser at college, and photocopied my arrest record from when I was a teenager in New Orleans. Burglaries."

What was the old saying? You could put lipstick on a pig, but at the end of the day, it was still a pig. She saw no sense in wasting valuable time by putting lipstick on that particular pig.

Cynthie raised an eyebrow but otherwise didn't change expressions. Sam bet she was tough as old boots and a damn good agent. "So he blackmailed you into coming here and looking for King John's crown jewels?"

"That's about it. And that's when Tom comes into the picture."

Cynthie set her coffee cup aside and leaned forward. "Tell me about Tom—everything you can remember."

They'd gone through the story so many times by now that it was easy to make it short but thorough. Brody propped his bare feet on the coffee table and did most of the talking.

Cynthie had been shaking her head through much of the story. Once they'd finished telling about their back-to-back phone calls from the previous afternoon, she pulled open her satchel and extracted a file. She pulled a sheet of paper from it and handed it to Brody, who looked at it with a tightened jaw, nodded, and passed it on to Sam.

It was Tom all right. Younger, fewer gray hairs, and not nearly as stressed looking. But the picture was definitely him. Sam stared into the blue eyes that had been haunting her nightmares almost as much as Gary's the last week and a half. "Who is he?"

Cynthie took a deep breath. "His name's Thomas Nelson, so Tom is his real name. He's a senior investigator with the National Crime Agency." She turned toward Sam. "Brody knows this, but you might not. The NCA was formed a couple of years ago as kind of an organized crime unit. Until that time, Tom Nelson had worked in MI5 and, before that, in a couple of different spots in the home office. A journeyman detective, I guess you'd call him."

"Fuck. I knew it." Brody stood up and walked to the window, his hands clenched into fists. "What would make a career detective get mixed up in something like this?"

Sam knew he had a lot of respect for the FBI guys who'd gone out of their way to save him, help him recover from the explosion, and set him up with a new life. He adored Cynthia Reid. To think all their work could be undone by the betrayal of one of their own infuriated him; he'd talked about it some last night. About how he'd almost rather Tom turn out to be a sleazebag hit man or mercenary than someone who was supposed to be one of the good guys.

Sam only knew that people did stupid, desperate things when they felt trapped. And being a detective didn't give you a pass on bad decisions. She wasn't excusing Tom Nelson, but she didn't find the idea impossible that a man, if trapped or desperate, could do something so heinous and against the law, even after devoting his life to upholding the law.

"How did you figure out it was him?" Sam asked, hoping that when Cynthie looked up at her from the folder it wouldn't be with anger or judgment. She was an important part of Brody's life, and Sam wouldn't blame her for holding Sam responsible for this mess. All the same, she wanted Cynthia Reid to like her.

But instead of a look of blame or recrimination, Cynthie's face was animated and she gave Sam a big smile. "He made the mistake of signing in at MI6 headquarters with his real name the same day Brody's file was pulled. We lucked out, really. Only two people named Tom signed in that whole day, and the other was the teenage son of one of the chief detectives. So he made it pretty easy to find him. I was able to use Brody's drawing and a simple Internet search to confirm it."

Bet that would piss him off when he found out. Part of Sam wished she could be there when he went down; the other part of her hoped to never see or hear from him again.

"So what do we do now that we know?" Brody squeezed Cynthie's shoulder on his way back to sit beside Sam on the sofa.

"I want to get back to London right away and turn him in. I've already set up an appointment with his supervisor—figured that was the best place to start. He doesn't know why I'm coming, of course, but I told his secretary it was urgent. Of course, I'm hoping that Nelson will give up his associate Gary Smith even if it means making a deal. Even if he escapes prison, his career's finished." She pulled her cell phone out of her pocket, looked at the screen, and laid it on the file folder. "Bloody phones. I remember when we used to wear wristwatches. Now we're tied to the damn things. Anyway, it's already after nine, so I need to leave right off."

"You sure? The Grainery is still serving breakfast." Brody smiled at her, and Sam waited to see if any pangs of jealousy kicked in, but they didn't. It was clear that Brody cared about Cynthie, and vice versa. Sam was glad Brody had had someone to lean on all these years when he'd been alone. And even after all the ugliness had been exposed, the feisty little agent still seemed to like her.

"Tempting, but no." Cynthie stood up and looked out the window. "I know it's just the fact of finding out something like this about a guy who has too much power and too much to lose, but I've been jittery since I left work yesterday. Like somebody was watching me."

Sam and Brody exchanged glances, and Brody told her about their trip to Boston. "Tom not only knew where we stayed but where we shopped and what we bought in the department store," he said. "Don't underestimate him. He might have screwed up by signing into headquarters as himself that day, but he hasn't made many missteps.

And this guy he's trying to screw out of the crown jewels definitely sounds like bad news."

Cynthie laughed, but not in amusement. More irony. "Don't remind me. If anyone knows how clever NCA agents can be, I do. I'm one of them."

"Call me when you get home so I don't worry." Brody walked her to the door and gave her a hug.

On impulse, Sam hugged her, too. "Thank you," she whispered, but inside, she thought, "I'm sorry." Yet another person whose life she'd gotten dragged into the muck.

"Talk to you when I get home." Cynthie headed toward her dark sedan, parked behind Brody and Sam. "Fingers crossed that by this time tomorrow, this nightmare will be over and both Tom Nelson and his mystery associate will be in jail."

Her lips to God's ears.

Brody stood behind Sam with his arms around her waist and his chin resting on the top of her head. "I hate that she's gotten mixed up in this," she said.

He nodded, his chin tickling her scalp. "Yeah, me too. But we never would've found out who Tom was without her. She came up with the idea of drawing the picture and had the contacts and the smarts to figure out how to use them."

They watched as Cynthie's car turned right and headed back toward the A52 to London. "Let's go out and see what we can find of Witcham House before—"

For the second time this morning, Sam thought she heard thunder. This time, however, it was heavier. More like a heavy thud, followed by a second and then a third.

They both ran to the edge of the courtyard and looked out toward the road. "Oh God, no." Brody's voice was a ragged whisper, and before he finished the last syllable, he began to run toward the highway, his feet still bare. A dark plume of smoke rose from a quarter mile beyond where Brody's drive turned onto Abbey Road. About where Cynthie's car would have gotten to.

By the time Brody was halfway to the road, he was already limping. Sam had been frozen in place, but now she, too, began to run. And prayed she was wrong about what they were going to find when they reached that line of smoke stretching like a finger toward heaven.

CHAPTER 33

Brody knew it was too late, but he had to keep running. Even when his knee buckled on him and he staggered, he kept running. When the rocks of the road slid beneath his feet, he ran. When the rough concrete at the edge of the road dug into his arches, he ran some more. Even when Sam caught up and flew past him. Even then.

Sam had stopped about twenty feet from the blackened husk of the car, but Brody had to try and reach Cynthie, no matter how bad it looked. If the FBI agent in charge of his case had given up on him, he'd be dead. He was proof you could survive shit like this.

He had to get closer.

He reached the driver's side door and stuck his hand through the flames to try and find the handle.

Something hit him from the side, and his knee collapsed on him again, sending him to the pavement. Instinctively, he rolled free of the fire and saw Sam climbing slowly to her feet. She'd knocked him away. She meant well, but she was wrong. So wrong.

He struggled back to his feet. "You don't understand!" His voice was hoarse, and he wasn't sure Sam could hear him over the pop of glass and the roar of the flames. "We can still save her!"

"It's too late, Brody!" Sam planted herself between him and the car, but he shoved her aside and lurched toward the driver's side door again. The flames had died back a bit, but tongues of fire still licked out the windows where the glass had burst into blackened diamonds on the pavement. The smell of burning plastic and liquefying rubber mixed with gasoline and an odor Brody remembered from the explosion at his apartment in Miami. It was distinctive. There was nothing else like it.

Flesh. It was the smell of your own flesh burning.

Brody dropped to his knees, frozen at the sight of a blackened figure inside the car, no longer a woman but just a charred human shape, twisted at an inhuman angle.

He was only vaguely aware of Sam putting her arms around him, rocking him against her.

He didn't know how much time had passed, but suddenly, people were there, firemen with a truck whose side was emblazoned with "Lincolnshire Fire and Rescue, Kirton Station." Police officers from Boston. Medical emergency workers who kept trying to ask him questions. Why wouldn't they leave him alone? He just looked at them, not sure what they wanted, only that he didn't have it to give.

A man in a dark-blue shirt tried to pull him to his feet, and he looked up as Sam shoved him and got between them. She was shouting, pointing.

By the time a truck arrived to take away the smoldering remains of Cynthie's car, almost everyone else had gone. What was left of Cynthie, that blackened shape whose image he couldn't get out of his head, had been taken away in an ambulance, zipped up in a bag.

Now only Sam was left, sitting cross-legged on the side of the road a few feet away, watching him.

Brody tried to stand, but after two failed attempts, sat on the ground again.

"Let me help you." Sam knelt beside him, pulled his arm around her, and much like she'd done after the fall off the attic ladder, she lifted him up without too much help from him.

The walk back to the courtyard seemed to take hours. Brody was shocked when Sam handed him a plate of food and told him it was for a late lunch. He set it aside.

She didn't ask him questions, didn't try to make him talk, just stayed nearby. Finally, he took a deep, shaky breath and exhaled. He had to get his brain reengaged. There would be time for blame and guilt later. For mourning. For the nightmares that had plagued him for a year after his own fire to return like old, unwelcome friends.

"I need to take a shower." He'd been sitting in the parson's old chair with his right leg stretched out straight but got slowly to his feet. Sam hovered nearby but didn't try to touch him.

"Do you need help with the shower?" He gave her a sharp glance, ready to tell her it wasn't appropriate to joke, but there was nothing playful about her face. It was covered with soot and ash, and tears had carved streaks down her cheeks, cutting through the grime. Her eyes were still shiny with them.

He shook his head. "I'll be okay." He got halfway down the hall toward his bedroom before realizing how vulnerable they were. He hobbled to the old wooden nightstand, got the big .45 out of the top drawer, and made sure it had a full clip.

Sam stood in the doorway, and he handed it to her butt first. "You know how to shoot, right?"

She nodded and stuck it in the waistband of her jeans. "I'll hold on to this one for you, and I'll keep the smaller pistol. It fits my hand better."

Cynthie's gun sure hadn't done her any good. It had just added some more material to feed the car bomb.

"Sit in the parson's old chair," he told Sam. "You can see both the front and back door from there. If anybody shows up, blow his head off." He wasn't joking.

Apparently, she didn't take it as a joke. "Gladly."

The shower cleaned more than just his own accumulation of ashes and tear streaks, although he didn't remember getting that near the fire and he didn't remember crying. There were a couple of burns on his right hand he also couldn't explain, but, slowly, his brain began to reawaken.

At first, all he could do was watch a parade of images and sensations march through his mind: the almost animalistic roar of flame, the pop of exploding safety glass, the smell of burning rubber, the dark-gray coils of smoke. But mostly the blackened shape that only a minute earlier had been his friend.

If Cynthie had left London when she'd originally planned, she would've been somewhere between King's Lynn and Swineshead when the bomb detonated—there was no doubt in his mind it was a car bomb and a powerful one. Nothing else could have done that kind of damage that fast. If the bomb had gone off then, it would have killed her before she'd been able to tell them about Tom Nelson, which meant her instinct that she was being followed was right.

Tom had probably managed to get her phone tapped as well, and based on her conversation last night with Brody, he knew exactly when she'd planned to be on the road, where she parked at night, and how much time he'd have to plant his little agent of death.

Only she'd left at least three hours earlier than planned, time to get to Swineshead, tell them what they needed to know, and leave. Barely. A minute or two earlier and the car would have exploded in Brody's driveway. It might have damaged his car and Sam's, but they'd have all been safe.

If, if, if. Such a big word.

Brody shut off the water and stood with his head resting on the black-and-white tile surround. What could he tell Wyland Reid about why his wife died? They'd only met once or twice, but, damn it, he couldn't tell him the truth—that Cynthie had been another sacrifice for the life of Nathan Freeman.

The only thing he could do was make sure Sam survived this, whether it was to go back to her life in the States or to start over with him. He was so damn tired he couldn't think about starting anything.

Brody dressed in a pair of loose sweatpants and a T-shirt and took the time to put on his running shoes. Because he seemed to be running a lot lately, and running in bare feet hadn't helped his knee any. He didn't have much optimism that the running would end anytime soon.

Sam still sat in the parson's chair, the gun in her right hand, resting on her thigh in much the same position as Tom Nelson had sat on his first visit. Brody didn't know how yet, but they were going to nail that son of a bitch.

It took Brody a while to get outside his own head enough to notice Sam's expression. "What's wrong?"

Stupid question. Everything was wrong.

"We have a new problem." Her face didn't look so much angry as . . . puzzled.

He was almost afraid to ask, but of course he had to. "What?"

"I got a call while you were in the shower." She stood up, handed him the .45, and gestured toward the chair. "Sit there, and you can stretch your leg out better."

"I guess it was from Tom, telling us about sending us a warning?"

She shook her head, her brows lowered in a deep frown. "That was the gist of the phone call. Kind of an 'if you don't do what you're told and find the jewels, you're dead' message. But it wasn't from Tom."

Great, maybe it was the anonymous guy who'd followed them in Boston. "So who was it?"

"It was a woman." Sam shrugged her shoulders. "She said she was Tom's wife."

CHAPTER 34

Brody collapsed in the chair, looking as tired as Sam felt. The clock might only say 3:00 p.m., but the past eight hours had taken a decade off her life.

"I can't even think about Tom's wife yet." Brody closed his eyes and let his head drop back on the chair's headrest. "Go ahead and take your shower. I'll stand guard."

He was more likely to fall asleep than guard, but Sam didn't share that opinion. Her stomach was tied in knots, and she'd only known Cynthie for all of an hour or two. She couldn't imagine how Brody felt.

God, it was bad enough that it happened. Did he really have to see it?

She expected Brody to be asleep when she reemerged into the den, but he was wide-awake and staring at the back door as if daring someone to walk in so he could shoot first and ask questions later.

Sam had no idea what to say to him. "I'm sorry" was so inadequate as to be meaningless. "How are you" was ridiculous because of course he wasn't okay at all. Instead, she sat cross-legged on the floor near his feet, trying to be a soothing presence if he needed her without invading his space—whatever that need might be right now.

"Before we talk about the phone call, what did you tell the police? I was out of it."

He'd definitely been out of it. Sam had feared he was in shock, enough to need medical treatment. Only Brody's occasional glance at something going on around him with a modicum of awareness convinced her to finally send the EMT away. The man had wanted to take Brody to the hospital, and he might still need it if his head didn't clear. But they needed to decide on their stories first.

"Basically, I told them as little as possible," Sam said. "I had to tell them who Cynthie was, because they'd have been able to find out from the car registration, and then they'd find out that she was NCA. We don't want to get caught in a lie. But they'll want to know why she was here. I suggest you just say we're all personal friends."

Her strategy had been blunt and simple. She obviously hadn't been very good at playing the legal system or she wouldn't have gone to jail on a juvenile ruling, but she'd still avoided arrest more times than she'd been caught. Rule of thumb in the Eighth Ward: tell as simple a story as you can so you don't get caught in an inconsistency.

"So, what, you said she was my friend, just dropping by on her way back to London?" Brody was totally focused now, his dark eyes watching her face. Which was good; it meant he was going to be okay. Or as okay as possible, given what he'd just been through.

"Right. I told them she had driven up from London after talking to you yesterday. You had some paintings for her to take a look at for a possible art show in the London area." She gestured toward the hallway. "There are a bunch of finished pieces in that room, stacked against the far wall. If they ask to see the paintings, you can use those."

Another faint smile, and this time it actually reached his eyes. "You've been plundering again."

She gave him an "aw shucks" shrug. "Former occupational hazard. Anyway, the story is that we have no idea what happened. She came, she looked at paintings, we chatted and had some coffee, and then she left. We'd just come back in the house when we heard the explosion."

"Can't really screw that story up. I have to admit, simple works in this case. Did the police buy it?"

"Yeah, but they were pretty gobsmacked over the whole thing, as the locals say." She paused. "I wonder what they'll make of it." The police and rescue workers had been almost as shocked as she and Brody, only without the emotional connection. This was clearly not a situation for which they'd been prepared. Training exercises can only provide so much realism.

Brody's voice was a flat monotone. "I'm sure it'll be chalked up to one of her cases. I'm sure I'm not her only assignment. I'm sure she's dealt with her share of scumbags over the years. The problem is that the real scumbag, Tom, will go free unless we can figure out what to do about him."

Or his wife, because that was one bizarre phone conversation. "Better let me tell you about the phone call."

"Okay, I think I can hear it now." He shifted the gun to his left hand and reached his right out to brush her hair off her cheek. She leaned into him instinctively, and only when she turned to kiss his palm did she see the burns.

She took his hand and turned it toward the window. This room was so damned dim with its ivy curtain outside the one window. The burn didn't look too bad, but it had to hurt. "Hang on."

Walking into the kitchen, Sam opened the pantry and pulled out a jar of honey she'd spotted on an earlier scouting mission. She folded a soft cloth, doused it in cool water, and spread a thin layer of honey on it before returning to the den.

"When you grow up one step from being on the streets and without health insurance, you learn a lot of tricks." She took his left hand and stretched out his fingers, then laid the cloth across it. She wrapped the makeshift bandage around the back side of his hand and secured it with a strip of masking tape.

He'd hissed when it first touched his skin, but his muscles eventually relaxed when the coolness eased the heat in his palm.

"That feels good. What's on it?" He held his hand up to his nose, then stuck his tongue out and touched the tip to the bandage. "Honey?"

"It's good for burns. Trust me. I'm not a doctor." Okay, bad joke but it got another hint of a smile out of him. "You ready to hear about Mrs. Tom?"

Brody sighed and groaned at the same time. The sound was one of total frustration. "Oh, why not."

"I answered the phone thinking it was Tom, so I was surprised to hear a woman's voice. She said she was Tom's wife and that she's working with him." Sam paused. "She said she hoped we'd heard about their message by now. If not, we'd be hearing about it soon."

The wording of the call had been strange—and the timing. True, the woman had sounded cold and emotionless, but she'd also implied that she didn't know whether or not they'd heard about Cynthie.

"She didn't say she hoped we'd heard it but *had heard about* it." Sam had been running the conversation around and around in a mental loop. "The way she said it made me pretty sure she didn't know the explosion had happened here. She thought it had happened somewhere else and we'd have gotten word about it. That tells me she isn't nearby. Maybe back in London."

"I was thinking about it in the shower, the timing of the whole thing," Brody said, staring out into space. Sam still worried about shock, but he seemed to just be thinking, and his conversation was engaged. "My theory is that they meant the bomb to go off while Cynthie—" His voice cracked when he said her name, but he swallowed hard and continued. "While Cynthie was on her way here. If they intercepted the phone call she made to me last night, they'd have known she didn't plan to get here until about ten a.m."

That made perfect sense. "And if they intercepted that call, they also knew that, as of this morning, she hadn't told you Tom's identity."

Brody nodded. "So chances are good that Mr. and Mrs. Tom don't know we're onto them. They think Cynthie never told us, which gives us an advantage. Except." He closed his eyes. "All the evidence was in Cynthie's briefcase."

Sam smiled, reached behind her to the coffee table, and held up a black cell phone. "Not all of it."

CHAPTER 35

"Get the fuck out of here. Can't you see I'm on the phone?"

As soon as the going-to-be-fired junior assistant had scurried out of the room, Brent finished punching the telephone "Send" button next to Tom Nelson's name. Brent's shoulder blades always itched when things weren't going right—call it intuition or nerves— and they'd been itching for the forty-eight hours that had passed since Tom had last called with one of his vague reports on Samantha Crowe.

This whole operation had become a clusterfuck, and Brent was ready to see it done, even if it meant forfeiting the full $30 million to the other C7 members, minus Tom Nelson, before the month was up. He'd gotten excited by the idea of owning King John's lost crown jewels, but he had too much work to personally oversee the job. With a little distance, he now saw what a long shot it had been from the outset.

Maybe it would still be salvageable if he had a reliable lieutenant on the ground in Pighead, or whatever the fuck that little town was called. But he had the mercenary, who had no imagination or ability to think on his feet, and he had Tom Nelson, a pathetic midlevel bureaucrat with balls of cotton candy.

"Good morning, Brent." Tom answered on the first ring but didn't sound the least contrite.

"I thought I'd made it clear that I wanted daily reports, Tom. Do you realize how much this little caper is costing me, and that you aren't going to get a cent? Not unless you can give me something I can use and do it in the next thirty seconds."

Tom cleared his throat. In Brent's experience, people who had to clear their throats before speaking were getting their lies in order. "Samantha is planning to visit the site of a place called Witcham House today, or the site where the house used to sit. There seems to be a great deal of agreement between her own research and the recollections of local historians. Her landlord, Brody Parker, was able to provide her with some previously unread journals belonging to the relative from whom he inherited the house."

Brent stroked his jaw, thinking. That was certainly a more detailed report than what Tom usually gave—albeit two days late. "What part of daily reporting do you not understand? You couldn't have reported in earlier?"

"I could have."

Brent closed his eyes. He was going to kill this pompous son of a bitch before all was said and done. "But you didn't."

"Brent, detective work—which is basically what you've asked Samantha Crowe to do—is a methodical process of slowly building evidence." Tom spoke as if he were explaining procedure to a first grader, for which he was going to lose at least a couple of percentage points off his cut. "I felt it a waste of both our time to issue the same report day after day. You're a busy man, are you not?"

He decided to abandon this line of argument. It was just pissing him off more, and if the girl was this close to identifying the site, maybe he could give her a few more days. "What about the big love affair between Samantha and Brody Parker? Are you sure they haven't shared information?"

This time the pause was too long for Brent's liking, but he waited.

"Well, I haven't exactly been in bed with them to hear their pillow talk firsthand, you understand, but since they're both continuing to do exactly as we've instructed, I see no reason to believe they have shared anything but body parts."

"Twenty-four hours, Nelson. I'll expect another report. That money I put in your account at the beginning of the job as a down payment? A hundred grand comes back to me every day that goes by without a phone call from you."

He ended the call and threw the phone at the wall. Insufferable Englishmen. No wonder the American Founding Fathers had routed them back across the pond.

Brent's shoulder blades still itched, and he hadn't liked those long pauses and throat clearings in Tom's conversation. He'd checked in with Tweedledee. Maybe it was time to check out Tweedledum's story. Felix Grummond had fallen in his estimation after failing to find information on Brody Parker beyond what Brent himself had learned on the Internet, which wasn't much. It's like the guy hadn't existed until seven years ago.

Retrieving his cell phone from beneath the conference table, where it had landed after bouncing off the wall, Brent called the reliable, unimaginative, but refreshingly amoral Felix, who answered with his own brand of annoying Britishness.

"Thought I'd be hearing from you yesterday, what with all the excitement in Swineshead."

Brent tried to count to ten but lost his patience at three. "And how would I know what was going on in Swineshead if you didn't tell me?" Jackass.

"An NCA agent from London got herself all blown up, she did. Right outside town not a half mile from High Street itself."

This time, he made it to four. "And this should interest me why?" An agent getting blown up anywhere, including Bumfuck, England, wasn't any kind of surprise. It was probably the fucking Irish Republican Army.

Felix's laugh, or at least Brent thought it was a laugh, came out more like a wheeze. "Well, that's the kind of information that's worth a lot of money to the high bidder now, isn't it? I can tell you it's information you'll be glad you have in your pocket, though, seeing as how it concerns the people you've had me watching."

One, two, three . . . "How much?"

"Well, I was thinking that the wife might like a bit of a holiday, you know. Maybe those Greek islands you see in the magazines, the ones with all the white buildings and blue domes what look out over the water. You know the ones I mean?"

That any woman would have willingly married this man confirmed Brent's belief that women were basically stupid. Samantha Crowe was another case in point. "How much?"

"Well, I was thinking, given the valuable nature of this information, that a million might do the trick. A million pounds, not American dollars. They ain't worth much these days."

Could anything Felix knew be worth a million pounds? Hell, he'd be saving more than that in what he wasn't going to pay Tom Nelson. "Deal. Tell me what you've got."

"You know I have a one-week payment policy."

Son of a bitch. "You'll get your money. Talk."

"So this lady agent whose car blew up has a good friend in Swineshead."

Brent might have an aneurysm. His head throbbed. "And?"

"Her good friend is Brody Parker. She'd been to see him for a couple of hours—him and Samantha Crowe—before she drove off and, boom, up in flames."

Why did he have to deal with idiots? Idiots should be outlawed. "Felix, if you want to see a penny of that money, you tell me why I should give a fuck that Brody Parker met with one of his friends just before her car blew up, even if she was a federal agent. It's not like you found any information worth a shit about Parker, and how does it involve me?"

"It wasn't the meeting that was so much interesting, you see, but who planted the bomb that blew up the agent's car."

Brent sighed. He'd just wait and not ask. The man would tell him when he was ready.

After a few seconds of silence, Felix broke the stalemate. "That would be me. I planted the car bomb."

Wait. What? "You blew up the car of an NCA agent?" If this was some misguided attempt by Felix to extort money out of Brent, he had chosen the wrong billionaire to cross. Again he waited.

"Right," Felix said. "And you might be wonderin' who hired me to do that?"

Whoever it was, he bet they paid out the ass and still ended up with hemorrhoids. He sighed. "Who?"

"Why that would be our good friend Tom, who normally considers himself all too high and mighty to deal with the likes of me. Guess he's slumming."

Brent had been swiveling his chair back and forth, working off nervous energy so he wouldn't try to leap through the phone and throttle Felix. Now he froze.

"Repeat that, please."

Felix did, with less embellishment this time. Brent's mind raced through the implications. Brent could only think of one reason to kill Brody Parker's friend, the NCA agent, and that was if Parker had confided in her and Tom had been found out. Nelson was trying to cover his ass.

But the hit happened after the NCA agent had met with Samantha Crowe and Brody Parker. Chances were that whatever the agent knew, they now knew as well.

Fuck. That was it. Game over.

"Felix, my friend, how much do you charge for a hit these days? You got a volume discount? Because I have some people who need to die."

"Well, Mr. Sullivan, the price of ammunition has gotten pretty—"

"How much?"

Felix paused, and he dropped the English version of the good-ole-boy act. "How many hits are you talking about?"

Crowe. Parker. Nelson. And, oh, why not? Mrs. Nelson.

"Four. As soon as possible." Then he'd have to kill Felix Grummond, the final loose end, and he'd do that himself.

CHAPTER 36

Brody pulled out on the road back to Swineshead from Boston. He'd spent the last ninety minutes making his statement to district law enforcement about the car bombing, not that anyone official had called it that yet.

Every question had twisted another knot in his gut that he didn't know how he'd ever untangle. He'd only cried twice. Bully for him.

At least until halfway through the drive back, when he got the call from Wyland Reid. Then he'd cried again.

He'd pulled off the road not too far from the Swineshead Railway Station, walking around the adjacent pastureland while Sam waited in the car. He could tell from the set of her shoulders that she was deliberately not turning toward him, not watching.

She'd been great through the last twenty-four hours, seeming to sense when he needed her close and respect when he needed space. Now, he paced around the field, lying to Wyl while the man wept over something he couldn't understand or accept.

Every question he couldn't truthfully answer. Every time Wyl said how much Brody meant to Cynthie and how much she loved working with him. How she'd been so pleased to give him a piece of Brody's art for their anniversary. How he couldn't believe he wasn't ever going to see her again. Every snippet of memory the man mentioned cut deeper into Brody's guilt.

He was as responsible for her death as if he'd planted the bomb himself.

When he ended the call, Brody knelt in the field, right then and there, and prayed for forgiveness, for protection—for Sam if not for himself. He hadn't prayed in a long time, and he wasn't sure he deserved to have anyone listen. But if ever they needed divine intervention, it was now.

A soft pressure on his shoulder brought him back to the present. "Let's go home, Brody." Sam held out a hand and helped him up, and they walked back to the car, the first clouds of another front moving in overhead.

Sam offered to drive, which left him free to stare out the window and watch the drab early-autumn landscape fly past, tormenting himself with very little brain activity. He was numb, and mindlessly staring out the window was about all he could handle.

He jolted awake when Sam turned onto Abbey Road. He'd slept all the way through town. But he felt like himself again, at least a little. Not like the zombie he'd been for most of the past twenty-four hours.

"How is Cynthie's husband?"

Devastated. Brokenhearted. In shock. "Pretty much what you'd expect. The funeral is day after tomorrow. He—" Brody swallowed down a lump of grief so big it almost choked him. "He wants to see her body, to help convince himself that she is really gone. I begged him to reconsider."

He'd have to live with the image of that blackened form the rest of his life. Wyl should remember his wife whole and vibrant and beautiful, not like that.

They rode in silence until they reached the drive to Brody's house.

"I probably should drop you off and go back to town to pick up some food," Sam said. "I doubt there's much at the house besides bread and peanut butter." She paused. "I guess everyone in town has heard about the accident."

"No doubt." Small towns were gossip hotbeds, and Swineshead was no exception. People were probably gossiping about it all over the village.

Of course, it was no accident. He and Sam knew it, and eventually, so would law enforcement. "Let's wait on the market. I'm okay with peanut butter if you are."

"Sounds good to me."

She pulled the VW alongside her car, killed the switch, and sat there, probably waiting for Brody to give her a clue as to what they did next. He hated that she was walking on eggshells around him.

"I'm not ready to face the house yet," Brody said. "Let's leave the car here and then walk to the back of my property, about a quarter mile. Maybe we can find the Witcham House site and look around."

"You sure you want to walk?" Sam looked pointedly at his legs. "Seems like your knee would be happier if we drove."

He got out and bounced on the balls of his feet. "It's a little better today. It'll be good for me to walk." He just needed to lay off running and climbing.

They pulled the metal detector from the trunk, and between them, they recalled enough of the parson's drawings to find the narrow lane leading around the edge of Brody's property. He'd been around this way a few times when he first arrived in Swineshead, but for painting he'd been lured several miles southeast toward the fens. He'd always be a swamp rat, he guessed. Mud and flat land and water were in his DNA.

"There's the abandoned farmhouse I hid at when I ran away," Sam said, pointing to the right.

Brody guessed it had been a farmhouse. Even after all these years in rural England, to him a farmhouse was the American version, a rambling house with white siding and a broad porch. But the Lincolnshire version, at least this one, was painted stone, sturdy and square, two stories tall with a chimney on each end and a steeply pitched roof. It appeared to have once been painted a sky blue. Now the house was faded to a kind of mottled gray with patches of blue shining through.

"So straight across that field is my cottage?" He hadn't realized any buildings were this close.

"Yep. There's a stone wall beyond the nearest tree line that I guess marks the property boundary."

A little beyond the farmhouse lay an unpaved road. More like a path. "I think this might be it." Sam turned down the overgrown strip of dirt and weeds, stopping at another farmhouse, which, judging by the ivy coating all the doors and windows, had been empty even longer than the first one.

They stood for a few seconds, looking for . . . he wasn't quite sure what.

"Look." Sam pointed to the far corner of the cleared lawn area, where a ledge-like hill could have camouflaged earthworks. "Does that look like it could be some kind of old structure to you?"

One way to find out. "Let's walk over there."

They spent the next half hour wandering the site, and even Brody couldn't help but feel a rush of excitement when they discovered the earthworks formed a large rectangle. The grass-covered land rose in spots and would run along a few feet before dipping again, only to rise several yards farther along.

"Let's mark what we think are the corners." Sam found an old tire nearby and dragged it to the nearest spot where the raised earth seemed to form a ninety-degree angle.

They took the metal detector from its packaging, and while Brody pretended to read the instructions and then look for the rest of the earthworks—he really was resting his knee—she walked back and forth over the corner spot near the tire.

Several times she gave a little yip of excitement when the detector found something. "Bottle cap," she called the first time. Then "nail."

"I remember seeing a concrete block near where we left the paved road. We can use that to mark another corner." Brody walked back toward the edge of the clearing, looking for the block he'd almost tripped over because it was surrounded by overgrown vegetation. He glanced up as a drop of rain splashed on his nose, then followed a strange cloud formation across the sky and stared, his mouth going dry.

"Sam!" His voice was hoarse from too much shouting, from too much crying. "We've gotta go!"

He looked back, gesturing, and she began walking toward him with a frown. When she spotted the sky behind him, she broke out in a run.

"Is it the cottage?" He was pretty sure the horrified look on her face mirrored his own.

"It sure looks like it. Let's cut through the fields."

What Brody had first thought was a dark, threatening cloud now had clearly become a column of dark smoke that sent his heart into his throat and threatened to paralyze him again.

His house. It was his goddamn house. He didn't even need to see it to know it was burning.

He ran as fast as he could, but by the time he reached the edge of the first clearing, he was already limping and Sam had pulled ahead of him. Every thud of his right foot hitting the spongy earth, still wet from the rains, sent a jolt of pain into his hip, but he couldn't let up.

The smoke now rose in graceful billows of gray and black against a pale-gray cloud-covered sky. With an awkward shove, he hefted himself over the low stone wall onto his property. Sam already waited on the other side, punching at the screen of her phone.

"I'm calling 999," she said. "Again."

Brody gasped for breath, his lungs compressing and expanding against his pounding heart. Over Sam's shoulder he could see the flames now, reaching orange fingers for the sky. The house had to be fully engulfed to send up smoke and flames that high. It wouldn't help that he had flammable art supplies in the house to act as an accelerant.

Kirton Fire and Rescue was the closest station, and it would take them at least ten to twenty minutes to get here. His house would be gone by then.

They started running again and finally came around the final corner. Brody slowed down, both horrified and mesmerized by the sight of orange flames sending up plumes of black smoke from his roof and fiery tendrils flicking out his den window.

He was wondering if they could find a way to save the garage and didn't realize that he'd left Sam behind until he heard her yell. "Brody, stop!"

He turned back. She was about ten yards behind him, breathing hard, looking past him. "Are you hurt? We need to get—"

"No, look!" He followed the line of her finger as she pointed to the right of the flames.

"Sam, I don't see . . . wait. What the fuck is that?"

"Not what. Who. It's a guy on the roof of the garage."

He strained to see and backed up a few feet to where she stood so he could get a better sight line. It was a man all right, looking over the peak of the garage roof with a rifle trained on the burning house. He didn't know who the guy was, but he was too tall and thin to be Tom Nelson.

"He thinks since the cars are there, that we're in there." Sam's voice was subdued.

She was right. "And he's just waiting to pick us off as soon as we come out. Or waiting to let us burn."

Son of a bitch. He'd been wanting to kill somebody; now he had a target but no gun. Sam still had her messenger bag, though, because she had Cynthie's phone stuck in it and refused to let it out of her sight.

"You got a gun in that thing?" He tugged on the bag.

"No, we were going to the police station. It didn't seem like a good idea to go in carrying it."

"Too bad, because I feel like some target practice."

"There's two of us, and if we can slip up on him, we can use those tire irons propped against the wall behind the garage."

He gave her a look. "Don't tell me. You were plundering."

"It's how I roll."

They walked now instead of running, and Brody hoped his knee would hold up to a confrontation. They'd gotten within a hundred yards or so of the back of the garage, about the length of a football field, when Sam stopped him again.

"Wait. We might need to rethink this."

Brody looked up at the shooter and his heart sank. There were two of them now, heads together, talking. Looked like both had rifles. "Great, an assassin for each of us, you think?"

"Looks that way. I don't like our odds with two of them and you injured." Sam squinted toward the garage. "This will shock you, but I'm not very good in a fistfight."

"This might shock you, too, but neither am I, especially on one leg." The idea of leaving his house to burn made him want to curl up in a ditch and hope it rained hard enough to drown him. The rain seemed willing to cooperate and do its part; it was coming down in a fine mist, which might at least slow the fire.

"Let's go to one of those farmhouses until it stops raining." Sam turned and walked in a westerly direction, toward town, at a slight angle from the way they came. "Then we can figure out what to do."

They'd almost reached the stone wall when Sam cried out and fell. "What happ—shit!" A chunk of mortar flew from the wall and sprayed them with small chunks.

"They've seen us." Sam got up and ran for the wall. "Come on!"

Brody zigzagged to the wall and rolled over right behind Sam. They collapsed on the other side as another spray of rocks and mortar went flying. Brody shook the stuff out of his hair and was surprised to see an old coin land in his lap. Probably a bad-luck penny, but he stuck it in his pocket. "Does this wall lead to one of the farmhouses?"

"Yes, the blue one we passed. It angles in at the back side."

"Let's hug the wall and go on the longest duck walk in history." After which his knee would be ruined, if it didn't give out altogether.

By the time they reached the farmhouse what seemed like a day and a half later, although Sam insisted it was fifteen minutes, Brody had to lean on her to make it up the back steps.

He reached out for the back doorknob and could have wept when it wouldn't turn. "It's locked. What a surprise. We can't catch a break."

"*Pffft.*" Sam let out an exasperated hiss of air. "Don't forget who you're traveling with. Plundering isn't my only skill."

She dug in her bag and brought out a pair of silver nail clippers and held them up. "You stand guard; I'll pick the lock."

"With nail clippers? Go for it." If she could pick a lock with nail clippers, he could defend them against two rifle-toting assassins armed with his wallet, a breath mint, and an unlucky penny, the total contents of his pockets. If he lived through this, he was going to start carrying a man purse.

It took her less than a minute, although the rain had intensified enough to soak them both. "It isn't even a dead bolt," she said, turning the knob and swinging the door open.

He followed her inside, and she closed the door behind them and locked it back. "If they find us, they're going to have to break in."

The house appeared to have been empty a long time. There was an old, dusty sofa in the middle of the front room, but they both decided they'd rather sit on the floor. Brody sat with his back against the wall, his legs stretched out, and his knee burning as badly as his house.

He knew he'd mourn it later because he'd come to think of it as his home, but in the end, the house was stuff. Compared to losing Cynthie, or the prospect of losing Sam, stuff just didn't matter.

He wrapped an arm around Sam and she leaned against him. He loved the way her shoulder tucked perfectly under his arm, with her head resting on his shoulder. This was what mattered, not a house. Home was the people you cared about, not the place where you lived. It had taken a long time and a lot of loss for him to learn that.

"You think those guys are working for Tom or for Psycho Gary?" Sam's soft voice echoed in the cavernous, almost-empty room.

Brody shook his head. "I have no idea. Tom, as well as Mrs. Tom, should know by now that Cynthie's car blew up less than a quarter mile from my house. I wonder how good their intelligence is. Will they realize the car was leaving my house, or do they think the bomb went off just in time to prevent Tom's identity from being revealed?"

As far as he knew, Gary wasn't even close to having his identity revealed, so his money was on Tom knowing Cynthie had gotten to them before they killed her. The detective must be in an absolute panic, and panicked people made mistakes.

As much as it galled him to think about it, panicked people also were open to making deals.

CHAPTER 37

Brody Parker sure knew how to kiss. "You're way too good at this." Sam snuggled against him, enjoying the sound of the rain and the quiet before the inevitable moment when they had to decide what to do and where to go. "You must've had a lot of practice."

It was her way of trying to plunder his past the way she'd plundered his house, but he didn't take the bait. "I'm just inspired by the present company."

"Uh-huh."

They froze at the sound of voices outside, and Sam barely dared to breathe. The shooters were looking for them.

They were not in view of anyone looking in windows, but they could see the doors, and Sam gave an involuntary gasp when the knob to the back door turned and the door shook in its frame. Had they left any telltale signs back there? Had there been enough rain to fill their footprints?

The door rattled again and then stopped. Only the soft sound of rain could be heard now. "I think they're gone." She kept her whisper as soft as air.

Brody's voice was equally soft. "Not yet, they'll try the front."

Sam shifted her gaze to the front door. The room lay in such shadows that it was hard to even see the knob, much less tell if it were turning. Had Brody checked to make sure the other door was locked? She couldn't remember.

A rattling noise came from the front, and Sam startled at movement from inside the room. Brody's arm tightened around her, holding her in place. Because she'd almost rather face a gunman than a rat, which is what it had to be.

Less than a minute later, a minute during which Sam barely breathed, they heard the voices again, closer to the window.

"Think they made it back to town?"

"I don't know, but I'm tired of fucking around in this rain. We'll find them later. Not that many places to hide 'round here. Plus, they're Yanks. Don't fit in, right?"

The voices faded into the sounds of the falling rain, and Sam felt Brody's muscles relaxing as he took a deep breath. "That was too damn close. We need to get somewhere safe."

"Without rats," she added.

"Problem is, I can't think of anyone else to bring into this short of calling my FBI contact. He can move fast, but we still need somewhere to stay for at least twenty-four hours." Brody stroked her arm as he talked, making her want to purr, not conspire or theorize. "The last thing I want to do is put anyone else in danger. There's been enough of that."

Sam weighed her answer. There was always risk, especially dealing with people who treated death like a move on a chessboard. "You think we can get to the professor's house in the dark? In the rain?"

Brody gave her a sharp look. "You want to bring old Miles into this?"

"No, no." Sam almost smiled at the idea of the old professor wielding a sword or a dagger at an assailant. "He's out of town, though. When I went to see him, he was leaving the next morning for a two-week trip to visit his grandkids. That house is pretty isolated. It would give us a safe spot to stay until we figure out what to do."

Brody was silent for a few heartbeats, then nodded. "It's a good idea. There would be no risk to him as long as he's out of town. By the time he gets home, we'll be gone. And I know a good lock picker."

Sam laughed. "Yes, you do."

"We'll have to walk, though, much as my knee hates the idea." Brody climbed to his feet with an awkward lurch and practiced pacing. His limp was pronounced. "Even if the cars aren't damaged, it's too risky."

"Agreed." Sam got up, wanting to stretch her legs as well. The gloom of this house was getting to her. "I hope Tom's nice and warm and dry right now."

Brody shook his head. "He must be desperate."

"Not to mention his wife." Sam stretched her back, stiff from sitting on the floor. "I mean, what's up with her?"

"I've been thinking about that. I haven't done much *besides* think about Tom Nelson the past twenty-four hours." Brody paused, looking toward the door. "One of the things that struck me the very first time I talked to him—the only time I saw him in person—was that he seemed, I don't know, *sad* about the whole thing. I can't move past that. It was like he was putting the screws to me but he genuinely wasn't enjoying himself."

Sam snorted. "Yeah, not like good old Psycho. From the tone of his little notes, he's totally enjoying himself."

She stood at the window, watching the rain and looking for any sign of lurking hit men, and thought about her own face-to-face with Tom. "You know, I remember thinking the same thing, at least about the tired part. He looked downright weary. You know, not like you're tired from a workout, but like you get after a long period of stress."

"Yeah, well, he'd be a lot less stressed if he'd quit trying to kill people." Brody walked the length of the room and back. "I think I can make it. That dive over the rock wall didn't help things. Oh, I forgot."

He reached in his pocket and pulled something out, then tossed it to Sam. "It fell on my head."

She caught it and turned it over and over in her palm. "It's some kind of coin. How'd it end up falling on your head?" She took the hem of her sweater and began to gently wipe at the coin, trying to remove enough mortar and dirt to get a better look at it.

"I guess it was embedded into that rock wall. It was in a chunk of mortar that also hit me in the head." Brody flexed his knee and winced. "This has not been a good day."

Sam watched him out of the corner of her eye. Damn it. If they kept having to run for their lives, he was going to do so much damage to that knee that he wouldn't be able to walk. She had a strong feeling knee replacement surgery lay somewhere in his not-too-distant future.

If they had a future.

Sam pulled out her cell phone and turned on its flashlight app so she could get a better look at the coin. Its shape was irregular—rounded but not quite round—which suggested it predated modern molds. A short cross covered one side, while the other had a crown and some worn figures or words on it.

She tried to tamp down her excitement. Just because it was an old coin didn't mean it was as old as the crown jewels. But it was something.

"What do you think it is?" Brody came to look at the coin with her. "Is that a crown or a head on that side?"

"I don't know. It might be nothing." Sam held it up and shone the light on it. "Or it might be a game changer."

CHAPTER 38

"I don't like it." Tom paced the length of his kitchen, back and forth, his shoes silent on the Italian tile. Another bit of evidence that he and Donna had lived beyond their means, and look where that had gotten them. "I don't like it one bit. He's up to something."

He'd been trying to reach Brent Sullivan for the past day, with no answer. Sullivan always answered his private line unless he was intentionally avoiding someone, so Tom could reach no other conclusion. And if Brent were avoiding him, he was up to some scheme he didn't want Tom to know about.

"Do you want me to call that Felix man again? Although I don't relish it." Donna had been sitting at the table for the last half hour, watching him pace, her brows drawn together in worry.

"For God's sake, no. He's done work for Brent in the past. If Brent knows we've been found out, and that we killed that NCA agent, it's Felix that told him. It was risky using him, but he's the only murder-for-hire I know."

Brent must have found out. Tom could think of no other reason Brent wouldn't take his calls. At first, he'd been hopeful that the man had perished in a plane crash or that a major earthquake had washed San Francisco into the sea, taking Brent Sullivan along with it. But the death of a young, vibrant billionaire or the destruction of a major American city would have made the news.

For all the tough, angry talk she'd spewed after Cynthia Reid had found them out, Donna had drawn in on herself since the agent's death. Hell, they both had. The guilt was eating them alive, from the inside. Murder sounded easy in theory, but it killed a piece of your soul. If you didn't find a way to forgive yourself, it killed more pieces, until you had no soul left. He'd seen too many of the aftereffects of violence in his career, and Donna was learning it firsthand.

Cynthia Reid had been so young, and she'd done nothing wrong except be smart enough to figure out it was detective Tom Nelson who'd been blackmailing her client. And for that, they'd had her killed.

"What do we do?" Donna's voice was scarcely more than a whisper of panic. "I feel as if we're in a guillotine with our heads hanging out, knowing that blade is going to fall but not knowing when, or who's going to be the one to release it."

Tom's guess was that the blade would take one of two forms. If Brent Sullivan wielded it, then he, at least, would be dead. If Brent didn't know that Donna had been in on everything, she might survive. But not likely. Felix would tell that it was Tom's wife, and not Tom himself, who'd been his contact. He shouldn't have let her make the call, but she'd insisted, wanting to prove to him that she was as willing to take a risk for their future as he was.

If the guillotine blade were wielded by Brody Parker, who most surely knew his identity since Cynthia Reid's car had exploded after she left his house, not before she arrived, then it would be a legal guillotine. Tom would find himself in one of the very cells into which he'd sent so many criminals over the years.

"I don't know what to do, love." He pulled out a chair opposite Donna and slumped in his seat. "I honestly am at sea."

Sitting on the table between him, his cell phone rang, its little screen lighting up with the words "International Caller."

"It's Sullivan calling back, finally." Donna leaned over and pushed the phone toward him. "Put him on speaker so I can hear."

"Right, but don't say anything. We don't want to set him off just in case he doesn't know you were involved."

He set the phone to speaker, then pressed the talk button. "Nelson."

The caller's voice sent his pulse racing, and he looked up at Donna. Her eyes were so wide she looked like a cartoon drawing. It was not Brent Sullivan.

"Hello, Detective Nelson. It's Samantha Crowe. Don't you think it's time we talked again?"

Donna jerked her head in a slight nod, and Tom closed his eyes. He'd been in hundreds of interrogations. He knew how to keep his cool. "Ms. Crowe. What do you think we have to talk about?"

She laughed, annoying woman. She'd gained the upper hand in this situation, and they all knew it. "Brody Parker and I would like to talk to you and to your wife. Alone. And we'd advise you to call off your hit men if you don't want us going directly to the police."

"And what would you tell the police? They'd require proof of any allegations you might make." He frowned at Donna, scribbled "Did U Hire Hit Men?" on a napkin and held it up. Donna's breath caught, and she shook her head.

Tom had seen the police report from the car bomb; the remains of a briefcase were found near the body. Just the metal fittings, but he felt reasonably sure Cynthia Reid kept the evidence to turn in herself. His best hope was that Brody Parker knew the truth but had no way to prove it.

"Funny thing." Brody Parker's voice boomed out of the phone, and Tom saw Donna flinch. "Cynthie was in such a hurry to get back to London and turn you in that she forgot her cell phone. She was a modern woman. Recorded all her notes on her phone. Kept track of all her calls. E-mails, too. And scanned every document in her file on you. Where do you think we got your phone number?"

A chill stole up Tom's spine, followed by a flush. "What do you want?"

"First, call off the hit men who burned down my house."

Tom's gaze shot up to Donna's again, questioning. Had she done something and not told him? Again she shook her head no.

"I don't know what you're talking about, Parker."

"Then it was your boss, the one who calls himself 'Gary Smith.'" He paused. "He's the one we really want."

If only it were that simple.

Samantha Crowe's voice came back on, soft and reasonable. In another life, she might have made a good detective herself. "Look, Mr. Nelson. And Mrs. Nelson, if you're there. Are you there?"

Donna swallowed hard. "Y-yes. I'm here."

"We want to meet with you, just the four of us. In a public place. Are you willing to play by our rules for a change?"

The way Tom saw it, they had few options. "We're willing."

CHAPTER 39

Brody parked the professor's ancient, hot-wired car two blocks from a popular riverside eatery in Boston. He and Sam kept their heads down, walking as fast as his knee would allow. They'd finally made it to Miles Thornton's comfortable home and, after a few minutes of guilt, settled in to lick their wounds and rest. They'd found the vehicle in the garage, looking as pristine as it had in the 1960s. Whatever the professor drove on his day-to-day jaunts, it wasn't the old blue bomber.

The respite had given them time and space to plot. The call to Tom Nelson had been the first move. They had agreed to tuck the mystery coin away, telling no one about it unless they needed it as a bribe to save themselves.

Once inside the café, they took a table with a good view of the door and waited. They'd come early so they had the advantage of seeing the Nelsons before the older couple spotted them. The café was one Brody had visited before; it was crowded during the lunch hour. Too public for a murder attempt or a scene, but private enough to be able to carry on a private conversation.

"There they are." Sam jerked her head in the same direction they'd come from, and Brody turned to watch them. Tom and Donna Nelson looked like any nice, middle-aged British couple out for a lunchtime stroll, at least if one didn't look too closely at their faces.

The stress of the last couple of weeks showed on both of them. Dark circles and sagging eyelids. Worry lines. Downtrodden expressions.

Brody would like to kill them both. It raged against everything in his being to offer a deal to the people who'd taken Cynthie's life. But vengeance was God's, wasn't that the old saying? All he could be concerned with right now was making sure she didn't die for nothing. He and Sam had to be safe, whatever it took. And if it really was Tom's boss who ordered the hits and burned his house, that was the guy who had to be neutralized.

Which meant they'd have to sacrifice revenge against the minnow in order to get the big fish.

Tom spotted them as soon as they opened the café door and pointed his wife toward them.

Donna Nelson was a slim, pale redhead who, if possible, looked even more miserable than her husband.

"Sit down," Brody told them. The time for pretending they were friends had passed. This was blackmailer turning blackmailee, simple as that.

A perky waitress bounced up to take their orders, but as if sensing this was not a table filled with happy people, she quickly brought their drinks and disappeared. Good. That made things a little easier.

"I'll get right to the point." Brody and Sam had agreed that he would start the negotiations, playing bad cop. If the Nelsons started any kind of emotional scene, Sam would step in as good cop. Those were roles and a tactic Tom Nelson should recognize right away. He'd probably played the good or bad role himself many times. Judging by his demeanor during their earlier meeting, he was very good at it.

"We have enough material to incriminate both of you for blackmail and, in Mrs. Nelson's case, murder."

Donna Nelson sat up straighter, and her thin neck seemed to grow longer as she assumed an indignant expression. "I don't know how—"

"I recorded the phone call," Sam said, and the woman seemed to deflate by half. "The one you made after Cynthie Reid died, where you identified yourself as Tom's wife and asked if we'd gotten your message. Remember that one?"

Tom gave his wife a sharp look, but Brody didn't feel sorry for either one of them. He might have to work with these people, but he'd never understand what they'd done.

"What do you want from us?" Tom looked at Brody, then at Sam. "Are you offering a deal?"

"We are." Even though it left a very bitter taste in Brody's mouth, one his soda didn't begin to improve. "We will keep your secret. The police assume Cynthie was killed as part of another case she's been working." They'd learned that much from the BBC news. "It will eventually end up as a cold-case file as long as whoever you used to do the dirty work wasn't stupid. That's out of our control. But if you're caught, it won't be because of anything we've done."

Tom didn't look surprised. He had to know they'd offer a deal. Otherwise, why meet? The next part probably wouldn't surprise him either.

"In exchange, we want your boss."

Tom blinked. He obviously was scared of the guy, and Brody didn't blame him.

"I'm not sure I can do that." Tom's voice held a slight tremor.

"I don't think you have much choice." Brody leaned across the table so his words wouldn't carry. "He has put a hit out on Sam and me, unless you were lying about sending snipers to lie in wait on my roof and burn down my house."

"We weren't lying," Donna said quickly. "We haven't talked to him in days."

"Then think about this," Sam told her. "If he has a hit out on us, probably because whoever set the bomb in Cynthie's car went to him for more money, chances are pretty good he'll try to hit the two of you as well. We're just harder to control and easier to isolate, so he'll go after us first."

Brody wanted that point nailed home. They had no choice. "And if he doesn't have a hit on you now, wait until you've been fingered for Cynthia Reid's murder. He'll take you out to protect himself, to keep you from using him to get a lighter sentence."

Tom closed his eyes, and Brody knew he'd made his point. He could tell that Tom believed it, maybe that he'd even come to the same conclusion himself. When the detective spoke, his voice was downright frail. "What do you want us to do?"

"That's your call," Brody said. "You can tell us his name, or not. But we'll know it eventually because he either has to be dead or, better yet, in jail with a long sentence, because we don't want blood on our hands. However you decide to take him down, we'll need proof. We'll not live the rest of our lives waiting for him to succeed in having us killed."

Donna spoke for the first time, sounding a lot tougher than she looked. "What's to guarantee that you're dealing honestly with us? What's to guarantee that once our contact is out of the way you won't turn us in anyway?"

"You have too much information on us," Sam said softly. "You can ruin us; we can ruin you. It's a stalemate."

And it was a hell of a lot better than they deserved. Brody felt as if he were making a deal with the devil himself.

Tom cleared his throat. "We spoke about it all the way up from London and anticipated this might be the type of scheme you'd propose. It's the best solution for everyone. You're right about our mutual contact. None of us will be safe as long as he is at large."

He squared his shoulders and looked Sam in the eye, then transferred his gaze to Brody as if to reassure them he was on the level. Only time would prove that true or false, though. Brody was beyond trust.

"I will take care of things," Tom said. "Do you have somewhere safe to stay until you hear from me? It might take me a day or two to make the necessary arrangements and, for what I have in mind, I will likely need your expertise, Mr. Parker."

He paused a moment, then added, "I don't want you to tell me where you'll be staying. It's better that way for everyone."

Brody looked at Sam, waiting for her to give the go-ahead. He'd made his decision but it had to be mutual. They were in this together for the long haul.

"We do," Sam said, placing her hand on Brody's leg beneath the table and squeezing. "We have a safe place."

CHAPTER 40

Tom Nelson looked out the window as white fluffy clouds tinged with sunlit gold gave way to blue sky, then a patchwork landscape, then dots of trees and hills and cliffside houses overlooking a gleaming blue sea.

"Ladies and gentlemen, if you'll look out the right side of the plane as you face the cockpit, you'll see the beautiful Golden Gate Bridge, one of the world's most iconic sights. Please fasten your seatbelts and prepare for landing. And an early welcome to San Francisco, California."

The bridge and the bay were every bit as beautiful in person as in the pictures he'd seen. Perhaps he'd bring Donna here for a visit, depending on how the day went. Brent Sullivan had transferred more than a million pounds to Tom's bank account at the beginning of this miserable venture, and so far, he hadn't gotten around to removing it.

Tom hadn't touched a cent of it. In fact, he'd left Donna with instructions to go to a local bank in Leeds, where she was visiting a cousin, and open a new account. He wanted their money separate from anything that had Brent Sullivan's taint on it. These days, with most business done electronically, having a bank in Leeds and living in London would be no hardship.

Tom stood in line and tried to still his racing pulse as he presented his passport to the US Customs agent. "Nothing to declare?" the man asked, looking up to verify that Tom and his passport photo matched.

"No, just a short business trip," Tom said, forcing a smile that he hoped came across as at least moderately genuine.

"And what type of business do you do, Mr."—the agent looked back at his passport—"Mr. Nelson?"

This time Tom smiled more easily. "I'm a detective for the British organized crime unit," he said, holding up his NCA badge and a form from his home office. "Just following up on a couple of leads here in the States. I do have special authorization."

Taking the papers and passport with him, the customs agent walked into a small room in back of the desk. Tom gave an apologetic look to the people behind him in line, who began shifting to find spots in other lines. It was like being the person in front of a long queue of people at the market checkout and realizing you were stuck trying to buy the one thing missing its price tag or bar code.

Tom wasn't concerned. His paperwork was legitimate, as was the excuse for his being here. His new caseload—the one not involving human trafficking—did include some international transactions.

"Everything's in order, Detective Nelson." The agent handed Tom's passport back and motioned him through. "Good luck with your case and welcome to the United States."

Welcome, indeed.

Tom checked into a small downtown hotel and adjusted his watch to local time. Donna should be sitting down to dinner, safe at her cousin's house, probably looking at her own watch and wondering about him.

He thought about calling to let her know he'd arrived safely, but he had a bit of business to attend to first. He'd chosen this hotel not only for its relative anonymity, but because it wasn't in one of the posher sections of the city. Which meant it had his next destination located within an easy walk: a gun shop. Not such a hard thing to find in America.

He walked into the shop armed with his passport and NCA identification. No one would wonder at a member of law enforcement purchasing a gun, after all, and he intended to purchase the most generic one available.

The transaction went smoothly. Tom was a little concerned about the store manager making photocopies of his badge and passport, but only a little. After what he'd already done, and what he planned to do, what was one more crime?

Back at the hotel, Tom lay on his bed and stared out the window at the steep hills of the city. He hadn't wanted to pay for a water view, and besides, building cities on the sides of cliffs and mountains had always fascinated him. Especially in a place like this, where a good rumble from a big earthquake could destroy it all within seconds and had done so before.

People put pleasure before practicality as a rule, he supposed. A good view versus a turn of the roulette wheel that one's home would remain stable. Tom would always go for stability from now on—his days of gambling, both literally and figuratively, were about done. He hadn't been that good at it.

He set the alarm on his phone and fell asleep almost immediately. When the soft pulsing chime woke him four hours later, he felt refreshed. Not because what he faced would be pleasant, but because he'd finally chosen a course of action. It hadn't been chosen for him. He could handle this any way he wanted, and that knowledge offered him a peace of mind he hadn't had in three long weeks.

He showered and changed into a dark suit, white shirt, and striped tie. Just another businessman walking the streets of San Francisco.

At 3:30 p.m., he dropped off an envelope to the concierge desk and paid a not-so-small fortune to have it delivered to Brent Sullivan's office promptly at 5:00 p.m. He'd written "Urgent" across the front.

Then he started walking—ambling, really. Stopping when he wanted to watch people going about their business. Enjoying the blare of horns, the clang of trolley bells, the smell of salt air and food, and the chatter along the waterfront. At a quarter till five, he arrived at Millennium Tower, a garish monstrosity covered in reflective glass.

Brent Sullivan had a big enough ego that he was quite accommodating of the media types who wanted to write and broadcast expansive stories of his brilliance, so Tom knew that the CEO of Millennium set aside the last hours of his business day to work alone in his conference room. "It's where the magic happens," he had told one of the leading business magazines. "It's where I change the world."

Woe to the underling who interrupted his magic time, he'd said. His secretary left for the day, he took off his shoes, locked the door, and figured out ways to make more money.

Today, so sorry, but his world-changing time would have to be interrupted. Perhaps if Brent had been willing to answer his phone calls, Tom might have handled things differently. He didn't like having to talk to the man on his own territory. But things were what they were.

He sat on a concrete-and-wood bench outside the building near a fountain, and at five minutes before magic time, watched the bicycle courier arrive, lock his bike, and go inside the building with Tom's envelope.

His only regret was not being able to see Brent Sullivan's face when he opened it, realized what it was, and saw who had done it to him. Funny thing about Brody Parker or Nate Freeman or whatever one wanted to call him. Tom had ended up rather liking the man. They'd worked together quite well for today's event. Having a common enemy created a bond. He wished he'd realized that a long time ago.

Tom took out his cell phone, praying things worked as he'd envisioned. He'd gotten international service in honor of this moment.

Depending on how quickly Brent opened the envelope, and how long it took him to understand it, Tom figured his phone should be ringing very shortly.

It took less than a minute. He let it ring a few times just to annoy the impatient brat upstairs, then answered with a voice so calm he knew it would madden his target even more.

"Good afternoon, Brenton."

"You goddamn son of a bitch. What have you done? I didn't issue that hit on you soon enough."

Oh my, good thing he was recording this conversation. "You might want to calm down, Brent Sullivan. It would be a pity for you to have a stroke at such a young age." And he got Brent's name on the recording. He likely wouldn't need it, but a little extra insurance never hurt.

"Undo this."

Tom grinned. He'd not enjoyed anything quite so much in a while. "I've been trying to call you for several days. You should have answered. Since you've been avoiding me, I needed to get your attention."

A few seconds of silence followed. "Fine, you have my attention. What is it you want?"

Tom had waited a long time to hear Brent ask that. "Well, why don't we meet and talk it over? I'm downstairs."

Really long silence. "Top floor, end of the hall."

And he was gone.

"Act one, scene two." Tom got to his feet and walked inside the sleek, modern building. The first-floor lobby was deafening, all hard surfaces of marble and glass that echoed and magnified every sound. By contrast, the elevator was quiet as a tomb, a glass tomb that glided along a vertical track in the open atrium fast enough to give Tom a touch of vertigo and remind him he hadn't eaten since the midflight snack.

He'd expected the penthouse offices to be plush and garish, but they were more like the lobby. Hard surfaces, gray-and-black-and-cream color scheme, modern desks of glass and metal. Very modern, like the CEO himself. At least on the surface; underneath, Brent Sullivan was an old-fashioned bully.

No one sat behind the reception desk, so Tom walked past it, down the hall to the end. A sign outside a plain brown wooden door read "Conference Room." The place where the magic happened, and where the world got changed. Especially today, Tom hoped.

He pushed it open. Thanks to the photos in the magazine article, he wasn't surprised to see Brent sitting alone at the head of the long black table, wearing his signature polo shirt and jeans. No suits and ties for this modern mogul.

Only Brent's eyes gave away his fury. Certainly not his posture, slumped back in the chair, playing with a red rubber band, stretching it and letting it pop from one hand to the other.

His eyes, such an odd color of deep blue, were hard as the marble floors in his building. "Planned all of this well, didn't you, Tom?"

Without being asked, Tom pulled out a chair and sat. "I should tell you, I suppose, that copies of all those documents showing you laundering money from drug operations are in a safe-deposit box with instructions as to their disbursement if anything happens to me."

Brent smiled, and Tom thought he looked rather like a shark. "Do you really think I'd kill you?"

"Of course not. You'd never get your own hands dirty. But I might run into Felix Grummond in a dark alley one night, and I'd hate for you to be ruined should he accidentally shoot me."

Brent didn't respond. He steepled his fingers in front of him and rested his chin on them. A thinker's pose. "What do you want?"

"Well, to start, I want out of C7 without a contract on my head or a worry about running into someone like Felix and being gunned down. I never belonged with your lot to begin with."

"Done, and for the record I never thought you should have been brought into C7, and I was right. What else?"

"A few million to buy my silence about C7 and your other unsavory dealings—in pounds, of course. It's pocket change for you and my needs are simple."

"Anything else?" If Brent's anger could be bottled, it would make a more powerful substitute for nuclear energy.

"You will never try to harm Samantha Crowe, either physically or in terms of her reputation." He didn't mention Brody because, as near as Tom had been able to tell, Brent had never been able to breach the MI6 sealed files. That was a skill set hatchet man Felix didn't possess.

"So you and that bitch were working together from the beginning. I suspected as much."

He was blowing smoke. If he'd even half suspected Tom was double-crossing him that early, Tom wouldn't be alive for this meeting. Brent had underestimated him. And perhaps would again.

Brent raised his eyebrows. "Is that all? Don't you want a fur coat for your murdering bitch of a wife?"

"That would be lovely. Thanks so much for thinking of her; she'll be quite pleased."

"Get out."

"I'd like the money transferred first, please. To the usual account."

The money was a bonus. If Brent reversed the transaction as soon as he walked out, well, Tom didn't give a proverbial rat's ass.

Brent opened his laptop, furiously punched in a series of keystrokes, hit the "Enter" key with a violent thump, and turned the laptop to face Tom. Ten million transferred.

"How very generous. Thank you." Tom stood up. "Perhaps we'll see each other again one of these days."

"You better hope not," Brent muttered under his breath but loud enough for Tom to hear on his way out. The smile he wore into the elevator was broad and sincere. That part had gone well. He couldn't trust Brent to keep his word, of course. The man had agreed too quickly and easily. Plus, he was a viper.

Back in the lobby, Tom bypassed the door he'd used to enter and instead walked out a back exit into an attached parking garage. Most of the workers had left for the day, and it was dark and damp, in the way most parking decks were, the odor a noxious mix of concrete and trapped exhaust fumes.

Tom had only waited for five minutes before Brent came striding out of the main lobby with a messenger bag draped over his shoulder. Of course the man wouldn't carry a briefcase like a proper businessman.

He bypassed Tom with barely a glance, then stopped cold a few feet past him. He turned slowly, as if he knew, and Tom saw the smirk try to inch across his features and falter. It was hard to smirk and look terrified at the same time.

"Tom, don't do anything stupid. We can all walk away without injury at this stage."

"Tell that to my wife, who I hear crying in the middle of the night over what we felt forced to do to that poor NCA agent. Tell that to Samantha Crowe, who's endured humiliation at your hands after working so hard to pull herself out of the mire. To Brody Parker, whose home your hired thugs burned to the ground."

"It's over, Tom, let it go."

Tom reached inside his coat pocket and pulled out the generic automatic from its discreet holster. It had already been fitted with a silencer, and Tom didn't hesitate. One shot to the head and it was done.

Before Brent's body hit the ground, Tom had blended into the shadows of the garage and was making his nonchalant exit through the Millennium lobby.

Now, I'll let it go, Brent. May God have mercy on my soul.

CHAPTER 41

"Sprechen sie Deutsch?"

"Ja-ha-ha-ha." Brody rolled Sam on her back and planted big, sloppy kisses down her neck and across her collarbone, headed south.

"Brody, you have to take this seriously."

He propped himself up on his elbows, his black hair tousled, wearing the sexiest five o'clock shadow in history. Scratchy, but sexy. *"Wer ist Brody?"*

Sam thought a moment, then closed her eyes. Damn. *"Was ist ihr name?"*

"Adam," he whispered. "You know, the first man. Lived in that Eden place?"

She smiled up at him. They were in Eden now. Paradise.

He sat up and held out his hand. "Come on, let's eat lunch on the terrace."

"It's kind of cold, don't you think?" She pulled on a sweater and followed Mr. Bare-chested He-Man onto the small balcony they'd dubbed the terrace because it so wasn't one. He leaned over the wooden rail and looked down. "The view is amazing today."

She glanced around him, marveling at how easy he was with her now, as if he'd forgotten the scars. He no longer flinched when she touched them, which was good because she touched them a lot.

Below, a tow truck revved its motor before hauling some guy's beater of a junk heap out of the parking lot. "Can't say much for that view, but if you look up, it's a whole lot better."

He pulled her against him and they stared at the Nordkette, 7,600 feet high and, this time of year, already covered in snow. It took the cable car twenty minutes to reach the top.

They'd arrived in Innsbruck, Austria, in the dead of night three days ago, after Brody had worked out some kind of financial hocus-pocus with Tom Nelson to set up Psycho. He'd spent two days falsifying financial records and creating fake paper trails of transfers and transactions, finally putting that cybersecurity expertise back to work.

The FBI and NCA had moved fast. They didn't know about Tom or the specifics but acted on the possibility that Cynthie's death had been related to Brody somehow. A silent man in a black coat had driven them from Miles Thornton's house in Swineshead straight to London, where another joined them on a flight to Munich. They'd been met at the Munich airport by a somber, monosyllabic driver, who took them to a safe house near the Austrian border while deals were cut, documents prepared, files sealed. Again.

Finally, Adam Garrett and Carole Preston, formerly of Atlanta, had arrived in Innsbruck on holiday. Whether it became permanent depended on what they heard from Tom and what they decided to share with Brody's new NCA contact, a sober and serious man named Jonathan. Sam could tell his calm demeanor made Brody miss Cynthie all the more.

If they stayed in Innsbruck, "Adam" would start work at a local bookbinder's shop and teach art lessons at night while "Caro" would teach at an English immersion school for privileged Austrian children while she finished the dissertation for Samantha Crowe, working through a secure intermediary.

They'd both be taking lessons in German and trying to remember their names.

Sam loved Innsbruck, where the modern city spread out reluctantly around the old central town of cobbled streets and picturesque pastel storefronts as if not wanting to leave it. Ringing the town on all sides were the Alps, the Nordkette and the Patscherkofel, which made her feel small but also made her feel incredibly lucky.

Innsbruck was relaxed, friendly, had enough tourists that they didn't stand out, and most people spoke English.

But it wasn't Swineshead. The apartment with the view of both a Dumpster and the Nordkette wasn't an ivy-covered cottage with spiders in the attic. Brody didn't say it, but Sam knew he was homesick for the place the new agent had told them was uninhabitable but repairable. They'd talked about going back, the pros and cons, and knew they'd have a lot of rebuilding to do. But the garage apartment was undamaged, albeit leaky, so they wouldn't be homeless.

Only one last loose end remained, and they expected an answer today.

The only part of their old lives they'd brought with them—no clothes or mementos—was a prepaid cell phone set up to work internationally and an ancient British coin whose origin was unknown but whose age, size, and markings set it in medieval times. It might be from King John's treasure and be worth a fortune. It might be a run-of-the-mill thirteenth-century penny and be worth about a hundred dollars. Only time would tell.

But no matter what they'd done today, whether cooking, making love in the odd little fold-down bed, kissing, showering, more kissing, they were mostly aware of that little black cell phone and its silence.

Once that silence was broken, they could move on.

At 3:00 p.m., Sam sat with earbuds stuffed in her ears, trying to wrap her Southern-born tongue around words ending in *ich* without sounding as if she were trying to throw up.

She eeked when Brody—make that Adam—touched her shoulder, and she could tell by the look on his face that it was time. Tom had finally called.

They sat at the tiny kitchen table with the phone between them. "We're here, Tom."

The detective didn't sound like the same man. His voice was younger, more buoyant. Which meant he'd succeeded in neutralizing Psycho. Sam felt a month's worth of tension drain from her limbs. Could it really be over?

"Samantha, Brody. It's done."

"Your associate?" Brody sat forward in his chair, his shoulders hunched forward.

"Is no longer with us, I'm afraid. It's all over the American news. You might look for a newspaper, wherever you are. His tragic story even made the front page of the *Sunday Times* this morning. Such a sad problem America has with crime, I'm afraid."

God, he was dead. Gary Smith, a.k.a. Psycho, was dead, and they were sitting in a beautiful little Austrian town talking as if they hadn't been part of his murder.

Remember what he did to you. The nag had been quiet so long, her caustic voice was startling, and she'd apparently turned vengeful. *Don't even give him the honor of buying a paper to learn his real name.*

She honestly hadn't thought Tom would kill him—not that he'd admitted to it, but it was pretty clear. From the shocked look on Brody's face, he hadn't thought so either. She'd expected blackmail and counterblackmail, ending in a stalemate that would free them. Sort of like their situation with Tom and his wife.

This was certainly more permanent. She knew it bothered Brody that Tom and Donna Nelson would never answer for Cynthie's murder, but he'd accepted that teaming up with Tom was the only way to bring Psycho down.

"So are you going to stay out of England, then?" Tom asked but quickly added, "Don't tell me; I don't even want to know and shall never try to find out. I just wanted you to know that you could come back should you want to. You have nothing to fear from us. I expect we won't be living here ourselves for long."

Sam and Brody exchanged glances. They needed to talk.

"Well, right then." Tom sounded reluctant to end the call. "I'm sorry the two of you got pulled into this mess, but perhaps some good can come of it. Samantha, I wanted to let you know that your mother is going to be well provided for. I've arranged with a local social aid agency to cover her financial and medical needs. She'll have counseling if she'll take it."

Sadly, that was a big "if." Elaine Sonnier going straight? Maybe, but Sam doubted it. Ironically, her mother was her greatest regret at the idea of going into protection mode with Brody. No matter how awful her upbringing, Sam hated that the woman who gave birth to her would live out the rest of her life thinking her daughter had abandoned her. But that was the only deal the FBI would agree to if they stayed in Austria.

"Thank you," she told Tom and meant it. "That makes me feel better."

"I've also arranged for a transfer of funds to your contact at MI6 on your behalf, Brody. It's half of what I received from Bre—from our acquaintance. I hope it will make your journey easier."

When Tom finally rang off, Sam and Brody sat looking at the phone for what seemed like forever. Then Brody took it, pried off the back, removed the battery, and tossed it in the trash.

"Do you trust them enough to go back to England?" Sam reached out and took Brody's hand. "Or would we always be looking over our shoulders?"

Brody stared out the window at the Alps and didn't answer for a while. "The FBI wants us to stay in Austria." He didn't look at her. "But they're willing to let me go back to Swineshead on a short leash."

Brody had said *he* could go back, not *we*, and Sam fought to keep the disappointment off her face. She couldn't blame him, after all the trouble she'd heaped on his doorstep, but it still hurt. They hadn't really known each other that long, true enough, but they'd lived a lifetime together, all compressed into less than a month.

Whatever future she'd envisioned, it had always been the two of them, together. But then again, she had a history of assumptions where men were concerned.

Her thoughts must have shown despite her efforts to hide them, because Brody leaned over and took her chin in his fingers, turning her face to his. "Of course I want you to be with me, here or there, but you do have a choice. You can follow your dreams, go back to LSU, and finish your degree. Samantha Crowe can become the world's foremost authority on King John."

She laughed and leaned back in her chair, relief washing through her. She might have a choice, but she didn't have to choose between Brody and her career. "Graduate degrees aren't necessarily done on campus; I can finish my degree in Swineshead. Besides"—she took the coin from her pocket and slid it on the table between them—"I have some unfinished business with a deserted farm and a metal detector. What does 'a short leash' mean, in FBI terms?"

Brody shrugged. "Pretty much like my early days in witness protection. Frequent follow-ups. Regular check-ins and protocols to follow whenever I travel. Nothing too intrusive; they might even place someone in Swineshead for a year or so to make sure there's no trouble." He picked up the coin. "Do you think this is really part of King John's treasure?"

She thought about the lost crown jewels, and about the earthworks of Witcham House, and where the materials might have come from to build that old rock wall. "I don't think the crown jewels will ever be found intact. I still think they're around Swineshead, but the land formations have changed so much they have to be deep underground by now. But you never know." More likely, they'd find more pieces like this: coins, bits of broken jewelry, whatever time and the receding tides had left behind.

"Let's say we go back to England. I'm not sure what to do about Tom's money." Brody gave her that little half smile that made her toes curl involuntarily, and quite a few possibilities popped into her mind. "Do we want to take Psycho's death payoff?"

Sam shrugged. She didn't care about the money. It would be a nice cushion to have, but as long as she and Brody were together, she wasn't going to worry about the future, or what they might feel for each other in five days or five years or five lifetimes. She hoped it lasted and planned to enjoy every moment of it while it did. Whether they did it rich, poor, or in-between? That didn't matter.

For now, he was sexy as sin, and she either had to pack up her Innsbruck suitcase and meager wardrobe for England or learn some new German vocabulary words.

"*Küss mich*," she said, moving from her chair onto his lap and hoping her invitation didn't sound like she was about to throw up. Those darn *ich* words. But *küss* at least sounded like "kiss."

"Okay." Brody cocked his head and watched her with more of that smile.

"*Berühre mich.*" She stroked her fingers along his jawline. How *berühre* related to touching, she wasn't sure.

Brody's gaze dropped to her lips. He might not understand the words, but he was starting to get the context. "Does that have something to do with books or milk?"

Or maybe he wasn't.

"Brody, I think we'll have to move back to England. I'm not sure you're ready to learn German."

He moved in for a kiss. "*Ja.*"

ACKNOWLEDGMENTS

As always, a huge thanks go to my editor at Montlake, the awesome JoVon Sotak, and my überagent, Marlene Stringer. A big nod to my alpha reader Dianne and fellow Mutineers Kat Latham and Moriah Densley for helping pull Brody and Samantha's car out of the ditch, figuratively speaking—you guys are the best. And to my A-list readers, for loving the characters I write and being willing to read those early chapters: a special shout-out to Miki, Roger, Liz, Sandy, Kat, Matt, Deborah, Bonnie, and Beverly.

ABOUT THE AUTHOR

© Studio 16, 2013

Susannah Sandlin is a native of Winfield, Alabama, and has worked as a writer and editor in educational publishing in Alabama, Illinois, Texas, California, and Louisiana. She currently lives in Auburn, Alabama, with two rescue dogs named after professional wrestlers (it was a phase). She has a no-longer-secret passion for Cajun and French-Canadian music and reality TV and is on the hunt for a long-haul ice road trucker who also saves nuisance gators. Susannah is the author of The Collectors series, whose first book, *Lovely, Dark, and Deep*, was released in 2014; the award-winning Penton Legacy paranormal romance series: *Redemption, Absolution, Omega,* and *Allegiance*; and the spin-off paranormal romance, *Storm Force*. As Suzanne Johnson, she writes the Sentinels of New Orleans urban fantasy series: *Royal Street, River Road, Elysian Fields,* and *Pirate's Alley* (2015).

FICTION SANDLIN V.2
Sandlin, Susannah,
Deadly, calm, and cold /
R2002512529

ODC

Atlanta-Fulton Public Library